Dear Joseph

by

T. S. Eure

authorHOUSE

1663 LIBERTY DRIVE, SUITE 200
BLOOMINGTON, INDIANA 47403
(800) 839-8640
www.authorhouse.com

First published by AuthorHouse 07/15/04

ISBN: 1-4184-6260-8 (e)
ISBN: 1-4184-4737-4 (sc)
ISBN: 1-4184-4738-2 (dj)

Library of Congress Control Number:2004092837

Printed in the United States of America
Bloomington, Indiana

This book is printed on acid-free paper.

DEDICATION

This book is dedicated to my parents, Albert and Dorothy Eure, for their love and to my wife Clarena, who has supported me throughout this process.

Illustration by:
Ron Sykes
mrszaire@hotmail.com

1.

I was only fourteen years old when I experienced the greatest challenges of my life. During the Depression years of the thirties, many fourteen-year-olds were doing adult tasks, and it was not uncommon to see children working in textile mills or coal mines. It is very strange how you can grow up in a few days. One day you're content collecting ants in a jar, and the next day you're struggling to keep a family together.

As a child in Fayville, Kansas, I remember my mother as a small olive-colored woman with a worn and tired face. The embedded wrinkles and graceful lines that fell upon her face were like a curtain of hurt that she wore. Like most women in 1934, she had only one good dress: it was a plain blue dress, not torn or spotted, that she wore to church only on Sundays. Yet deep within my mother was kept a constant well of understanding and love from which she let us children drink.

At one time our house was filled with much love. My father worked as a Pullman Porter for the railroad. He was a tall, light-skinned, gray-haired man with a very impressive look, a mixture of Greek and Turkish characteristics. He did not fit the mold of the average Colored man of the time. Perhaps he could have passed for other than Colored, but his wool-like hair and broad nose were identifying characteristics that could not be hidden.

Dressed in his Pullman Porter uniform, I used to imagine him being the captain of a luxurious ocean liner. He was so proud to be a Colored porter; for it was the kind of job that people in the community respected. He kept telling us that there were opportunities regardless of what color you were. He was meticulous in his job, serving the people on the trains and living as if his color did not matter. He lived in a dream world, refusing to see the signs around him that said, "Colored Only." He walked as if discrimination was an unnoticeable fact or that it did not touch him, but the Depression was slowly eating into every fragment of society.

When he would take us to the train station, it was exciting to see so many people walking and moving about with large and small baggage or carrying great bundles in their arms–an ecstatic river of life, moving and dignified with briefcases and newspapers. Their expressions were serious and their eyes were filled with destinations as yet unseen. Great and magnificent chandeliers hung in the station like sacred lights in some ancient temple. Doors of shining, polished brass were like the entrance to a majestic, golden kingdom. Fashionably dressed people, men wearing neat pinstripe suits, women with hats decorated with peacock feathers, paraded through the station.

My father walked around the station as if he owned the whole place, pointing out the different kinds of trains, telling us stories about each train. Big and black trains came into the station, heaving like uncontrollable giants filling the loading area with white, beautiful smoke.

Those were good and happy times when we could afford a real Christmas tree and presents wrapped in silver and gold paper, awaiting us on Christmas morning.

Then everything changed. My father lost his job. The Depression was like a plague eating and devouring everything. Fewer and fewer trains were running: people did not have the money to ride them any longer.

Gradually the proud man began to change too. Drinking and smashing furniture, he was no longer loving or caring, but hateful. He stayed drunk all the time and, worst of all, he started beating my mother. Nothing remained of the gentle man who spoke with kindness and wisdom. Perhaps it was the reality of prejudice surrounding his every move. That which he had kept so far from himself now surrounded him. He began to realize that he too was nothing more than a poor Colored man.

I will never forget one night when my father came home drunk. My mother was asleep in the small room next to ours. He yelled at the top of his voice, "Where is my food, woman!" Mama sprang from the bed, ran down the stairs to the kitchen, and began to heat the baked chicken and mashed potatoes and gravy she had prepared for him earlier. I crept from the bed that I shared with my brother David, sneaked down the stairs, and peeked around the kitchen door. Father lifted his fork, took two morsels of food, and then flung the entire plate against the wall. Thick hunks of mashed potatoes splashed across the wall and floor and porcelain shattered into a thousand pieces. Then his fist came down on her face. Her small body collapsed from the force into a huddled mass of pain.

I ran to my mother's rescue as she cried out in terror as he tried to kick her. One of the blows from his foot caught me in my stomach. I too cried in pain while David and our two sisters, Ruth and Sarah, came into the room and huddled around us, crying in fear for our lives.

Sometimes at night I would pray for him to die, or that he would never hit my mother again. But the drinking and beatings continued, until one day he won a large sum of money from gambling and walked out the door to be seen no more.

My mother suffered greatly through those years. Her deep smile vanished, and in its place grew a beaten and destroyed countenance. She was fortunate to find a job cleaning the homes of rich ladies who were untouched by the Depression. The money that she earned was barely enough for her own needs, let alone that of a whole family. She made one dollar and twenty cents a day; and when she came home late at night, she was often too tired to do anything but sleep or pray that she had enough strength for the next day.

She used to cry herself to sleep every night, praying to God for a miracle for her family–a miracle that never came. She sewed and patched our tattered clothes to the best of her ability, yet we still looked like orphans. Many times she would not eat dinner so that we could have a little more food to survive. I cried at night, listening to my mother in her room pleading that God would help her soon.

Then my mother became sick, so sick that she had to stay in bed. One day Dr. Johnson reluctantly came to the house even though Mother didn't have any money to pay him. As I pressed my ear against the door, I heard him saying, "The bone cancer has spread and consumed most of your body. I am sorry but you don't have much longer. There is nothing that can be done now."

Now I knew the reason why Mother cried every night. She was in pain, but she did not want us to know. Things went from bad to worse. The landlord threatened every day to evict us. Mother pleaded with him to let us stay just a few more days, because a miracle was coming.

Then it happened. I heard a loud cry come from Mother's room. I ran up the old wooden stairs of our little frame house with David, Ruth, and Sarah following close behind me. My mother was smiling; it was the first time I had seen her smile like that in years. She held out her hand to me.

"Joseph, come closer to me. God has given me my miracle. I have spoken with the Lord. I touched His hands. And he told me not to worry anymore, that he has given each one of you, my children, a special miracle and a blessing. Joseph, my son, you are chosen for a great work. I must leave you now for a little while. I love you, my children."

5

Her eyes became clear and bright, like the sunlight reflecting off the bottom of a lake. Then she died. We gathered around the bed, all four of us weeping and holding the dead body of our mother.

As the hours passed, I finally arranged for the Gentleman Funeral Home to come and take her body to the mortuary. It was a terrible day, raining and thundering outside. It seemed strange to look at my mother's dead body, the body that once had such vigorous strength, energy, and enduring kindness. A strange stillness settled around the room, as though something had been removed, some unexplainable force or beauty taken from the atmosphere never to appear again. That small body that moved from room to room cleaning, washing these old walls, now lay huddled in silence, with a deeper secret, now untouched forever.

The mortician arrived in his long black hearse. I had never heard a man's voice so dignified and poised, like whispering in a whining song of sorrow that made me feel even worse. But the soft, trembling, compassionate mask that he wore became twisted and distorted upon his face when I told him that I had no money to bury my mother, but that in time I would repay him. His whole appearance changed, turning into a grotesque figure of outrage and insult. In a whining voice, he said, "I am sorry son, but your mother didn't have an insurance plan with us. And it is our policy for customers to have the money in advance. Maybe you can borrow the money from someone to bury your mother. I am sorry but we cannot take her body."

I was devastated. Looking at my mother's body, I worried about how I was going to bury her in a decent way. I thought about my relatives, but they were poorer than we were. Then I remembered the church; surely there was someone there that could help.

Reverend McDaniels was the pastor of the Brownstone Methodist Church. He was a big, round, roly-poly man with a deep, loud voice. His sermons were terribly boring and usually put me to sleep. But my mother's nudging became a constant reminder to me to stay awake during his Sunday torture sessions.

I ran over to his beautiful home out of the slum area of my neighborhood and pounded as hard as I could on his door. When he finally opened the door, he was in a rage saying, "Who in the hell is making all that noise out here? My family is trying to eat their evening dinner."

My tattered clothes were covered with rain and mud, and I cried, "Reverend McDaniels, my mother has just died. I called the funeral home to come take her body, but they refused, because I didn't have the money to bury her. I need your help." I fell exhausted into the rain-soaked earth, my fingers groping through the mud, seeking some meaning to life.

A brief silence erupted between us as he stood staring down at me. I rose slowly. As if my eyes had the power to peer through flesh and bone, I could see him looking at me very annoyed and impatient. All that really mattered was that I had spoiled his dinner.

He bent down and touched my shoulder. Like an actor reading a script, he spoke saying in that pious, loud manner, "Your mother was a good member of our church. The Lord has his own ways in dealing with us. You have to accept whatever will come. The church cannot be responsible for each of its members. We must be responsible in life and also in death. You cannot use the Lord or his church for your own use. God will show you a way. There are many others suffering greater misfortunes than you. However, I will perform my duty by doing the eulogy for your mother, but we cannot assume such a financial obligation or burden. Call me when you need me. I will be here to do what I can. May the Lord guide you on what to do. Now, if you will please excuse me, I must go back to my family."

Then he shut the door as the rain fell upon my face. No one could see my tears except the Lord.

That night I covered my mother with a blanket and shut the door of her room. A whole day and night had gone by and Mother still lay dead in her room. That night all four of us children slept together on the floor of the living room. A year ago the electricity had been turned off in the house; since then we had used candles for light.

With the small candles burning in the room, I lay thinking about the happy times my family had enjoyed–the times we laughed and shared Christmas and special days together. Then I remembered my mother's wedding ring. I felt a cold chill run through me. I felt joy and sadness at the same time. Who was I to take the only thing that signified her marriage–that endless and eternal time that lived forever within her heart and was symbolized by this sacred ring? I could not bring myself to do it. But it had to be done.

I ran upstairs and stared a great while at my mother's lifeless, gray body. Touching her hands, I said, "Please, forgive me, Mother." Then I removed the ring that she wore for so many years.

The next day I sold the ring for two hundred fifty dollars. I called the funeral home and told them that I had money. The mortician arrived, asking first for the money, and then counting it. "We usually charge three hundred dollars, but we will take this," he said. They told me that the casket would be just simple wood, nothing fancy. I felt hurt that I could not afford flowers, but neighbors brought some early tulips.

Two days later we had the funeral at the mortuary. Reverend McDaniels came wearing his long black robe, saying that he had come to deliver the eulogy. I told him in front of everyone that I didn't want him to say anything over my mother. The mortician told me to be quiet; he didn't want a disturbance in his place. Then Reverend McDaniels asked, "Who do you have speaking the Word of the Lord for her?" I replied, "I am." He left in a great huff, his robe flying in the breeze as he walked away in anger. He resembled the flapping of a bird whose wings were broken.

I was surprised at the number of people that had come. People from every walk of life were there. I didn't know that my mother had known so many people. They were all shocked when I rose to speak.

"My mother was a woman that knew God, not just a person that talked about God. You could see God in her. She would clean a floor the way God would clean a floor. She would wash dishes the way God would wash dishes. She would cook a meal the way God would cook a meal. Many times I felt God in her life. We should pray that we find God in us that way."

Tears rolled down my face, hitting the floor in great drops. I had often considered my mother a quiet, very withdrawn woman. On the contrary, her life was full, vibrant, and radiant with meaning.

As time went on, the state people sent us to orphanages and foster homes. We tried to write to each other and keep in contact over the years, but there were too many miles between us to ever become a family again.

2.

I was placed in the most terribly depressing orphanage ever built. It was a ruined Victorian mansion where some fifty children struggled for existence. Large pieces of plaster had fallen out of most of the walls, lying in shattered fragments on the decaying, creaking wooden floors. None of the housemothers thought it was necessary to clean up the debris that cluttered the house, for in a sense we were no more than debris to be gathered and dumped in an obscure corner, void of affection and compassion from those who ruled and disciplined us. The cold wind of winter swept through every crack of the house. The bitter drafts caused sickness and disease to infect many of the children with outbreaks of whooping cough and polio.

I still remember the tasteless, cold, and skimpy meals that we received. I was so hungry that oftentimes I would become dizzy and fall into brief periods of unconsciousness. The constant noise of children whining and fighting for food and warmth and for tattered blankets to cover their shivering bodies gave me a feeling that I was losing my sense of reality. I would lapse into periods of dreaming and would imagine myself eating until I became full. At night I would lie awake crying silently on a mattress stuffed with old rags and newspapers.

In my heart I cried out to God, asking him what my life's purpose was–to suffer endlessly without hope? I used to pray that I would die, or go to sleep and never have to return to this life, or to assume someone else's life and destiny; for I believed that my life had been set for failure.

In winter they marched our cold, feeble bodies over barren railroad tracks to look for lumps of coal discarded from moving freight trains. We would tote the coal to the furnace bin of the orphanage. It would provide barely enough warmth for us to keep from having frostbite. It was so cold in the orphanage that you could see your breath.

The constant feeling of being trapped in a web of suffering and despair almost drove me to the point of breaking. I tried to escape from an environment that sought to entangle my very spirit into hopelessness, where I was no longer perceived as a human being having potential to accomplish or achieve anything. But in the eyes of the orphanage people, our humanity was reduced to something that needed food and clothes.

When Sunday arrived, they made sure we were clean. They gave each of us a rough, dried, white shirt and a pair of old, coarse, corduroy pants to wear. Then they marched us into the dining hall. A huge, broken, dusty chandelier hung from the ceiling, almost as a symbolic resemblance of our lives in the orphanage. If only the children in the orphanage were polished with love and restored with affection, and not broken with hatred and taught only to distrust. But no one took the time to polish their brilliance.

When foster parents would come to pick children to adopt, we all secretly prayed that we would be one of those chosen to live in a beautiful house where we could escape the daily struggle for food and warmth. I hated this Sunday ritual. I felt like a piece of property to be felt and handled. Yet I desperately wanted someone to adopt me. I smiled stupidly and tried to appear cute, but each week I was passed over. Only the children who were three and four years of age were adopted from the group. And it helped to look like little cherubims that had fallen from the throne of God. I hated the foster parents as much as the housemothers, because they never wanted to look further than the physical surface. They cared little how we felt, what we thought of, or what our aspirations were. I heard some of the housemothers talking about me, saying I was too tall and I was almost sixteen, too big for anyone to adopt.

The women who worked at the orphanage were called housemothers to give the impression of a home environment, but often the children were slapped in the face for the most trivial reasons. They were beaten and brutalized to the extent that they could not laugh or play like normal children, and in their expressions was a dead lifelessness. I felt like a prisoner of war, forgotten in a dungeon of hate and prejudice. I felt an empty void in the depth of my spirit, that my life no longer had a purpose or meaning. I was dead to all that I understood of life. I stared like a slain ghost out of the shell of my body, desperately seeking someone to love me.

Mrs. Bradenkins, the superintendent of the orphanage, was a tall, ugly woman with a long, crooked nose. With bony knees protruding from under her dress, she looked like a deformed chicken when she walked. She was constantly reminding herself, when she approached me, that I was a troublemaker, because I had fought so long trying to keep my brother and sisters together. She would point her bony fingers at me saying, "You little crumb snatcher. You need to be in reform school, not in an orphanage." She hated me because of my defiant spirit. I would not respect her just because she was an adult. Examining her motives and how she related to the children in the orphanage, one could see what a harsh, cold, callous person she was.

Every day I endured the daily degrading of my self-worth. I remember the day before I left the orphanage for good. We were all gathered in the dining hall, being served our evening meal. The dinner consisted of a cold, creamy wheat batter that clung thickly to the spoon. It was almost like trying to swallow lumps of paste. And the rolls that they served were so hard you could have played baseball with them. We were all gathered around the old oak table waiting for Mrs. Bradenkins to give us the gesture with her hand that we could eat.

A small boy, who had just arrived at the orphanage that afternoon, was seated next to me. He was unfamiliar with the kinds of food served in the orphanage. Looking at his bowl of wheat paste, he flung it to the floor not realizing the severity of the crime for disobeying the rules. He had jarred the table, knocking down my bowl of food along with his own. Everyone became paralyzed with fear, scarcely breathing.

I felt a stinging hand against my face. Mrs. Bradenkins hit me so hard that I fell out of my chair and broke a front tooth. Before I had time to tell her that I didn't throw my food on the floor, another one of her crashing blows struck my head. I tried to tell her that I was innocent, but all she saw was my food on the floor. She didn't even see what the small boy seated next to me had done. Yet another part of me believed that she knew what had happened, and she had been waiting for the opportunity to hit me. I began spitting blood from my mouth.

She was now on top of me and driving her long fingernails into my throat. I was weak and dazed from the first blows. Then she began gripping my throat and smashing my head against the hard wooden floor until I could feel warm blood on the back of my neck. I heard her screaming in a loud, shrilling voice. "How dare you throw away this good food that was given to us! How dare you upset this house!" Her grip tightened around my throat, and I could feel pieces of my flesh being torn away by her fingernails.

As we rolled across the floor, I strained all of my muscles trying to break free of her strong grip around my neck. Somehow I was able to break free and grab the tablecloth, pulling everything to the floor. I heard a loud clang on the floor. A butter knife had fallen next to my head. We both wrestled to get to the knife. I broke free from her grip and plunged the knife to within an inch of her throat. Everyone was silent now as I contemplated taking her life. From deep within me, I knew that I could not sacrifice my principles and beliefs. I would not accept the hideous beast that she had tried to create in me.

The children started screaming in terror and hate saying, "Kill her, do it now. Kill her!" My hands trembled uncontrollably. I felt another blow to the back of my head. One of the housemothers had hit me over the head with a broom handle, leaving me almost unconscious. The housemothers dragged me back, hitting and kicking me, until I was a mass of bruises.

Mrs. Bradenkins rose to her feet like a demon, her eyes rolling strangely in her head. She rushed at me, scratching and hitting me even more. Finally one of the housemothers restrained her. For a long while she stood, screaming and cursing at me until they took me away.

3.

Mrs. Bradenkins decided that I was too hostile to remain in the orphanage. The next morning she called the sheriff and had me arrested and transferred to reform school. She suggested that I serve a four-year sentence at hard labor in the textile mill without compensation, so I could learn how to behave like decent people.

My body was a collection of bruises, and I could hardly find the strength to walk. I needed medical attention for my head, for it was still matted and wet with blood. I was given a mop and a bucket and told to clean up the dining hall where I had fought with Mrs. Bradenkins. The housemothers watched me closely as I tried to mop up my own blood as it dripped on the floor in a speckled array of pain. Inside my heart, I cried out to Mama, "Why did you have to die? Why did you leave me alone? I didn't know there were people like this in the world." I crawled through the debris, picking up broken dishes and bowls and pieces of bread, and scooping up the wheat paste meal from the floor. I scraped it off my fingers into a container to be eaten later by the children.

As I reached into one of the bowls to scrape out the portions of wheat paste, I felt something inside the bowl. It was a key with a string tied around it. Mrs. Bradenkins' key! She had lost it during the fight when the bowl of wheat paste fell on the floor. I finally knew this ungodly food was good for something, for the wheat paste had hardened around the key, forming a perfect camouflage. I had seen Mrs. Bradenkins shove children into closets and lock them up with a key similar to the one I now possessed. I slipped the key into my pocket, as a smile of triumph broke over my bruised face.

Having completed cleaning the dining hall and with my arms twisted around my back, I was thrown into a basement closet. In the dark, cold room, I heard a small boy whimpering. He was shaking with fear. When I finally reached him, he clung to me as if his next breath depended on me. He whispered in my ear, "There are rats in here. One has already bitten me."

I jumped in terror as something ran over my feet. I ran to the door pounding on it with my fists and screaming, "Let us out, you bloodsuckers! Damn you! Damn you!"

The silence and darkness of the house was not disturbed by the fear and pain crying out from the basement. Something clung to my sock, and I kicked it until it squealed in pain and scurried off. I took off my sweater and began hitting the floor and swinging at the shadows moving quickly around my feet. I cried out to the boy, "We are getting the hell out of here!" I reached into my pocket, and finding the key, jammed it into the keyhole of the door; but nothing happened. I tried again, but nothing happened.

The rodents were beginning to regroup and stage another attack on their evening meal. Then I remembered the key was covered with wheat paste. I began peeling the dried meal off the key with my fingernails. The boy was crying again, "Mister, they are coming back again. I can feel them under my feet."

Then something bit me, and the key dropped with a loud clang in the consuming blackness of the room. I tried desperately to find the area where the key had dropped. I reached down on the floor, my arms swinging wildly, sweeping the floor in a flurry of motion, knocking the squealing creatures away with my hands. Thank God, I found the key! I rushed towards the door like a madman trying to escape from a nightmare. Hearing the soft click of the key turning the doorknob, I grabbed the boy, almost ripping off his shirt as we both stumbled out of the closet into the dim light of the cellar.

I found a window that was partially open and kicked it out. We crawled out of the basement to the side of the old house. It was late in the evening and the wind was softly blowing through the old oak trees. The leaves had turned brown and reminded me of withering hands; the trees protruding from the darkness were like skeletons in the ominous night.

As we ran up the dirt road away from the grim mansion, my body was so weak that I thought I would fall dead any minute. The small boy ran, crying and trembling as I dragged him along. He would fall running and I would pick him up and we would continue again. I do not know how long we ran, but we had gotten a great distance from the house when I twisted my ankle. We both fell down a hillside, rolling into a clump of hedges.

We resembled two tumbleweeds driven by the winds of life, rolling to exhaustion and despair. My eyelids strained to open, but I had consumed every ounce of my strength. I closed my eyes there in the haven of the hedges and slept, at peace for the first time in a long while.

4.

As the morning light stretched forth, the softness of its curtain in colors of gold rose across the countryside; the sound of morning doves singing in the trees resounded like trumpets of freedom. In the distance crickets chirped with the clear resonance of an orchestra. The grass was soft and the leaves offered me a more gracious bed than the one I had in the orphanage.

In my arms the boy lay shivering and soaked with sweat. I could tell he was burning up with an intense fever. As he stirred, he groaned, "I feel sick, terribly sick." I placed my hand on his forehead and a deep hot warmness penetrated my fingers. I believed being confined in a damp basement closet by the housemothers and running all night in the cool evening air had caused the fever. His condition was weakening, and I knew that he could travel no longer. What he needed was food and warm blankets around his shivering body. I stood broken in spirit, wondering what our fate would be. I knew they would be searching for us as soon as the morning approached.

I could not let him return to the orphanage in his condition, where the damp basement closet meant certain death. I stood trembling in the morning coolness, wondering how I was going to preserve this child's life. I tried to reason within myself on the cruelty of a world that would condemn a five-year-old child to a basement closet for doing something so trivial and unimportant. I was too hurt to cry anymore, but I was too strong to give up.

In the distance I heard the noise of an old truck coming up the road. As I hid on the grassy hill, my heart was beating in a racing panic. Could it be the reform school officer or one of the housemothers who had been persecuting us? Realizing that the boy would die without food and warmth, I had to take the chance.

I jumped out in front of the old truck moments before it drove by. It veered to one side, barely missing me. I fell down on the dirt road in a rolling fashion. The truck came to a screeching stop. An old man sprang from the truck, racing toward me. He cried in a startled voice, "Oh, God, Betsy, I hit a child. Lordee be!" He was picking me up in his large, calloused hands, almost like a giant gathering a pebble.

His wife was a silver-haired, gracious woman with soft lines of age streaking across her face. The round shape of her body reminded me of a tugboat in motion. The voice of the giant that cradled me like a baby cried out to the old woman, "Mama, hurry up. I think I hit and killed this child."

I tried to tell him that I was quite all right, but my voice was lost in his shouting. After they thoroughly examined me, making sure I was only bruised, I told them how we had escaped from the orphanage because of the cruel and severe beatings that Mrs. Bradenkins would administer.

They found the small boy shivering in the hedges and wrapped him in some wool blankets that they had in their truck. All of their life belongings were loaded on the truck, tied down in a cluttered array. The old woman opened a trunk, found a bottle of cough syrup, and with a large wooden spoon gave a big dose to the boy. Then she went to the back of the truck, opened a large basket, and came back with apples, oranges, and baked chicken.

It was almost like Christmas. I slowly took bites of the baked chicken, not wanting it to dissolve in my mouth but last forever. It was the first time I had eaten real food in almost two years. They told me that they were going to California to try to start a new life, because the mills had closed down in the region.

"Don't we have room, Pa, for two more? For God has never blessed us with no children, and I think it's time for us to have some."

The old man looked at us and then smiled in a gentle way, "You don't know where you might find your blessings. Son, you and your friend can stay with us as long as you want. We will do all that we can to make you happy."

I pleaded with them kindly, simply stating that I appreciated their offer to take me in, but I wasn't ready to become a part of anyone's family. I longed now for my independence. The hatred and cruelty of the orphanage had taught me all the necessary skills for survival. I told them that if they gave me a lift to the next town, I would appreciate that very kindly.

As the old truck began moving down the dirt road, the small boy slept in the back of the truck on a cushion of blankets. The sound of the tires moving along the road and the humming engine caused me to meditate on the past experiences of my life.

Just then a sheriff's car drove by with a pointed-nosed woman frantically pointing at the truck. Oh, no! Mrs. Bradenkins had found me and brought the sheriff with her. I looked around in a terrified panic as the sheriff's car whipped around and turned sideways to block the road.

I shouted at the old man to stop the truck right away. "I got to get out and run away. I am not going back to that orphanage no matter what!"

The siren of the sheriff's car continued to get closer and closer. I grabbed the steering wheel of the truck, shouting in a piercing voice, "Do you hear me? I am not going back!" Everyone in the truck screamed in horror as the truck rolled in the ditch.

Then I heard a calm voice saying, "Son, wake up. Everything's all right. You were dreaming. You are in Mason City now." I did not realize how exhausted and physically drained I had become. I had slept for hours, they said. Yet I was still being tormented by the demons that I had lived with for two years.

The truck came to a heaving stop. As I slowly got out of the truck, the old, round-faced woman followed me. She gave me a comforting hug, "I will pray for you, child." The old giant came out of the truck, dug down into his endless pockets and gave me a dollar bill. "Be careful, Son, this is a mean, old, dirty world."

I took one last look at the small boy with whom I had escaped that terrible night. He reached out a weak hand and smiled from his bed of blankets. The old couple reentered the truck and disappeared down the dusty road. I turned away quickly and felt something wet on my face and realized that I was crying.

5.

As I began to walk toward the small, lonely city, the morning shadows crouched on the plains in mysterious shapes. An old, dilapidated cemetery lay on the outskirts of the city. The dirt was hard and rocky beneath my feet. I could sense the generations of life that sought to find sanctuary in the soil. I could feel the dust of dead men on my lips as I walked through pasture land. Slowly I began to breathe in the fragrance of farms and cultivated fields. The sweat of their broken backbones poured into the depths of my soul.

Yet I knew that my destiny would lead me beyond the pulse of this small city. My mother's voice echoed her prophecy through my pores. I had not understood this miracle which she spoke of that would descend upon me.

The city was void and desolate. Ancient wrinkle-faced men with hollow eyes huddled by small fires in the darkness trying to keep warm. Their expressions, empty and beaten, resembled dead trees consumed by termites gnawing through their souls.

The wind began to blow in a whirling motion against my face as I stumbled over the aging streetcar tracks in the cobblestone streets. The paper and debris of the city whirled around me in a graceful ballet of splendor–the fragments of life disintegrating in the wind, bearing the memories and dreams of men. As I moved in this storm of humanity's clutter, I whispered to myself, I am like the papers in the wind, thrown away and forgotten. I too am left only in the hands of earth's cruel elements. Maybe I am nothing, like Mrs. Bradenkins said. I am just poor trash blowing around without any home.

Just then I felt a piece of paper blow under my shoes. I reached down and read what it said: "Young men needed now for military duty. Help the Allied Forces. Join today." I reasoned within myself that the military would be the perfect escape. No one from the orphanage would ever look for me there.

I was able to locate the recruiting office as the morning burst across the sky in a tabernacle of color. I sensed a positive excitement and felt the door-of-life swinging open on its hinges. When I arrived at the recruiting office, there was a group of young men all about my age. They were talking and laughing loudly. There were two lines, one for Colored and one for White. I lied about my age because I looked older than sixteen. I raised my hand, took an oath and became a soldier in the Army.

The weeks that followed were an endless nightmare. I lost my identity and my compassion to feel. I was completely ignorant of world events and the war that was raging in Europe. I had been kept in isolation for two years. I was fourteen when I entered the orphanage, and now at sixteen, I felt as though I had already lived a lifetime. I didn't know who Hitler was or what he was doing or why everyone hated him so. I had heard only rumors of him building an army in Europe, but it had meant nothing to me at the time.

I stood in bewildering awe when they marched us into an old airplane hangar for dinner: I could not believe that there could be that much food in one room. I gobbled up plates of food and smiled in ecstasy. After dinner we were taken into another old hangar and fitted into different uniforms. I had brand new clothes! I felt the material as if it would deteriorate with my touch. The old orphanage clothes that reeked of hurt and pain were gone now.

With the passing days and nights, the timid, unsure youth died and a heartless being emerged from the ashes of hatred. I became vicious in my demeanor. I had learned my lessons of hatred well. I was determined to rise from the scrap pile of human failure, no matter what the cost. I would be relentless in my purpose to attain the riches of life. I tried not to think about the family I had lost, but deep within me I wanted to believe there was a miracle that would bring us together again.

I knew that my brother David and my sister Ruth were strong enough to survive any foster home. I remember David when he was in the third grade. A big, fat, sixth-grade boy named Othello used to steal the lunch money from the third-grade boys every day. At knife point he would line them up in the hallways, spread their hands against the wall, search their pockets, and take their lunch money. David never cried as Othello took the fifteen cents for which

Mama worked so hard. If I had known what he was doing to David, I would have beaten him long ago. But David never told me.

One day during lunch time (as the story was told to me), Othello was in the cafeteria eating four lunches. He had robbed the third-grade boys early that morning and was sitting like a king, eating two mashed potato plates, three chicken salads, and drinking four cartons of milk. All the third-grade boys looked at him from a distant table, their heads bent in silent humiliation; but resentment could be glimpsed in some of their sideway glances. David rose up calmly and walked over to Othello's table. He took a carton of his milk and poured it over Othello's head. Before he had time to even rise up, David dug his fingers into the mashed potatoes and flung them into Othello's face. Like a ferret, he moved around him and began to pound on his head. It took three teachers to restrain David that day.

The principal gave David a beating with the large wooden paddle that hung in his office. You could hear the air whistle through the drilled holes in the paddle as it was swung. David didn't care what the principal might do to him, because he had become the hero of the school. The next day the third-graders were pushing Othello up against the lockers, taking his lunch money.

My sister Ruth was the best rock thrower I had ever seen. I remember one time some kids followed us home from school, laughing at the way we were poorly dressed, calling us names, yelling, "There go the Holie Molies," because we had so many holes in our socks and shoes. Ruth could not take it anymore. As we walked near an alley, she picked up a smooth, curved rock and threw it at the leader of the group. They had to be almost a block away. The rock began to turn and twist in the wind, pirouetting in slow motion. It was like watching the throw of a great pitcher at the World Series; it was a beautiful sight to behold. It landed perfectly with a boing-g sound on the point of the kid's head, who was making the most noise about us, and bounced off with equal accuracy. He stood shocked and amazed that it had landed on his head. We broke out laughing. The boy cried out loudly, "I'm gonna to tell my Mommy." We ran for home.

Ruth could outrun any boy in the neighborhood. She could climb to the highest part of the tree, and she wasn't afraid of the dark. I knew that David and Ruth could survive anything. But Sarah was the youngest, only five years old when Mama died. I used to lie awake at night, wondering what would become of my baby sister.

I promised Mama that I would take care of our family. Over the years that promise had begun to vanish. A thick darkness grew over my heart and hatred burned with fury within me. After Mama died, the foster homes we went to were only to be temporary until they found a place where we could all live together again as a family. They said that we could see each other anytime. But all the things they said were soon forgotten.

I only received one letter in all my years at the orphanage. The letter was from my brother David. I kept this letter with me the rest of my life; it was one of the few fragments that I had left of my family. I must have read the letter over a thousand times.

Dear Joseph,

I am quite fine. I was placed with a kind family of missionaries. Mr. Jacob Mitchell and his wife Marian have adopted me; they never had any children of their own. They have treated me very well.

You will not believe where I am. I am in Calcutta, India. This is the most beautiful country I have ever seen. The waterfalls are spectacular.

The Mitchells are doctors who work long hours every day, giving food and polio vaccinations. The little children seem to suffer the most; they are crippled and deformed and very poor. Every day they come to the mission waiting to be healed of this dreadful disease. I am learning how to care for the children; I wash their small bodies. Some of them have never seen soap before. Mama would be proud of the way I am helping the poor people who come to the mission. The heat, dust, and flies are unbearable at times, but it is worth it.

I never imagined that I would be in India. On May 22, 1935, we left a strange and beautiful place called San Francisco on the West Coast. We boarded an ocean liner, the size of a dinosaur, a gigantic mountain of steel. It was unbelievable that something that big could stay afloat.

Joseph, you must see the ocean. I felt as though it would crash against the shore and swallow me in one breath.

When I first arrived in California it was like the Garden of Eden. I could not believe the number of orange trees that grew on the side of the road. Dr. Mitchell's father owns a large vineyard: he earned his money by making wine. The vineyards were like a beautiful sanctuary. I ran for miles, eating grapes and chasing red and blue birds that swooped down to eat the grapes. The vineyards were between two little mountains in a quiet valley. There were so many places to explore and so many trees to climb and fruit to eat. I remember the first time I saw the orange trees in the orchard: I ate so many oranges that I got sick and had to be carried into the house by the Mitchells. Dr. Mitchell is very rich; yet they act like ordinary people. They treat me like their very own son.

We sailed from San Francisco and traveled on the sea for thirty-three days before we finally reached India. The name of the ship was "The Restless Lady." The ship itself was a gigantic city. There was a ballroom with shiny mahogany floors. An orchestra played in the ballroom and people danced and drank liquor. The rooms on the liner had expensive furniture and thick, soft carpet. The waiters followed you wherever you went, holding trays of fruit and sandwiches.

I will never forget what happened on June 8, 1935. That morning as I lay sleeping, I was suddenly thrown out of my bed. Everything in the room crashed onto the floor. Dr. Mitchell came into my room saying that there was a terrible storm outside. He put a life preserver around me and then rushed me into the ballroom. Everyone was huddled together in silent fear as the storm raged outside, rocking the ship violently back and forth. As the water began to pour through the hallways and cover my ankles, I could hear the screams of the crew outside trying to fight the force of the sea. It was only 9 o'clock in the morning, but it looked like midnight, for the sky was black and filled with clouds. We all huddled together whispering silent prayers. That was the longest day of my life. There was no sun or stars, no sign that anything existed. I finally fell asleep in Mrs. Mitchell's arms.

The next morning the sun was so bright and the clouds were white like the wings of angels. A large group of dolphins began to follow the ship as though nothing had happened the day before. One passenger had been swept off the ship by a wave, and Dr. Mitchell was asked to give a eulogy for the dead man. I remember him talking about the swiftness of life and how we are but fragile beings blown around like pieces of dust out into the sea of life. I never knew Dr. Mitchell could speak so eloquently and inspiringly. Everyone was crying.

Finally we arrived in India. As we unloaded our baggage and traveled through the marketplace, there were thousands of people talking and selling fruit and things that they had made. They were selling crickets in jars, snakes of every description, and charms to wear around your neck. Everywhere we went there were thousands of other people dying of hunger. The people were lined up on the streets crying out to us as we walked through the crowds. I was afraid and began to panic until I realized I was screaming at the Mitchells that I wanted to go back home.

However, I have come to love this land with its beauty and poverty. Once I went to the sacred river called "The Ganges." I started to make soap bubbles and blow them through the air. It was the first time that many of the people had seen soap. As the bubbles floated over the people lying in the dust, they started shouting and screaming loudly, and a great crowd of people came running towards me, singing and laughing. They called the bubbles "angels." And from that day on they called me the "angel maker."

I met a boy about my age named Kahlil, with whom I became good friends. His father owns a herd of elephants in the forest. They use elephants to knock down trees and take the wood to the lumberyard. When Kahlil's father is not around, we have elephant races in the river. We have water fights with the elephants; and using their trunks, they spray water at each other.

I wish that I knew where Ruth and Sarah are living. I pray every night that God will take care of all of us wherever we are. I pray that we will get together to share Christmas again like when Mama and Dad were with us.

I must leave now. There is a line of people waiting for medicine and food at the mission.

Your brother with love,

David

In my spirit I was still a surging well of pain. The military gave me a way to release my inner hostility. The six weeks of basic training was a continuous assault on my senses. We were as clay figures shaped and molded to exact specifications. We were young men full of energy and adventure, ready to carelessly run into the dark and mysterious arms of death. And when the work was completed, our personalities were ground under the dust of our combat boots. The rigor of the military was a haven compared to the physical brutality and deprivation of the orphanage. Over the years, I had written a dozen letters to my brother David, but I never received any reply.

The war that had begun in Europe had escalated into a global holocaust. Hitler was determined to purify the earth with his madness and genocide. This deranged lunatic was piling bodies in graves like pennies in a jar. There were rumors of atrocities within the isolated camps for Jews. We were being marshaled into fighting units and preparing to join the battle.

It was raining the day they marched us into the huge aircraft carrier and transported us thousands of miles to a beautiful field in Belgium. This field had once known the calm winds of an August harvest, had embraced the soft cooing of morning doves eating seeds scattered neatly in perfect, quiet rows. This field was to be held in reverence by all who walked in the light and shadows of its celestial sunrises and holy afternoons.

And then the rains came. It rained for weeks at a time as though God was already crying for the blood that would soak through the ground, for now the field became a muddy graveyard. The dark trenches we clung to, like children upon our mother's lap, would become our caskets. The smell of death filled our nostrils and choked our lungs.

Our objective was to move southwest and converge with troops driving through Western France toward the Rhineland. We began to question our orders. We were only miles from the German border, and it was only miles farther to the towns of Bergen and Belson, between which it was rumored there was a concentration camp for Jews. Why not push to the west and do some real good? Why endure this seemingly futile effort to the south? Years later it would be called the Battle of the Bulge–all we knew that it was a blood battle.

For more than thirty days we lived in the muddy trenches. Eating mud, breathing mud, allowing the military undertakers to drill holes in our consciousness, and then fill those holes with mud till sucking mud was into our very spirits. Since I had arrived, I had not seen the Nazis, but my pores had tingled, prickling like the sound of bees building their hive inside of me. Then everything went extremely quiet.

The quiet was disturbing and deceiving. A fog descended on the field consumed with the rumors and whispers of terrified men. I held my rifle in my hands as if it was some sacred artifact that would restore my life. The mist of the clouds started to appear on the surface of the ground. The clouds resembled angels calling men to their graves. The fog had hands in it, eyes and faces, calling and crying out.

Then I saw my mother walking in the mist of the clouds. I cried out to her, "Mother, what are you doing here?" She walked toward me, her flesh transparent with clouds. It seemed as though I had stopped breathing; everything began moving in slow motion. She told me, "You shall not die for you have been chosen to give the miracle to others." Then she became cloud-like and dissipated into the surrounding whiteness of the air. My breath seemed to suffocate in my lungs, struggling for meaning. The clouds bathed my soul in contentment and the dark shadow of death withdrew from my trembling heart.

It occurred to me that this would be the last glimpse of earthly beauty that some of the men in the trenches would see, for death crouched over the next hill. Death stood grinning, waiting for endless hours and days in the mud. I reassured myself that it was only my exhausted mind forming images of the past. Maybe I really didn't see my mother before me; perhaps out of my fear, I resurrected her from my heart. For the first time in my life, fear consumed every cell in my body.

I had endured the hatred of the orphanage and survived the cruelty of Mrs. Bradenkins' beatings, but now I was afraid. When I was a child in the orphanage, I wanted to die. Now it did not seem right to overcome the torturous events of my life only to die in an empty, muddy field. But this dream, this apparition of my mother, would not die. It appeared again staring in mysterious wonder at me out of the mist.

An unspeakable disturbance hung over the soldiers in the trenches. The uncertainty of life created a quiet distance between each one. We were afraid to become close friends with anyone in the platoon, because creating friends in war did not last. And now this haunting beast of fear disrobed itself from the skin of our bodies and stood before us, jeering at our fragile armor.

The deep, gravelly voice of the Captain brought me back into startling reality. I could hear him saying, "All right soldiers, we didn't come over here to have a Sunday school picnic. There is a city beyond this field that we have to take. And those Nazis in the trenches are standing in our way." Then his voice yelled louder, "Put your bayonets on your rifles. We are goin' in!"

At his command we arose from the mud-covered trenches. An unearthly cry rose from our terrified throats as we rushed toward the enemy. I heard the sound of bullets piercing the bodies of men, like raindrops falling into a gutter. As legs and muscles, consumed with shock, continued to run, body parts lay strewn on the soil. Explosions ripped through the air causing the very earth to rock and shudder. I swallowed noise and smoke as my pores became clogged with insanity. I ran screaming in the darkness, crying as I sprayed the atmosphere in a glitter of bullets. Then I felt an explosion of pain. I did not know why I was covered with so much blood. When I fell upon the ground and looked at my leg, everything below the knee was gone. I yelled and screamed, "Where is my leg? Somebody has to find my leg!"

Blood squirted out of my artery like a red flowing fountain. I was in shock, crying out like a madman, enclosed in a nightmare that I could not escape. I squirmed on the ground like one of the night crawlers I used to put on my fishing hook. Finally two men from my platoon pinned me to the earth. One of them jabbed a hypodermic needle into my leg, while the other soldier tore off my shirt and tied it tightly above the bleeding stub of my leg. I felt my youth fleeing, escaping through my pores.

It felt as though every molecule in my being instinctively knew that the precious ointment of youth and mobility was evaporating eternally. My freedom would now forever be bound to a wheelchair, a cane, or a walker. I would be labeled a cripple, forever abused by those who could run faster and stronger toward the door of opportunity. Shadows now filled the atmosphere; men moved in slow motion around me. My heartbeat boomed in my chest mimicking the echo of forgotten cannons in a graveyard. I felt old, with the winds of death heaving like locomotives rattling on broken and dilapidated tracks. The piercing winds of unlived dreams blew through the cracks of my soul. I was dying, but I was not sad. I was ready to leave this beat-up body, to abolish this world, this pit of misery that had become my life.

I wanted to close my eyes forever and never wake up. But, still I cried out in the smoke and fog, pleading in vain for my comrades to find my leg. My soul moved through the black holes of rifle barrels and bathed in the dark and terrible silence of men's tears, exploring the quiet room where each man meets and embraces himself for the first time. My leg had shattered into a million pieces, and in that terrible second, my youth had also shattered into irretrievable fragments.

I was dying; yet I felt warm and secure. Somehow the pain was gone. Nothing mattered anymore. Everything became quiet and comfortable. I heard choirs singing out of the voices of soldiers and trumpets rather than bomb blasts. So this was death. I felt at ease. I felt like running and dancing. I wanted to burst out laughing for no reason. Perhaps my mother would now come and take me home, or I would ask God to give me a new leg.

6.

I awakened to a nurse standing over me in ghostly white clothes. Her eyes were piercing and bright, yet filled with wonder. It was the eyes of a child staring at this empty shell of a life. She had a pure, soft, loving face imbued with honesty that enslaved my thoughts. It was this sincerity that flowed through all physical matter and touched my soul with a healing love.

In the midst of this there was a consuming atmosphere of death that lurked like a hungry beast with the corpses of men in its mouth. I felt a love so powerful that tears began to wet my eyes. In the distance I heard the crying voices of dying men struggling with twisted faces to leave their bodies on blood-soaked beds. Now this angel was hovering over me, gently stroking my forehead with fingertips as soft as sunlight penetrating my aching soul.

I reached down, trying to feel for my leg, since the pain of it being torn away from the kneecap caused it to resurface in my nerves. And then the kind voice said, "Please, don't move, everything will be all right if you don't move." She was one of the nurses who cared for the dying and wounded. In the large medical tent, the constant cries of death horrified me. Then my angel left me quickly as a doctor in the distance called for her help with another soldier, who was in the last stages of death.

I became angry. Why did the doctor call her away? Can't you see, I thought, this man is going to die anyway? Perhaps the doctor just wanted something of the earth's beauty to be with the soldier as he drifted away from the earth. As they lay dying, I heard grown men call out for their mothers. I felt as though I were just waiting for my time to come next. Why didn't death come and take me?

The sound of explosions rang out from distant hills, and I began to relive the whole event, running over the hill with the men in my platoon, many of them falling to their deaths, as the smell of smoke and blood began to fill my nostrils again. The pain intensified in my leg with sudden contractions. All my muscles tensed with pain, arching my body into violent, deformed shapes. I tried tearing off the huge blood-soaked bandages that were wrapped around my knee. It felt as though my leg was still there and I wanted to see what piece of humanity remained. The mind can play cruel tricks on your body. I kept reaching for a leg that wasn't there. I tried not to cry by holding my lips together until my teeth were biting so hard that my mouth was filled with blood. Then a cry broke out from my lips, a loud bitter, angry cry like the sudden collapsing of an old building that lay in a mass of dust and debris.

I cried with a heaving breath like a locomotive struggling to turn its wheels on broken and worn tracks. I cried because my father left one night without saying goodbye–not a word from him all these years. I bet he didn't even know that Mama had died. I cried because I wished he were dead and that he suffered like we did, and that I would have beaten him up. I cried for every time his fist fell upon my mother's frail body. I cried because I would never have a chance to play basketball with David, or teach him how to hold a baseball, and how to throw a curve ball. I lost my brother forever. I cried for my sisters, Ruth and Sarah, because I could not protect them from the state people, who lied and gained my confidence, and then separated us. I cried because I should have plunged that knife down Mrs. Bradenkins' throat rather than leave her to inflict her cruelty on the rest of the children. I cried because I was still alive, deformed, and alone.

The medical staff caring for the dying and wounded came running towards me. There were around two hundred men in the biggest tent I had ever seen in my life and only about thirty nurses and four doctors. People were constantly running back and forth in panic, carrying bags of blood and medical supplies. Now a small group of nurses came over to me. It took three nurses to try to restrain me. I became enraged and was swinging my arms frantically. I became consumed with hatred and pain. I fell out of the bed and began ripping tubes and bags of clear liquid out of my arms and leg. Everyone came hurrying towards me with anger in their eyes, for exhaustion had overtaken them. As I fought off the nurses, my fist struck the jaw of one of them. She was knocked out cold on the floor for a few minutes.

The nub of my leg began to bleed again in a flowing stream. I was picked up like a sack of potatoes and dumped on my bed. A doctor ran over and grabbed me by my white gown and pushed me down in the bed saying, "You only lost a leg. There are some here that will be dead before the day is over."

I screamed at him, "The pain. I can't take it anymore!" I was shot again with more needles in my arm and leg. Slowly the pain began to ease up, but it still felt like a bee was wrapped up in the bandage around my leg. I didn't care about what the doctor said: I prayed that I too might be one of those precious dead.

In the distance I could see the rows of bodies lying in the comfortable body bags. The nub of my leg was an ugly sight. The knee was still there but the area right below it resembled a dried up prune. The tissues of skin were blackened and wrinkled, reminders of the shell. If I could only go back on that battlefield, I could find my leg and let them sew it back on.

As the days passed, they strapped me down to the bed, because I kept removing the bandages to stare at the ugly nub. A few times they found me outside my bed crawling near the door, trying to find my leg. I lost track of time with the medication I was on; the days and nights all seemed as one now. I heard the doctor muttering, "We must do something to control his fever. If the fever does not break soon, he will die."

Then I had a dream about my father. I was ten years old again, and my father was showing us the trains as he used to do. Everything was just like it was before. We were all so happy, as we walked through the white clouds of locomotive smoke. I became separated from the rest of my family as the crowds of people filled the station. I was pushed off the dock by the flow of people rushing to catch their trains. As I stood up, my shoe got caught between two tracks. I screamed for help but no one heard me. I screamed and screamed but no one paid any attention to me. As a large train started coming in the distance, getting closer and closer, my father came running out of the crowd and jumped down on the tracks. The train was almost upon us when my father freed my foot, with only enough time for him to hoist me onto the dock in one motion. But before he threw me to safety, he smiled and said, "I give you my legs."

The fever broke. I cried for a nurse in a weak voice, "Can you give me some water, please?" It was the same nurse that I had seen when I was first brought in. She leaned over and rubbed my head and said, "You finally decided to come back to us. We thought we might lose you there for a while." She was a small brown-skinned woman, with eyes that spoke more than her lips. The water flowed down me like a well being revived. I looked around the room. The men were still there, wrapped in an assortment of bandages around their heads, legs, and arms.

When I first joined the military, there were two lines one for Whites and another for Blacks, but now here, it made no difference as men struggled for life. Color was no longer important, for death did not discriminate. It took all the hands of the living to build the door of hope to lock death out of our reach.

Sunlight began to stream through the holes of the tent. It felt good on my face. The sound of bomb blasts in the distance had temporarily subsided. "What about the war?" I asked, in a hopeful voice.

As she sat down on the bed next to me checking my temperature, she replied, "Your division has taken a large part of the land near Bergen, and now they are moving toward the city. But there have been casualties on both sides. Many men will never go back home; they only had time to put them in a common grave and move on."

"How did a woman like you get to a hell place like this?" The question made her move away. I reached out toward her to make her stay, saying, "Please, talk to me. Take my mind off my pain. Tell me about yourself. Just talk, please." She sat on the chair beside my bed and began her tale.

"My name is Claudette Borders. I asked to come here. I am from a small town in Topeka, Kansas, where there are only a handful of Black people. I came from a large family of five brothers and five sisters; I was the seventh child in the family. My father tried to make a living as a farmer, growing corn and soybeans. All of us were required to work the farm as soon as we were able to walk. I knew that life had something better for me than that. There were ten Colored families and all the young men about my age expected me to choose one of them to marry and carry on the tradition of their mothers." She stopped and looked around. "You need to rest. I have taken up too much of your time."

I was afraid she would leave and not return. I wanted to know all about her. I reached out again pleading, "No, please. I want to hear how you got here. Please, just go on talking." She looked at me for a minute and then continued her story.

"I just did not want to be another Colored woman, cleaning house. I remember one church dinner when I was introduced to one of the Johnson boys. I shook his hand and then left the matchmaking arrangement abruptly. Later that day my mother gave me a verbal beating. She said, 'I don't know who you think you are, trying to be Miss High and Mighty. Mr. Johnson's boy is a nice young man, and you just walked away from him as if he had the plague. You are almost seventeen years old and you should be looking for a husband. Me and your father can not afford to feed you forever.'

"I tried to tell her that I didn't want to be like her, with a whole life of changing diapers and wiping running noses. I reasoned with her, saying, 'Mama, I want to see the world. You have never set foot out of Topeka your whole life, but I know there is a wider world out there. I want to discover it.' She slapped me across the face saying that I needed to get those foolish notions out of my head.

"But I persisted anyway. I became the valedictorian of my class. My counselor at school suggested that I write to Hampton Institute in Virginia. It was a Colored girls' college, and if I would write to them and send my grades, they would help me go to college. I waited every day for the mail.

"My mother threatened that if I did not get serious with one of the boys in town, she was going to call the Johnson boy over and arrange a day for a marriage. I remember the day I got the letter from Hampton Institute stating that I would be eligible for a full scholarship, and they would also give me a job on campus. Everyone became speechless. My mother didn't talk to me anymore after that day. Yet she was glad I was leaving town.

"There were many other girls my age, all studying to be something. It was a whole new world for me. There were girls studying to be teachers, doctors, and nurses. The whole atmosphere was unbelievable. I began to study to be a nurse and after graduation I joined the Army. I have not been home for over five years.

"I didn't want to be another sixteen-year-old girl with a house full of children. I have not missed that beat-up old farm or the people there at all."

I did not think it was unusual that she would talk about her own family as if they were strangers. However, there was a deep hurt when she spoke of the farm. I did not question her as to why she had not seen her mother or father during all these years, for I had my own hurt.

Her skin was the color of honey. Her thick, black hair hung down her back like a rope against her neck. Whenever she spoke to me, her smile filled her whole face. Her eyes were like brown, dirt roads that led to a quiet place where shade trees protected the sacred power of her love. They seemed to behold a future place where a white frame house with a picket fence would preserve the concept of family.

The rain fell outside for endless days, washing away the mud sides of the trenches, causing them to fill in where we had been hiding and waiting to fight and die. It washed the blood of the fields until the green grass began to peek out of the dirt—the dirt that had felt a thousand combat boots grind its beauty into nothingness. Beauty tried to reappear; nature struggled to digest human bodies and evaporate the tears left in graves under the earth.

I drifted into the arms and thoughts of Claudette as she talked with me for hours about her hopes and dreams. I was blessed to have a personal angel to stay by my bedside and care for my needs. Often in the middle of the night I would awaken to see a soft form praying nearby. I asked her one night: "Why are you praying for me? You don't know me. Why are you doing this?"

She answered: "There is something inside of you that is hurting, even as there is something inside of me that is hurting. Nothing is an accident. It was meant for me to meet you at this time, to perhaps heal myself while I seek to take care of you."

One day one of the nurses brought me a letter which she said came when I had the fever, but became lost among the other mail. I could not believe that I had received a letter. Who would be writing to me? No one knew I was here. Perhaps they got the wrong name;

there was no return address. I was so excited; I examined the letter slowly. My name was beautifully written in cursive. I felt the weight of the letter in my hands, measuring it as if my hands were a scale. I slowly opened it to find that there was another envelope inside the first. The second envelope was smaller, and the return address had been torn away. The first letter began,

Dear Joseph,

You probably do not remember me, but I was one of the housemothers at the orphanage. My name is Betty Van Horn. I am writing to give you this letter that was found among Mrs. Bradenkins' things. First of all, you should know that the state people knew you went into the military, but they regarded you as one less mouth to feed and clothe; no one is seeking you anymore. The letter, I believe, is from your brother or one of your sisters. I know you will be happy to receive it.

I am also writing to tell you that I am ashamed of the way the housemothers treated you and the rest of the children at the orphanage. I want to apologize for what happened back then. You should be told that Mrs. Bradenkins died about three months ago.

All of the children were in the dining hall eating their wheat meal. Everything was quiet as Mrs. Bradenkins was overseeing the dinner and steadily watching to make sure they were eating. Everyone was surprised to see her begin eating the wheat meal, because she had never eaten it before. She started coughing quietly, until the coughing grew louder and louder. She started screaming in a high-pitched voice, trying to tell the housemothers that she was choking and needed water. Mrs. Bradenkins drank the water but it did no good.

All the children stood in silent awe. The housemothers began hitting her on the back, trying to dislodge the food but to no avail. Then she screamed at them saying, "You fools are trying to drown me," as they tried to force water in her mouth. She started running and stumbling through the house saying that she couldn't breathe. All the housemothers followed her in panic and fear.

Mrs. Bradenkins then ran up the old stairs, holding her throat, saying "I can't breathe." As she leaned against the railing of the stairs, the weight of her body caused the railing to break and she fell and broke her neck. The housemothers tried to revive her but it was useless.

The children stared at her body, still afraid that she might rise up and kick one of them or pull one of their ears or hair and slam them down on the floor.

After her death, everything changed. It was as though the evil force that directed all of us had left. First, the housemothers began to actually clean up the house. All the wheat paste was dumped that same day, and a cook was hired. I went to the agency and asked for donations of real food. All of us began to examine our own hearts and souls and were kinder to the children. I am ashamed of myself and for the years I allowed this devil woman to go on. I wrote letters to the State Commission for Children and complained about the Mrs. Bradenkins' brutality and how the house was a living nightmare for children.

Please, Joseph, please forgive me and the other housemothers for our actions. I will pray for your safe return.

Betty Van Horn, Superintendent

Home of the Good Shepherd

I was glad for the children. Mrs. Bradenkins deserved worse. I could never forgive her. I hoped that she was eating wheat paste in hell for the rest of eternity.

As I held the other letter in my hands, I pressed my nose against the paper, hoping I could smell the warmth of one of my sisters or my brother against me. Slowly and carefully I opened the letter and unfolded the old paper. The paper made a creaking sound as if it had been exposed to moisture and then had dried.

The handwriting was the beautiful cursive style of my sister Ruth. I would have known that handwriting anywhere. The way she made her letters reminded me of some ancient script. I gently touched the paper as if it might disintegrate in my hands. I began to wonder what she looked like now. What kind of experiences had she gone through? Had she become as bitter and filled with pain as I had?

This small patch of folded papers now became my family. They were the closest thing I had to connect me to my past. I had refused to be a statistic of the state, being wiped out and erased forever without a past or a history.

Now I knew that we could speak to each other even if we never saw each other again. There is a force of love that moves over hillsides, across fences, and enters closed doors. A power that even separation could not overcome. Our love for each other had the strength to survive.

My body trembled. It had been a long time since I had spoken to my sister. I would allow her words to soften the hardened shell formed by the orphanage's brutality. I would meet Ruth again as I read her letter.

Dear Joseph,

I prayed last night that this letter would reach you wherever you are. I have written you dozens of letters but have never received any response. The only address that I have for you is the orphanage called the Good Shepherd. I am going to keep writing and praying no matter what. At night I walk and look up at the stars and pray that they will look down on you, David, and Sarah and carry my love.

I used to cry a lot at night. The nights were the hardest part of all; I kept seeing all of your faces at night.

Your faces haunted me and then spoke to me of your pain. I miss all of you so much. There is not a day that goes by when I do not think of all of you. I believe that David, from the little information I received from the state people, is living in California. And Sarah went to a state orphanage in Sioux Falls, South Dakota. I never should have let any of them separate me from Sarah.

I just turned eighteen a few days ago, but I feel about fifty. I would not even recognize all of you now. Time is moving so swiftly these days that I realize the mental image I've held onto of each of us is a picture of the past.

When I was taken away, they put me on a train with a matron and didn't even tell me where I was going. Every time I saw a porter I kept seeing the face of Father and hoping the next one that walked by would be him. I used to wonder how Father felt when our faces would appear out of the dark night.

We rode the train for two days, me and this fat matron. She kept me like a prisoner. All she needed was some handcuffs and a chain and I would become an official prisoner. She watched me like a hawk expecting me to run away. I guess she really thought I would jump off a moving train. She wore an old, soiled, gray skirt and blouse and looked like an old nurse somebody dug up from a graveyard. When she walked, the weight of her body shifted causing the hump on her back to shake. She sat looking at me in disgust, as we traveled for hundreds of miles until we reached a mountain town called Tuscaloosa Ridge. It is an old and dirty coal mining town.

Then I met my foster Father and Mother, Mr. and Mrs. Austerberry. I remember when she delivered me to them; it was little more than a business deal. Mr. Austerberry walked around me examining me like he was buying a piece of property. He commented, "She is kind of small and don't look too strong." Then he reached into his pocket, pulled out some crumbled dollars, and gave them to the fat matron, who immediately broke out into a smile and started giving some kind of speech about how much he was helping the homeless. It was nothing more than an act of child slavery. I was bought and paid for, to be nothing but a maid, servant, and nurse for Mr. Austerberry's sickly wife. He could not afford a nurse or nanny to care for his wife and children, but he learned he could get a Black girl from an orphanage for a very low price.

Mr. Austerberry is a tall, pale, dirty-faced, brown-toothed man that is forever chewing tobacco and spitting it everywhere. He hardly speaks, but when he does everyone in the house jumps with fear. His three sons hate him and wish that they could kill him, but they are too young to stand up to him. He slaps them in the face and curses them until they are in tears. The vocal lashings of his tongue are like a whip beating these children down mentally. He never calls his sons by their first names, but just says, "Come over here, fool. Hey, stupid, what are you doing now?" I have entered another house of fear and violence.

Before dawn breaks, Mr. Austerberry takes his three sons, Mirch, 16, Bill, 14, and Hamilton, 11, to the coal mines. They are only children but they work in the mines just like men. Hamilton is his favorite target, because when he tries to talk, only stuttering sounds and slow jarring words come out. His father attacks him from every angle. One day he was telling Hamilton that he was nothing but a freak and a stuttering misfit that could never become a man. Hamilton was struggling, trying to tell him that he was a man. His small, bony body was shaking with fear and tears streamed down his face, saying, I am a man.

Mr. Austerberry spit out a large wad of tobacco that hit Hamilton in the face and said, "You are nothing, boy, nothing at all." Then he walked away. I hate that man more than I hated any person in my life. I see this pale, rotten-toothed, bowlegged man who always has an odor to his body, who does not appreciate or deserve these beautiful children.

Mrs. Austerberry is paralyzed. She contracted some kind of muscle disease so that she can only sit in a wheelchair and move her head slightly. One of my main duties is to care for her. I wash her body, cook her meals, and then hand feed them to her. She is really a nice lady, who stares silently angry at the raging of her husband.

Coal dust is everywhere. I wash all the clothes in the house and make sure everything is clean, but it is so hard to keep a house clean near a coal mine. The coal dust filters into the house, and in a matter of minutes the house is just as dirty. If you leave a window open, it will blow onto the table and right on the food. A lot of people in town walk around with scarves over their mouths, protecting themselves from the blowing dust. The faces and teeth of the men who work in the mines are so stained and blackened with coal that when they smile and laugh, they don't look human anymore.

The Austerberrys live in a two-story, clapboard, company-owned house. All the houses are fitted in neat little rows along the roadside. They look like little wooden cubes; some have small porches, and some have three bedrooms rather than two. Mr. Austerberry has a three-bedroom house. There is a small barn in back of the house where a room was made for me to sleep.

Mrs. Austerberry is the nicest woman you could ever meet. She can hardly speak because of her sickness, and you have to be very close to her to hear what she is saying. The Austerberrys also have two daughters, Mary, who is 7, and Laurie, who is 5. My days are full of washing clothes covered with coal, combing hair, making beds, and caring for Mrs. Austerberry. The children like me very much. I have taken over the duties of their mother.

I remember one day last June when Laurie lost her doll and she came crying to me because she could not find it. We searched everywhere in the house and still we could not find that doll. Then I remembered the doll I had when I was a little girl and I gave my doll to Laurie.

When Mr. Austerberry came home and saw Laurie on the porch playing with the doll I gave her, he had a fit. He cried out saying, "Who gave Laurie that nigger doll to play with?" The color of the doll did not even matter to me at the time when I gave it to Laurie. He snatched the doll from her hands and tore it in half. Laurie is his pride and joy and to think that this little blond-haired angel was playing with an old Black doll was enough for him to have a heart attack. When he found me, he unloosened his belt and beat me on the back. I tried to run away but he caught me by my hair and dragged me back to the house. I swore from that day on if he ever touched me again I would kill him. Mr. Austerberry's eyes are twisted and crazy-looking when he starts yelling and cursing. His mere voice causes his children to start trembling in fear wherever they are in the house. There have been times on payday when he has come back to where I sleep and has tried to touch me and use my body. But I am too fast for him when he is drunk. I don't know how long I can keep living like this. I wish there were some place for me to go where I could run away and begin a new life.

There was a mining accident last month. An official from the mining company came to the house and said that Mr. Austerberry was trapped in the mine. His three sons were not in the mine at the time of the accident. He and fifty-seven other men were trapped in the mine and they didn't know how long they could survive without air in that condition. All the families with husbands and sons trapped in the mine were there. But Mrs. Austerberry and all of her children were smiling and perhaps hoping that he had been buried in the mine. We waited all night until they dragged his dirty, coal-covered body out of the mine along with fourteen other men who managed to survive the tragedy. Shock and sadness came upon their faces when they learned that he was still alive. It seems strange that the evil people live on and on.

Please pray for me, my brother. I love you and always will.

Your sister,

Ruth

7.

I was exhausted after I had read her letter. I began breathing hard, trying to hold back tears as a deep hurt moved across my body. My hands were trembling in anger and frustration. Sweat had formed on my forehead and was flowing down my face; my eyes burned as I lay helpless. A deep sadness unfolded within me and then pierced the silence of the air with screams only heard in my thoughts. I was powerless to rescue my sister. Her letter was an epistle of pain and survival. The letter had destroyed any sense of hope that lingered in my being for her. At least I was grateful that I knew where she was. I did not know the state or address of the house, but she had mentioned that she was in a coal mining town called Tuscaloosa Ridge.

When my leg was better, I would go to the orphanage to seek more information as to where the letter had originated. It did not seem strange that the return address had been torn away, for I knew Mrs. Bradenkins' tactics only too well. She sought to isolate the children from their families so she could control them mentally and physically. I would search a lifetime if I had to, to find my family. I planned to write the state orphanage at Sioux Falls for information on my sister Sarah. I could only imagine what horrors she had gone through.

As I lay on the hospital bed, I imagined how I would arrive in Tuscaloosa Ridge. The dust of the city would be blowing upon me. Clouds of black smoke would move through the little dirt-road town. The dark, coal-stained faces of the people would be staring at me from their bleak little houses along the roadside. The children would be pointing their little fingers at me, asking their mothers, who is the stranger among us? I would walk in the stores and marketplaces reading and feeling their thoughts. I would ask, "Where does Mr. Austerberry reside? I have come a long way to see him." In haste and terror the people would flee from my presence, sensing clouds of danger that would threaten their degrading and damning traditions. I would come perhaps during a thunderstorm as lightning would be striking 300-year-old trees.

"Excuse me, kind Sir, but can you please tell me where I can find Mr. Austerberry's house? I would appreciate it very much." A nervous and fearful man would speak to me saying, "You must be new around these parts. There is a storm coming across the mountains, and if you don't take cover soon you might be hurt. The house is just right down the road near the pond with the shade tree." I would now walk towards the house, over the creaking evil bones in the segregated cemetery. I would come with the rain blowing, with thunder and lightning cracking.

I would go to his house and perhaps find him in one of his moods of cursing his son Hamilton. I would politely walk up to him in a humble way and speak to him in that apologetic tone I saw the Colored porters use when they were trying to get a tip from someone. "Why, excuse me, Sir. I am looking for a Mr. Austerberry. I hear he is taking care of a Ruth Potter."

And then he would look at me in that glaring and twisted stare, chewing on a piece of smelly tobacco, his face covered with about two weeks' of dirt and coal, standing with his hands upon his skinny hips in a pair of greasy overalls. I would hear him say to me, "I am taking care of her, boy. Now, what are you doing on my property? And what business is it of yours?"

Then I would drop my head down toward the ground and act like I was frightened of him. I would pretend like I was stuttering, so afraid of him that I could hardly talk. "I, I, I did, didn't want to, to upset this household and things, Sir. But it has been a long time, sin–, sin–, since, I, I, I, seen, my sister Rut–, Ru–, Ruth…and I, I, wou–, would think it, it would be a, a kind thing, if you wou–, wou–, would go, go, get her for me."

Mr. Austerberry's blood would flow into his pale, spotted face. The fat under his neck would start to wiggle like a chicken, and purple and green veins would start to pop out on his transparent skin. He would speak in that saliva-splattering drawl, saying, "Ain't no Colored boy tells me what to do. And I'll be darl garn if none is gonna do it in my own house."

I would drop my head down like a tree that falls so easy by the first blow of an axe. I would speak to him in that muttering language created by fear and intimidation. "I, I, I didn't mean to up–, up–, upset you, Sir. But, sin–, sin–, since you wo–, won't get my sis–, sis–, sister for me, I, I, I want to give you this." Then I would come up with a right cross smack in the middle of his tobacco-smacking face. I would watch as he would start to choke on the tobacco. Then I would hit him with an upper cut. I would watch that dumb expression of surprise come upon his face as he would slowly crumble to the ground.

Next, I would call his family to come out of the house. His sons would come out and look in joyful surprise as they saw him pleading for mercy from me. Ruth would also come out, pushing Mrs. Austerberry in her wheelchair. I would drag him screaming and kicking and pleading to the pond. All the children would be laughing and skipping about on the green grass as the sun would now break out in the skies. Mrs. Austerberry would be smiling and nodding approval. I would tell one of the children to get a bar of soap. Then I would throw it to him, kicking legs and all, into the pond and order him to bathe that nasty body as the children snickered and grinned in amusement.

As I lay on my bed, a smile broke over my lips. I would have my own revenge on him in my mind. There I was lying on the bed with one leg, smiling and crying at the same time. I knew the kind of personality that Mr. Austerberry had. He had been poor his whole life, a victim himself of an oppressive society that stained his teeth with coal. A victim of the coal company that consumed his strength, mocked his humanity, and provided him with a meager salary to support his family. He had now developed a hatred for living. His cursing and raging at his family had become his sense of fulfillment. It was his way of restoring and redeeming his purpose. He was a weak man hiding behind a screaming voice. I had known these personalities before. Poverty and exploitation had left him with no life accomplishments. And now the only redeeming thing that he had pride in was his skin color. Yet, even that was now permanently stained black with coal dust.

His house was owned by the company. The very food that he ate was given to him in credit by the company. He was in a depleting cycle of debt and credit. He was afraid of his bosses and he would not speak out about the injustice that plagued him, but he would come home and beat and curse his children. And he hated his wife who was too sick to comfort him. I had known many men like him my whole life, for the lashing of Mrs. Bradenkins' tongue still haunted my thoughts. I knew he was a coward for he preyed on the weakness of the innocent. Children were his victims, a prey he could manipulate and enslave.

I would have my revenge on Mr. Austerberry, even if it took a whole lifetime to find him. I was determined that his crimes would not go unpunished. I would make him pay for what he did to my sister. I would only be satisfied with his death by my hands.

All of us had been scarred by the separation of our family. I was placed in an orphanage of brutality operated by a vicious woman. Ruth was living with an insane lunatic, and David was thousands of miles away surrounded by disease and despair. I could only imagine him being infected by one of the diseases brought into the mission station. And I did not even know where Sarah was for sure or what horrors she was enduring.

Now as the weeks continued, my leg slowly began to heal. The barren and blackened skin slowly peeled away to reveal new skin, but the mass of scars permanently clung near my knee cap. Through all the inner conflict, Claudette began to pour hope into my being. We continued to talk for hours at a time about life. It was a special time to share dreams and touch the quiet in each other's eyes, even though death was all around us. Voices of pain, hatred, and suffering interrupted our conversations with "Nurse, please come over here and talk to me." Still she came back and rested her thoughts in my awaiting embrace.

All of the men in the compound were attracted to her like nails clinging desperately to a healing magnet; this glow of hope moved through her whole being. There was a way Claudette touched you and talked to you that went down into the very depths of your pain and filled your body with sweetness. She was like summertime and badminton. She did more than put a bandage on a bleeding wound; she was a source of comfort. She had the kind of eyes that would wait quietly, listening to your every word, slowly examining your expression, hearing more than your words, because she would listen to your heart. And when she spoke she added hope and constructive building branches of understanding, sacrificing a piece of her, so that you could stand in the world again. She made many wings for the dying men, letting their thoughts drift and taste the fragrance of home and front yards before death swallowed them up. Claudette was a torch burning away despair and doom. When she was around, you could no longer hear the bomb blasts. The pain in our bodies had a way of silencing itself. She developed a sense of caring: it was her power to transmit a personal love to all those who cried out to her.

I wanted her all to myself; no one else had a right to the peace that covered me so completely for the first time in my life. After the death of Mama and the separation of my sisters and brother, love was a force I had not felt in some time. Every day I began to fall more in love with her, even as I was beginning to learn how to love again. Each time she came near me, my mouth would break into a silly and stupid grin. It felt strange and wonderful to find myself laughing at something Claudette had said, or the way she winked at me as she made her rounds, checking the condition of other men. The smell of her perfume opened up all my pores and filled each one with sunlight, until it was becoming harder to remember the smell of the orphanage or the smell of bullets and smoke and burning bodies. Whenever Claudette came around my bed, I would cover up the nub of my leg. I was ashamed to let her see me like this.

I wished she had known me before when I had both legs, for she would have liked me better when I was truly a man. Now I considered myself more a misfit. I didn't know the exact day when

I first loved her. I knew that I wanted to tell her that I loved her so very much and that I needed her in my life. But I was ashamed and afraid of the way I looked or what she might say. I felt a spiritual connection with her. I could sense her moving like a thousand hands in my heart calming the constant ache. Slowly and methodically, she began sweeping out the hatred in my heart that I still held for Mrs. Bradenkins, the orphanage, and everyone that had hurt me. Yet, I was afraid that somehow, in some way, I would be burned, and I would seek to hate all over again.

The day Claudette came to me and said, as the tears glistened in her eyes and her lips trembled, "I didn't know how to tell you, but I have been transferred to another unit to help with more casualties coming from the front. There is something I want to tell you. I have been afraid to truly get close to you. I am afraid. I will miss you always." She leaned over and kissed me on the forehead, and then she quickly left the room.

Once again the fog came around and voices began to surround my bed, laughing, devilish voices. Voices like Mrs. Bradenkins saying, "You will never have any peace. Do you hear me, boy? Get in the closet. Get in the closet and shut the door." Inside my tears, the fragrance and the light of Claudette rolled down my face.

I was transferred to the Veterans Hospital in Springfield, Missouri, for further therapy. I was put with a group of men who were all crippled and lame, missing some vital body part. We were victims of the war seeking to restore our lost humanity and identity.

Each morning we rose, exercising and strengthening the remaining parts of our bodies. Color again was unimportant. As the morning light stretched over the quiet field, we were reaching out hands towards the skies like some pleading prayers, exercising limbs, hoping to awaken the man who had died when we lost our body parts. Now we were all second-class citizens. We were dead men living in dismembered bodies.

All of the one-legged men were gathered together and were taught how to use their one remaining leg. Everything had to be learned again: how to put our pants on, tie our shoes, and walk up stairs. We were a strange sight hopping across the field like a bunch of deranged rabbits running a race. Every day we had rabbit races, and the winner would get the coveted carrot.

But I didn't care. Everyone in the group was growing stronger, physically and mentally, but I was becoming less involved with the group's activities. I still felt I didn't belong here. We were all in our twenties, yet I felt I was part of an old folks' home. There were rumors that we would be receiving the legs in a few days. "The legs?" I asked one of the men that I shared a room with. "What kind of legs are we going to be given?"

"The artificial legs that we are going to have to learn how to use in a few days," he said.

I yelled at him in anger, "Who wants an artificial leg? That is nothing to be excited about." I didn't want any artificial leg attached to me, because it symbolized that I was something different and inferior. I was quite content to walk around for the rest of my life with my crutches, letting the baggy part of my pant leg flap in the wind. They all waited in anticipation, wondering when we would receive the artificial leg.

The rabbit races were serious affairs. It was a way for us to release the hostility of losing our legs and feeling like we were still men. The hospital scheduled Rabbit Relays and even invited the public to come. There were about forty men, and we were divided into groups of ten with each group competing against the others. Each group trained for a whole week. My group had the fastest hoppers, and everyone knew that we could win the race if we worked together. Everyone was serious about the races except me: I could have cared less whether we won or not. I thought they were a bunch of fools hopping around on one leg. But we were a group and they all decided that we were going to do it together or not at all. I then felt compelled to join them as part of the group.

On the day of the races, everyone was tense. Each group wanted to win the small trophy of the carrot. The whole thing was stupid and silly. But it was something that the men could find meaning in a small measure of renewing their humanity. As the races began, the shouting grew louder as the men cheered on their groups.

The relay races now began. Our group beat everyone but a strong group of all right-legged men who swore they could win the races hands down. We were fortunate to make it to the final three.

The first group we hopped against was all fat and out-of-shape and it really was no challenge. One man, in the next group of hoppers, got sick and had to leave the race. Now everyone was gathered around for the final race, wondering who would carry off the precious trophy. In the first two races, I really didn't have to hop too hard to win. We had to hop a hundred yards around a tree and back and touch the hand of the next hopper. My group had gotten a big early lead when their second hopper tripped and fell. I was the fifth one to take off hopping. I was around the tree and on my way back. Their man had just taken off when I turned and twisted my ankle and fell to the ground with a thud. All my teammates began yelling at me to get up. I just lay there as their hopper got closer and closer. At this point my teammates had surrounded me, screaming at me to get up. I lay there with my face in the dirt, not trying to move as each man passed by me. The last one hopped past me and a loud cry rose up from the group that beat us. My teammates stared at me in silence.

8.

After the rabbit races, everyone left me alone. I represented their worst fear–the fear of being empty and alone. I had accepted myself as inferior. There was no use pretending anymore. I was truly now a second-class citizen and all these motivation tactics meant nothing to me. I felt hideous, stupid, and broken. Who cared about the stupid rabbit race anyway? I said, as I tried to reassure myself for my failure. For the men in my group, what did life have in store for them now? What was the use of trying to achieve anything in life now? I was not going to try to change myself in some dumb race. Perhaps they were trying to train us for life, trying to push us beyond our limitations.

My lack of trying was the symbol of death to all the men. For so many had haunted visions of being in a one-room shack, dying in poverty and loneliness. I represented a vision of their future that they did not want to see. I thought about all the running I had done as a child. The times when I got into a fight with one of the older kids at school. And how I could only get a good lick in and then take off running and laughing. Moving like a flash, leaving the battered kid dazed, trying to catch up with me. Or the times we would be stealing apples in someone's backyard and we would jump out of the tree and run for our lives in mischievous glory with apple juice dripping happily from our mouths. Or the time when I had to run all night after I had escaped from the orphanage. It was the strength of my legs that gave me the power to flee from the injustice of Mrs. Bradenkins. My legs were the symbol of life and survival and youth. Running was the only way I knew how to escape from oppressions. Running was the symbol of youth, a small freedom now lost forever.

The day finally arrived when they brought us the artificial legs, and all the men were excited. They were fitted to each man's specifications and measurements. Everyone listened intently as they instructed us on how to strap the dead corpse to our body. The leg was a cream-colored, hard shell that looked like it was left over from a funeral home. I asked myself, how am I supposed to put a sock and shoe over this thing? Now there were more classes on how to walk–without making the leg look so obvious–and how to bend and pick up objects. I felt retarded as I tried to walk on the leg, and sick to my stomach every time I strapped it on my body.

As a child, I remember visiting my father at the train station and seeing an old Colored man who didn't have any legs, sitting on a box, selling pencils. He cried out as loud as he could: "Pencils for sale. Pencils for sale. Someone, please buy a pencil from me." Everyone ignored him, not wanting even to look at his deformed shape, like some twisted and misshapen form curled up in a corner, pleading for life. And this would also happen to me, I assured myself.

The artificial leg was stiff as a board and heavy to lift. The only movement was at the ankle joint that only moved up and down. Every time I strapped the leg on, I didn't feel human anymore. True, it was a pleasing sight to see the leg filling up the empty part of my pants, but the leg felt unreal and restricting.

We were getting closer to returning to the world. The days of military service were over, and each of us would have to fight a new war, an inner conflict—the struggle to find a sense of purpose and meaning. Each man had to go through a series of maneuvers: picking up objects, bending over, and lifting. It was more therapy and motivation, trying to get us used to our new legs. There was a sense of celebration, for it was like a graduation as we watched each person going through the various routines. There was laughter and joking about this new walking device. It was a nervous laughter, the kind that men make when they are about to enter the unknown.

Then it was my turn to walk and go through the routines. When I came into the room, the loud celebration slowly quieted. I had made no friends among them. They all detested me ever since the day of the races; I was an outcast among them. I hated them because they were not dealing with reality. They believed that just through determination they could conquer any problem or overcome the emptiness of their legs. To me, their futures were bleak. Some would be living off small military pensions for the rest of their lives. Employment would be hard to find for men with one leg. They would all learn what discrimination was all about. As I began to go through my maneuvers, everyone fixed their eyes on me. I became nervous having the group staring at me in hatred. As I climbed up a small flight of stairs, I missed one step near the top and came crashing down in a bouncing motion on my bottom. Everyone in the group broke out in thunderous laughter.

I did look comical bouncing down the stairs, but now my weeks of anger found a cause to explode. "You're all a bunch of sick fools, thinking you have a life left. You got nothing left…but this ugly leg," I shouted. I unhooked the straps of the leg and beat it against the floor with tears streaming down my face, crying out, "You have nothing but a fake leg. I wish I had a hacksaw. I would cut up all of your stupid, wooden legs and start a campfire and roast some marshmallows. I've had enough of this therapy. I've had enough of this stupid, fake leg. And I've had enough of all of you."

I quickly stormed out of the room in a hopping motion. One of the therapy nurses shouted at me in a concerned, motherly tone: "Young man, you come back here right now and get in line. You're out of formation. If you don't come back this minute, I will have to report you."

I didn't care what happened to me now. I began spending the rest of my time in bed. To avoid humiliating myself in the therapy classes, I used every ailment I could think of to report in as sick for four weeks. My room was my tomb of self-pity. I learned that self-pity was a satisfying, soothing pacifier. In desperation, I held on to my pacifier, believing its hollow promise could liberate my shackled soul. I stayed away from the therapy and all the men in my group.

I spent my days in an endless routine of self-hatred. I didn't have the desire to dress myself or comb my hair. All these efforts were too exhausting for me now. I walked around in my bathrobe, complaining to all the nurses about how unjustly I had been treated. With curtain drawn and blinds shut, I peered every once in a while at the men out on the exercise field as they went through their daily therapy drills. I hated them for having the will and desire to try and improve their condition. I hated them because they were not afraid of failure.

The Allied troops were making great progress. Along with the Russians, they were now converging on Berlin, and the surrender of the Nazis was imminent. I was becoming an emotional wreck. I was constantly complaining and arguing with the nurses and the medical staff, talking about all my illnesses and their lack of medical attention. As the days turned into weeks, I became a wearisome, irritating nuisance to everyone.

Often I sat thinking about Ruth and her foster parents. Her pleas for help haunted my mind, and then I could not even sleep through the night.

Then one day, for a brief instant, I thought I saw a familiar form moving up the hallway, checking on the patients in each room. It could not be possible. But the soft stride of her walk and the thick, black hair laying flat against her neck bore a striking resemblance to

Claudette. In an unsure voice, I cried out to the distant figure down the hall: "Claudette, is it you?" There was no response. Perhaps, it was not her. I yelled so loudly that everyone in the corridor was staring at me in alarming wonder.

And there, staring at me with those "big, old, homey eyes" was Claudette. As her lips parted into a large, summertime smile, she exclaimed, "My God! What are you doing here?"

I burst out into a little laugh, and then a beaming smile erupted over my troubled face. A brief silence interrupted our first words to each other as we examined each other's face and touched the quiet that surrounded our beings. In my excitement, I stumbled for words. "I was transferred here for therapy."

She stared at me in wonder and shock, saying, "I thought I would never see you again. When I was assigned to a medical unit closer to the front, I tried to erase the feelings I had for you." She stopped and stared at me again. "You look like a wreck! What happened to you? Are you the Joseph that all the nurses hate? The one who is a troublesome nuisance? How did you get like this?"

I looked at her in stark betrayal. She was the only person I thought might possibly understand me and sympathize with my cause. I wanted her to be on my side and go to the nurses, saying, "Leave him alone. You just don't understand him." Now I pleaded with her. "Can't you see? I only have one leg. My life is ruined. I have already been through a lot. My mother died when I was just a kid, and I had the responsibility of trying to keep my brother and sisters together. And I couldn't do it; I just let everything fall apart. Now, they have been distributed across the country and I may never see them again. I can't live anymore in this world. I have nothing left to give. Do you hear me? I have nothing left!" My voice was weak and frail, beseeching her to fall down at my throne of self-pity.

She looked at me angrily. I could hardly bare to speak as my lips trembled in fear. "What's wrong, Claudette?"

As she stood silently, her thoughts pierced through me, wringing out my soul. Her eyes began to see beyond the physical walls that surrounded us and to another landscape as if ignoring my words and pleas. Slowly she spoke. "When I was near the front, there were hundreds of men whose body parts were torn away. We worked sometimes for eighteen-hour stretches with hardly any rest. So many young men had to face the agony of death as I watched them slip away. They were brave men. Not brave because they had been wounded in combat, but because they stood before the wings of death and did not flinch, but faced it courageously. Nothing more could be done. Some of them were no older than twenty. None of them cried or pleaded for life: they were strong men, who faced the unknown with the knowledge that they had tried to help change an unjust situation. I held many in my arms before their final breath was pulled out of their bodies. I wondered how I was able to go on day after day as men without limbs were brought in for surgery. And for most of them, surgery would do little good. But it was their capacity to have the strength to die that gave me the power to do what I could for the living. I realized that each day is a miracle and nothing is to be taken for granted.

"Joseph, you are acting like a spoiled brat. How dare you say to me that you can't live anymore in this world! You should be ashamed of the way you're talking. I am surprised you didn't learn anything when your leg was blown away."

In a high-pitched shrill of self-pity, I uttered, "I need somebody on my side. Of all the people in the world, I thought you might understand me. But you are just like everybody else. Claudette, how could you turn on me? How could you?"

Claudette's eyes began watering and softening as she continued. "I met one soldier who only had a torso. He and his buddies were walking around a field after engaging the Nazis all day. It was a bloody battle and both sides had taken heavy casualties. They were successful in driving the Nazis out of the city, and the fighting had temporarily subsided as the Germans regrouped for a final fight. They decided to walk through a flower-covered field. Laughing like kids, they picked brightly colored flowers, seeing who could gather the prettiest ones. They were laughing and chasing around until one of them stepped on a mine that blew him into bits.

"The other two men began crawling on their hands and knees, inching their way through the field. If they had their bayonets they could dig through the earth, but now they had to use their hands to inch their way out. For nearly three hours they tried to crawl through the field making just a little progress, calling out to each other when a mine was found. Then as other explosions shook the earth, another soldier's body fell mangled to the ground.

"After seeing his two buddies die a grisly death he stood crying, unable to move one inch from his position, his body filled with shock and fatigue. Overcome with grief, he sat down looking at the remains of his once laughing friends. The darkness of the night forced him to maintain his solitary position. When morning came, he took a chance in trying to walk out, because he could no longer use his hands that were so sore and bleeding from digging. Then he also stepped on a mine, yet he survived the blast. When they brought him to the medical unit, the only thing left was his torso; his arms and legs were nowhere to be found. They brought in just a lump of a body, yet he was shouting with the loudest voice he could that he was going to live no matter what it took. That he was going to live…for his friends that could not. All he has left is a burned torso and he is fighting to live each day."

Now, I made my last pathetic plea. My words sounded unconvincing even to my ears as I cried in frantic urgency. "I thought you liked me, Claudette. I thought you would be on my side. Claudette, I thought you cared. I've been through a lot."

Claudette's voice rose like the piercing quickness of an archer's arrow flying into a sliver of light. Her words were like beating window shutters trying to keep out the coming storm. Like a sparrow fluttering its soft wings against the door of my heart, her sculptured body began to tremble as her words raced across her lips. "Let me tell you something, Mr. Be-sorry-for-me. There was a reason why my mother tried so hard to have me marry the Johnson's son. For years my father tried to abuse me. I was the youngest of four girls in our family. One night when I was twelve years old, I found my father on top of me, but I was able to throw him off. You see this was a tradition in our family: all of my sisters had been raped by him and two of them became pregnant. One had a miscarriage and the baby died. My other sister had her baby by him and the baby was deformed and retarded. The baby lived on the farm until it died at the age of three. All of my sisters left the farm and were married to boys around the area at a very young age just to get away from him.

"I remember the night he attacked me again when I was sixteen. I scratched his face so hard that I blinded him in one eye. But it did not stop him. As my body continued to grow and develop, his attacks became more frequent. But year after year, I was getting stronger in my fighting ability.

I pleaded with my mother for help, but she simply ignored the whole situation. She began to act like it did not exist and then to blame me for not getting married and moving away. Not once did she approach my father for the vile things that he did to all of us. She told the neighbors all her girls were loose, and they were having babies with all the boys in town. At church she said a cat had scratched her husband's face and they had to destroy it. She gave her life for that no good man, having his dinners on time every night, never questioning his way of life or the things he did. She was just as sick as he was. He was a little man on a beat-up farm, treating everybody as his servants rather than his family. And my mother was sick with the idea that nothing would blemish their marriage. There would be no public scandal about her family. Nothing would stop her from staying the sweet little wife trapped in a pleasant hell. My mother began to believe her own lies until her world of lies became more real to her than the world of reality.

"You see, Joseph, I once lived through my own kind of hell. I was able to push him away for years. Eventually his good eye started to become blind until one day he could not see. My scholarship was my ticket out of this nightmare. But for my mother, my scholarship was not enough; she wanted me married, not just going away to some school. She was afraid that I might have to return home. My mother is now a slave running to the cries of a lunatic. My father is completely blind, yet he yells more now than he did before and my mother fulfills his every need and comfort. All of the children are grown and none of us ever want to go back and visit them. Even my two brothers disappeared at an early age to seek new horizons. We're scarred for life because of our parents' sickness, and we feel a sense of security not having to see them again. For in our isolation there is a peace and safety.

"So, Joseph, don't you tell me you're the only person that has lost a family. I lost my family also. Don't you tell me you can't live. Each day I'm living. You are not the only one that had to get up from the scrap pile of life. So if you think I'm going to pat you on your big head and say don't nobody understand my poor baby, you better think again. You better grow up and grow up fast. There's a world out there that will push you down faster than you can climb back up. It's about time you grew up."

Claudette's body was trembling, her hands were shaking, and tears were running from her eyes in luminous streams. I stared at her with mouth wide open, gawking like an ostrich, startled and lost. In the troubled, dank dungeons of my heart the darkness broke into pieces and I spit chunks of foolishness out of my soul, saying quickly, "Claudette, I didn't know. Please, forgive me."

"I am living. Everyday I have learned to live a little more. I have lived through my pain and sorrow too," Claudette angrily responded.

Words now were useless. I found my fingers pleading for the companionship of the angel I once knew. I held on to her, believing that she could heal my insecurity. Her body was quivering and trembling and her heart was beating rapidly. Her breathing became soft and heavy, and I heard her whispering to me, "I love you, Joseph. Hold me, please. Don't let me go."

As the days continued, Claudette was by my side once again and everything was right with the world. Slowly she began to rebuild the fallen blocks of my soul until I could break through this ceiling of clouds and see the miracle of living again. I finally returned to the group with renewed self-confidence and an unshakable determination.

The day I arrived to complete my therapy training, the whole class was standing with rabbit ears on their heads and waiting for me. I had resolved that I would tell them I was sorry for acting like an ignorant fool, but seeing them wearing rabbit ears, I broke out laughing at the ridiculous sight. One of them spoke in a very dignified voice, "We, the Brethren of the Rabbit Society, hereby give the Sacred Rabbit Ears to our Brother who has triumphed over obscenities and adversities. May he hop with dignity every day of his life."

Then one of them stepped forward and fitted the ears on my head. As everyone burst out laughing, Claudette came in the room with rabbit ears on her head too, carrying a cake inscribed with "Welcome Back."

They had forgiven me for the way I treated them. Now as I stood looking at them, I knew that love can change the most stubborn hearts.

9.

The wheels of the war machines had left twisted and mechanical shapes on bleak, grassy hills. A thousand caskets waited ever so patiently for the last group of soldiers to be fitted in them and buried so perfectly in neat little rows. It was all ending quickly now–this hell that the world had lived through over the past years. It was ending in a bunker in Germany. The dreams of a madman, who committed suicide, put an end to a terrible vision.

The war was ending as if God had commanded death to stand still and gather no more lives and as a weary humanity searched for lost loved ones whose memories lingered on. Mothers from every station of life walked through the deafening blackness of death trying to feel a moving pulse of life, asking the inevitable questions: "Have you seen my son? Is he all right?"

Cottonwood trees filled the days with soft, white puffs and tulips shot their colorful heads from the black nourishing earth, which always becomes greener with the sacrifice of bodies to feed its hunger. And once more women become pregnant and babies sleep in their arms under cool shade trees. As they grow, they play with toys that were left by their fathers.

A quietness hummed over the earth as a cool, spring wind filled an afternoon with shade and patches of sunlight. It was the kind of sunlight that starts out dim in the shadows and slowly illuminates everything in dazzling brilliance. The church was quiet and still as everyone stood up when Claudette walked slowly toward me. Her beaming smile was like a clean, transparent window that reflected the joy of God.

We were married in a small baptist church in a rural area. The wedding was simple and quiet. Claudette asked a kindhearted preacher, who counseled patients and showed so much love and patience to the soldiers at the hospital, to perform our ceremony. One of the nurses she worked with at the hospital was her Maid of Honor. I borrowed a tuxedo from a medical student, who had just graduated and worn it to a graduation dinner. There was no one to give Claudette away. We spotted an old man fishing by a riverbank and asked him to escort her down the aisle. He said he would be honored to participate at such a grand affair. We were surprised that the shabby, old man spoke so eloquently. Claudette wore a simple white gown which she had sewn herself. She looked like a little princess as she walked toward me.

She was the angel that brought me back from the dead and refilled the canister of my soul with peace and contentment. Together, we were a family. We talked about our dreams of having a big family, a white cottage-style house with a sun porch and a backyard swing, and a small garden and an apple tree for shade and fruit in the summer. We both longed for a family life that had been taken away from us as children. We were wounded souls seeking a sense of wholeness and belonging.

Everything was quiet in the world. Thousands of men would lay buried forever in full military dress. Their guns would be collected and stored in museums and their medals would be chewed up with their bodies by the lips of the dust. A new generation would write about the old generation that had passed away. Books would be written about battles that had been fought. And those books would be stored on dusty shelves for children that do not know how to read.

With Claudette as my wife, I was no longer afraid to face the new world. I was ready to challenge this raging overseer called life. After the wedding we rented an upstairs flat from Mrs. Biesely; it was our perfect little love nest. We didn't have a lot of money and she only charged us thirty dollars a month. With the Army pension from my leg and Claudette's income, we barely had enough to cover expenses for our food, clothes, and just the basics.

After the war, everyone was searching for employment. I was fortunate to find work as a janitor at the Continental Missouri Life Insurance Company. It was a growing company that was expanding their markets across the country. I truly felt like I was part of the company, and the salary I was paid was a comfort to us. But as time went on, my co-workers demeaned me to be nothing more than a one-legged, Colored man with a broom and a mop.

Every day I felt hurt and dejected as the young White men my own age walked past me with their briefcases, selling insurance and making deals for the company. Yet I took my job seriously. I mopped and waxed the floors to a brilliant shine. But that was not enough. My supervisor was a fat slob named Joe Washington, who smoked stinking cigars. He hated Coloreds and would fire any of them without so much as flexing a muscle. Even more degrading was his calling all of us George instead of by our names. Many times I asked myself if the reason I lost my leg in that bloody battle was to have this fat overseer blow cigar smoke into my face.

When Mr. Washington approached, all the Black workers ran in fear. He would come waddling down the hall yelling, "Hey, George. You're puttin' too much wax on dat floor." Or he would say something else like, "If ya don't clean them floors better, George, we can always find another of yur kind in the woodwork."

I tried to hide the hatred and animosity I felt for him, but somehow he detected it. Even though my floors were the cleanest and the brightest, he still found fault with my work. Worst of all, he would yell at his workers in front of others.

However, there were ways of getting in the good graces of Joe Washington. Tall Boy, a tall, thin, Black janitor was his favorite worker even though he did the least of all of us. Every time Mr. Washington came around, Tall Boy began growling and barking like a dog, which made him laugh so hard that he forgot everything he was going to say. He kept on telling the rest of us that we should be like Tall Boy. "He's a good George," he used to say.

Tall Boy always wore his pants high with his bony ankles protruding from his beat-up shoes. He had dyed his hair blood red and had a perm in it, so it stood straight and stiff as if he had just stuck his finger in a wall socket. Tall Boy was nothing but an undernourished clown. He talked about all of us, laughing at our appearance and how hard we were working. Then when Mr. Washington came around, he put on an act that would outshine any actor in the movies. I often wondered how a society could allow something as dumb, fat, and stupid as Joe Washington to have such power over the lives of men. I was not satisfied with spending my life listening to Tall Boy jokes and being called George by a man who could not even spell the word.

Tall Boy had mutated to a thing–no longer a human seeking equal treatment and dignity for himself. He had become a ridiculous cartoon figure, something out of the mind of Joe Washington. It was utterly sickening, watching Tall Boy perform before Joe, who was thoroughly entertained by Tall Boy, his personal jester. The only thing that was missing was a costume fitted with bells.

One day as Tall Boy was going through his daily performance, Mr. Washington began laughing so hard that his stomach bounced up and down like a ball. Tall Boy commented to everyone, "Hey, look everyone, Jelly Stomach."

Mr. Washington exploded. "You just watch yur mouth ya stupid nigger."

Tall Boy froze in his tracks. He tried to change the subject quickly, but the hurt in Mr. Washington's face would not let him forget what had happened. For the first time in his life, Tall Boy had to deal with the reality of his insane world. He could not find another joke to replace the shame he had brought his god.

Mr. Washington looked at all of us and said, "I mean he's a simple George. All of you Georges are a lot of talk and no work."

I froze with the mop in my hand. How could he say a thing like that when we would work almost non-stop in the huge office building? We cleaned over forty offices a night, and only had a fifteen-minute dinner break. I refrained from exploding the rage of my heart. I didn't want to lose this job. I didn't want to live in dirt-poor poverty. This job provided all the extras that we needed to survive. We were fixing up the broken-down apartment into a thing of beauty. We painted the walls and hung new curtains. Through determination and love, we transformed a dark apartment that no one wanted into a new home. Mrs. Biesely was so impressed with what we had done that she gave us a five-dollar reduction on the rent. I just didn't want to quit the job–this job that gave me a sense of pride. I never graduated from high school. Claudette was an educated woman, and I didn't want her to be struggling to pay all the bills by herself. I endured the daily humiliation from Mr. Washington and quickly accepted the childish behavior of Tall Boy.

I remember the day I was buffing one of the offices when Mr. Washington came to me, puffing on that cigar, looking like a chimney with black smoke coming out of his nostrils. He reminded me of a medieval dragon as the smoke curled around his nose and came out of his mouth when he talked–like a creature from hell that was permitted to roam upon the earth. He had a heaving, garbled voice that sounded demonic, as if he had swallowed Tall Boy who was crying out for help. Mr. Washington approached me saying, "Ya been a little too lazy lately. And ya need ta move a little more faster with yur work."

I had been working there for over two years and he still did not bother to know my name. I turned around and said, "My name is Joseph."

"That may be a fine and good name somewhere else. But as long as ya work for me, you're a George."

I shut off the buffing machine and repeated, "My name is Joseph."

"You're a smart-aleck George, aren't you?"

I approached him and said, "My Mama put down Joseph on my birth certificate. I don't know who George is."

He flared back, "You're fired, George. Get yur things and get out."

I walked out of the building as the rest of the crew watched. In their silence, I could hear a thunderous roar of applause.

I didn't know how I was going to tell Claudette that I had lost my job. We really needed that job to make ends meet and I ruined it for both of us. Why did I have to open my big mouth? I should have just remained quiet and let that fat pig waddle in his own slop. I didn't want to be a failure for Claudette now that everything was going so right for us. I had just received a raise and was looking forward to buying her a china cabinet that she had always wanted.

When I arrived home, I told Claudette everything–how Mr. Washington refused to address us by our own names and called us George, and occasionally the word "nigger" would slip from his lips. Claudette was upset that I had endured such humiliation for so long without doing something before now. She suggested that I return to work the next day and talk to the personnel officer or explain the situation to the company administrator.

The next day I went to work dressed in my best suit and walked into the personnel office. I politely asked the receptionist to let me see the supervising administrator. She asked if I had an appointment, and I admitted that I didn't have one. When she called his office, he found time in his schedule to speak to me. I slowly walked in the finely trimmed, chestnut-wood-paneled office. As the shining mahogany desk loomed in front of me, a tall, thin man with a warm smile stood up and reached out to shake my hand. "I am Mr. Henderson, the head administrator for Missouri Life. It seems as though we have met before. Oh, yes," he paused to stare at me,

"You are one of the men who finely cleans the floors around here. How may I help you?"

I then explained my story of how Mr. Washington refused to call any of the Black workers by their own name, just calling them George, and how he had occasionally used the word "nigger" in a joking way, or apologized right after he said it, claiming that it had accidentally slipped out. I told him how I was fired because I wanted to be called by my own first name. All the color faded from his face as I talked, then a deeper red color filled his face. He proceeded to pick up the phone and ask his secretary to page Joe Washington.

When Mr. Washington arrived, his face was red and flushed. He was heaving and taking big breaths as if he had run all the way. Mr. Henderson did not waste any time. He tore into the frightened rabbit, trembling before his presence. He spoke with the voice of authority as if life and death were created in him. "What's this I hear that you have been calling our Colored workers George, rather than by their own first names? Who in the hell told you to do such a stupid thing? How would you like it if somebody called you 'idiot' every time they saw you? If I hear one more incident like this against you, Washington, you are fired. This is a growing company and we will not tolerate anything like this. Furthermore, I believe that you owe Mr. Potter an apology before I let you return to work."

Joe pleaded with an abundance of "Yes, Sirs" and "It won't happen again."

Mr. Henderson interrupted him and said, "What about the apology?"

A deep silence fell upon Mr. Washington. He turned and looked at me with a pitiful stare. He tried to speak and moved his lips but nothing came out. He tried again and still nothing came out of his mouth.

Mr. Henderson interrupted, "Mr. Washington, speak up. We cannot hear you."

And then a weak, childlike voice came out in a trembling voice. Like the voice of a child afraid to go to sleep in a dark room at night, he said, "I'm sorry for the things dat I said. It'll never happen again."

And with that, the meeting was over and we both walked out of the office. A triumphant smile spread across my lips.

The next day I returned to work. Mr. Washington never raised his voice to any of us again. He called us by our own first names and even complimented us on our work. I sensed a fear every time he came around me. Even Tall Boy could not make him laugh anymore. Tall Boy was now useless to Joe Washington, and eventually he was fired by another supervisor who evaluated his work performance. Now as I mopped, a new dignity erupted within me. I truly was somebody.

I now realized that I could change the situation and help alleviate a little of the world's evil, if I would only use the power to act. I did not have to sit idle and fall into the deceiving winds of change. This determined spirit was always within me even when I was in the cruel hands of the state people: I would not succumb to being a submissive pawn. Even at this job I was destined to be a fighter, and I would not allow an ignorant fool such as Joe Washington to control my life and corrupt my soul.

We now received a thirty-minute lunch break, not just a quick fifteen minutes. I viewed my fellow workers with respect and dignity, which they showed as well. We were no longer just Georges working in degrading silence. Even the supervisors realized we were men and treated us with respect.

Yet I was not content spending the rest of my life mopping floors and having men like Joe Washington evaluate me. Realizing that everyone can make a difference, however small or great that might be, I enrolled in reading and writing courses at night school. Books now became my constant companion. On my breaks at work I would read my assignments. I was determined to rise from the depths of a mop bucket. Eventually I earned enough credits to get my high school equivalency certificate.

I remember when I walked in front of the small class to receive my certificate. I could hardly believe that I had accomplished something in my life, that I was not some orphaned misfit who would spend his life in a janitor closet. When you have always been told you are nothing, you reach a point where you start to believe it yourself. Many of my fellow workers had believed the lie about themselves and that their future and destiny really did not amount to anything. When I lost my leg, I let self-pity build a room of inferiority in my life. The janitor closet would have been a good place to hide for the rest of my life, peeking around the corners, hiding from the Joe Washingtons and not knowing the power of determination that flowed within me. Determination has to be learned; from early childhood, someone has to assure you that you are special and important. Mrs. Bradenkins destroyed children's minds. I wonder how many of the children who left that orphanage ended up in prison or were killed by the violence that was inflicted on them. Somehow I was saved from the destructive forces that surrounded me. I could have easily killed Mrs. Bradenkins that day with the knife. And I could have spent the rest of my life in prison being further diminished and twisted by evil hands.

After graduating from night school, I attended a community college to study business and marketing. The whole world was slowly changing. Black men were no longer afraid. Neither police dogs nor fire hoses could stop the civil rights workers who were demanding integration. A whole generation was being forced to change.

Word spread that I was going to college, and some of the workers would not talk to me anymore. They thought that I was becoming uppity and considered myself better than many of them. Fear causes people to believe so many misconceptions. I read and pushed myself to the limit. I kept a dictionary with me at all times, constantly looking up words and reading the meaning and definitions to myself.

One day on my break, another janitor told me, "Man, you really think that you are something, always reading the dictionary. Let me tell you something, just because they don't call you George anymore, don't think that you are nothing but a nigger. And don't you ever forget it. This broom and mop is going to be with you for a long time. So you don't have to be acting like no big shot around here, 'cause you are just the same as we are, a janitor, and that will never change."

Hearing him say that caused a cold chill to shoot up my back and a deadness to descend to my feet. He sounded just like me when I had lost my leg and told all the men in my class that they would become nothing. However, we truly do have the power to change our world for the better.

When I was in the eighth grade, I had to drop out of school to take care of my mother. Now I had gained an appreciation for learning and made the Dean's List in college. Only two more years and I would receive my degree in business. All of the cleaning crew was excited about my going to college. They, too, had been beaten down mentally but watched me slowly improve myself. Those who whispered against me were motivated by fear. Change is always a frightening, upsetting, disturbing experience, and to change the thinking of the oppressed is always difficult.

Many nights Claudette helped me with my assignments until we would fall asleep in each others' arms on our old worn sofa. Outwardly everything within me was reaching skyward. Slowly, I began changing, tearing down the walls of poverty and humiliation. But the voices of the past would not leave me alone.

A deep void began to consume my thoughts again. Sometimes while working or studying, tears would stream down my face. The pain of the past began to speak to me daily, asking for relief. It had been ten years since I first read David's letter. He would be about twenty-two years old now, perhaps studying medicine. Can you imagine that? I used to say to myself, my brother is going to be a doctor. I wondered how he survived in India and prayed that he would not fall victim to some foreign disease or that he was not killed in a storm at sea.

Ruth had to be about twenty-three years old, a grown woman. Perhaps she was married and had a large family of her own. How I wished that I could see her again. We would not even know each other–I was but a skinny kid with a big head who had a smart mouth, and she was nothing more than a tomboy with a head full of pigtails.

Sarah would be about eighteen years old now. I prayed that she grew up in a loving home wherever that might be. I had written dozens of letters to the state home in Sioux Falls, South Dakota, and they kept saying that no such person had ever lived there.

All the writing that I was doing was in vain. I told Claudette that I wanted to go back to the orphanage and talk to Betty Van Horn and ask why she had not responded to all my letters. Each morning an inner voice woke me up telling me to go back to the orphanage. Claudette heard me speaking to this voice in my sleep, saying, "Yes, I will return to the orphanage." She was quite sympathetic and agreed that I could use our small savings to travel to Fayville, Kansas, and visit the orphanage. Something there was beckoning me, something I needed to know. I now felt that searching for my family was a spiritual mission and was no longer directed by my own power.

The day finally arrived when I bought a ticket to Fayville, Kansas. The bus ride was a strange and wonderful experience. I felt like I was going back in time, to a period of my life that I had pushed aside and tried to forget. But with the passing of each mile, it was all slowly coming back as my heart began to beat faster and harder.

When I arrived in Fayville, all the same shops were there but they appeared much smaller. The town looked as though it had been put together with Legos. Many of the older people I remembered had long since died, and their children were now adults. The orphanage was only about one mile from the city so I decided to walk there.

While walking along, I met an old lady working in her yard. She paused, looked at me, and said, "I remember you. You were one of the children that lived in the orphanage. I used to chase you and the rest of the kids away from eating all the apricots off my tree. What are you doing back here?"

"Well, Ma'am, I wanted to visit once more the orphanage where I grew up and remember something of my past."

She looked at me for a long moment in silence. "You don't know, do you?"

"Know what?" I asked.

"The orphanage burned down ten years ago. One of the housemothers had carelessly tossed a cigarette butt into a closet–she was afraid she would be fired if she were caught smoking. It was one of the worst fires that ever happened around here. Seven children were killed and two of the housemothers."

"What?" I exclaimed in a loud, startled manner. Then what about the voices that woke me at night? "Are you sure this happened? It can't be."

In a quiet and sorrowful voice, she said, "It's all gone now; only a shell remains. I am so sorry to disappoint you."

Now I felt like a fool coming this far only to learn that the orphanage had burned down ten years ago. I used our savings to come back here for nothing. I wanted to turn around and board the bus for home; yet, I wanted to at least look at the old building, even if it was only a shell.

I thought to myself, I must be awfully stupid, listening to some voice and walking down a dirt road in the middle of nowhere. I was surrounded by the fresh green leaves of summer corn standing in neat little rows. As I journeyed in the quiet and almost sacred air, I looked at the old oak trees whose branches were twisted in sanctioned shapes showing me the way. Then I saw the old orphanage. A cold chill moved down my back, turning my feet into sweating pools of fear, and causing my fingers to tremble.

It looked so different now. The red bricks were covered with blackened soot, and every window was broken out. The roof had a big hole in it and leaned to one side. Large flocks of pigeons, some gray and white, made their home in the roof. As they flew out of the roof's hole, it looked as if the fire had engulfed the whole building, leaving only blackened walls covered with ash. A large sign stood before the porch that read, "This building is condemned as ordered by the state. Entrance is forbidden. It is dangerous and unsafe."

10.

Having come so far, I could not turn back now. This shell of a building stood like a barren ghost calling to me. So many unpleasant memories hung within its deep dark walls. So many tears had soaked through the wooden floors and even deeper into the very depths of hell, creating a huge black pit through which many lives had fallen.

When I walked near the front of the building, I saw two children throwing rocks at the broken windows. My sudden appearance in this isolated field caused a disturbing panic that filled their hearts with a need to escape. A tinkling sound of broken glass filled the air as one of the boys got in one last throw before he ran away. Out of a childhood yearning, I picked up a good-sized rock and hurled it at one of the third-floor windows. The rock disappeared into the deep and dark silence of the house. As the faint sound of broken glass made that sweet tinkling noise, I felt a small sense of accomplishment, having knocked out a piece of the window with my first throw.

As the dull thud of the rock fell into the dark window and the depths of the house, pigeons flew out of a hole in the roof, forming sweeping circles in the sky. The old house did not look as frightening as it did when I was a child. As I approached the door, I saw dark and ominous shadows stretching themselves like human figures with grieving faces racing down the corridors. Within the house, I began to look around. The dining hall was still intact and didn't look very different from when I was a child. The wallpaper had fallen off and the smell of charred wood and mildew hung in the air.

Walking from room to room, the voices of the children still pleaded in the cracks and crevices of my mind. I could hear them repeating the daily ritual as we were gathered in large groups before every meal or when we were out in public. "We will be good citizens. We will not steal any food out of the kitchen. We will obey Mrs. Bradenkins with all our hearts and at all times. Mrs. Bradenkins is our nanny and provider, and God put her over us. We are thankful for the Home of the Good Shepherd and those who will some day adopt us." The rigor of the house rules and regulations restricted any kind of freedom.

Everything was quiet now as I walked down the pain-filled corridors, chasing these disturbing shadows in the darkness. I believed that somehow these old burned walls would speak some message to my soul. I touched the walls like an archeologist trying to read some forgotten hieroglyphics in the Victorian mahogany paneling. Most of the walls were blackened with soot and the few pieces of furniture that remained were strewn around the room. I looked down at my hands now covered with black soot.

Then I found Mrs. Bradenkins' old office. Surprisingly, most of the furniture was still intact. Soot and dirt covered every piece of furniture, and the color of the cherry wood desk was no longer recognizable. It was in this room where the housemothers would hold an unfortunate child while Mrs. Bradenkins would beat the child with a large wooden paddle that hung on the side of her desk. Sometimes the beating would last so long that the child's buttocks would bleed and remained bruised for weeks. I wondered how I survived in such a tormenting place. Now all that was left of that world were a few charred pieces of furniture and the memories that lived within me.

Looking down I saw Mrs. Bradenkins paddle on the side of the desk. I held it in my hands, swinging it in the air, listening to the wind moving through the holes that were cut in the paddle. Taking a handkerchief out of my pocket, I brushed off the old, torn, leather chair with the stuffing protruding from it. I sat in the chair, pretending I was Mrs. Bradenkins saying, "Look at me when you talk to me, you little crumb snatcher."

I stopped playing this sickening game with myself, for even the very thought of acting like her caused a sense of fear to surround me. Examining the old desk, I noticed three drawers on one side. I began pulling on one drawer, but it would not open because time and moisture had warped the wood. I pulled and pulled at the drawer until all at once it flew open and folders full of old photographs fell to the floor. Upon inspection, I realized the old, large, black-and-white photographs were of Mrs. Bradenkins when she was young.

I could hardly believe it was Mrs. Bradenkins–it seemed as if the person in the picture must be somebody else. But it was her, and she was actually smiling and holding two children in her arms. There were other photographs of her lying in a seductive pose in the arms of a young man on a checkerboard blanket in a picnic setting. Another picture of her was with him on an archery range with his hands about her little waist. She adoringly looked into his eyes as he apparently explained how she should hold the bow.

Next there was a series of wedding pictures in which she was eating cake and joyfully laughing with friends in dance poses. It must have been a very big wedding, because her dress had the longest train I had ever seen. There were also pictures of bridesmaids, flower girls, and little children carrying the train of her wedding dress.

Still, more photographs depicted two babies with curly blond hair, taking a bath together and splashing water as Mrs. Bradenkins watched smilingly. There seemed to be more than thirty photos of these curly-haired babies being pushed in their strollers, eating birthday cakes together with icing and cake smeared all over their fingers and faces, and dressed in pajamas, playing with Christmas toys. Mrs. Bradenkins had a set of twins when she was young, I whispered to myself; she had such a beautiful family. As I looked at the two little girls dressed up for church with their patent leather shoes and white Easter bonnets, it seemed to me that Mrs. Bradenkins had had a happy life. What could have caused so much hatred to consume her? The woman in the pictures took on a different form–

even the structure of her face was pleasant, not stretched tight with sharply angled bones protruding under the flesh.

Then I saw a newspaper article attached to a sympathy card which read:

A violent rainstorm took the lives of three individuals last night. Twin eight-year-old girls, along with their father, Mr. Bradenkins, drowned after he lost control of his car on the Madison Bridge. The lightning storm was violent and visibility was poor. The 1932 Packard broke through the guardrail and fell thirty feet into the Murry River.

Mr. Walter Jackson was one of the first persons to arrive at the scene of the accident. He had been checking the safety of his livestock when he saw the car veer and then plunge into the river during the height of the storm. He called the local sheriff, and dredgers were enlisted to help, but to no avail. Scuba divers were then called; they secured a chain to the bumper of the car and pulled it out. All three of the victims were still in the vehicle.

The accident occurred about twelve o'clock midnight when the family was returning from a weekend visit with the children's grandparents. Funeral services will be held Saturday, the 12th of June, at 1:00 PM at the Risen Savior Baptist Church. Mr. Bradenkins and daughters, Lorraine and Lucille, leave behind wife and mother, Mrs. Jane Bradenkins of Fayville, who is a public school teacher.

111

I stood looking at the fragment of Mrs. Bradenkins' life in my hands. The sudden loss of her whole family must have caused hatred to manifest itself through her. Years of hating and despising life ate away the gentle smile and sparkling eyes of the woman in the pictures, leaving a haggard and deformed façade. I have witnessed how hatred can disfigure faces and age the best and most beautiful soul.

In her own way of living, she was mad at everything and especially at God for allowing death to seize her precious loved ones. Hatred had caused her to divide and become two women. Perhaps Mrs. Bradenkins hated the orphanage children because the pain of living every day surrounded by children and knowing that her own were dead tormented her too much. If she had only found the compassion to love, how different and better her life would have been. God did not leave her without children. We could have been her extended family, her children, but she rejected our love and continued to live in sorrow and bitterness. She had allowed hatred to become her god and to destroy her mind.

I vowed that day that I would no longer allow sorrow or hatred to consume my life or grieve my soul. As I searched through the drawers, I found the old coal receipts, electric bills and plumbing bills, some paid and some unpaid. Then I discovered another folder filled with children's adoption papers. I could not believe that these precious records had been left behind. It was like finding a treasure chest after all these years. These papers held the secrets of happiness that lay hidden in this dark old house. Maybe one of these pages contained some information about where my family was. I searched frantically through all the names, trying to find records about where my sisters could have gone. I looked over all the pages, but there was nothing about my family.

As I held these pages in my hand, I felt the pain of those who had been separated from brothers and sisters, never knowing where their relatives were. A great void must have consumed their spirit, drilling a hole in their lives. Then after searching and searching there still was nothing. I flung the pages in the air and watched as they drifted down onto the black soot-covered floor. Out of anger, I screamed, God, why am I here?

Then in the far back corner of the drawer, I spotted a large packet. I wondered why I hadn't noticed it before. The notation on the packet read: "Please send this material to Joseph Potter, as he requested it about his family." It was signed by Betty Van Horn. I quickly grabbed it and, like a child with a Christmas package, tore it open. Out fell a series of newspaper articles.

The Tuscaloosa Herald, July 9, 1940

A brutal and unprovoked slaying occurred on Sunday the 9th of July, just shortly after midnight. Mr. Hector Austerberry, a long-time resident of Tuscaloosa Ridge, was savagely slain in an ambush-style killing. He was left for dead by his assailant, Ruth Potter, a Negro orphan girl who was living at the Austerberry home. The girl killed Mr. Austerberry as he took his evening walk in the woods.

Potter had apparently taken a large rock and hit him in the head. The coroner's report said that death occurred at one o'clock in the morning. Mr. Austerberry's body was found by a neighbor's dog about fifty feet from his house.

The County Sheriff organized a search party, and, with their dogs, the brave men hunted for the savage killer in the darkened woods. The violent and crazed woman was hiding in a tree in the orchard area of the property. The dogs had chased her and surrounded her for apprehension. The savage girl, kicking and screaming, was finally bound and gagged and taken to the courthouse jail for arraignment and hearing.

The citizens of the County of Tuscaloosa have been filled with rage and shock at the senseless act which ended Mr. Austerberry's life. It has been reported that the killer has had a history of mental problems. She has been described as a very difficult girl who had lived in a reform school and had escaped from there numerous times before Mr. Austerberry had taken her in.

Ruth Potter had constantly shown disrespect and contempt for the Austerberry family while she lived with them. Mr. Austerberry had kindly opened his door for this unfortunate person and now he has paid the price of death for his act of kindness.

The compassion to help the unfortunate appealed to Mr. Austerberry. It was apparent that his generous act was not accepted by the killer, Ruth Potter. She could not deal with the realities of finding a family so committed to the care for one another.

The hatred of this maniac has left a permanent scar on this community. The sheriff and his deputies had a hard time keeping the search party from taking justice in their own hands. Mr. Austerberry was a fine example of Christian living, a fine and upright citizen of Tuscaloosa Ridge. He will be sorely missed by this community and the many people that loved him.

More newspaper articles lay before me with secrets that beckoned me to read. I didn't want to touch anything in this dirty house of death. Maybe it would have been better not to know what had happened to Ruth. But it was not by accident that I was here now. Surely God had brought me here. This house could have been torn down, and my sister's demise would have remained forgotten in the dust of Fayville. Now I had to be strong to read the other materials.

In huge letters from the <u>Tuscaloosa Herald</u>, issued July 10, 1940, the headline story read:

MOB KILLS NEGRO GIRL AND 14 HURT AS
HOODLUMS STORM THE STREETS

It was shortly after midnight when the mob that had been gathering all day began storming the city jail, demanding that the Negro girl, Potter, be given to them. Potter was arrested yesterday for the brutal slaying of Mr. Hector Austerberry. His body was found in the wooded area near his house with his forehead bashed in. As word spread through town yesterday, the crowd began gathering from early that afternoon.

Some had been drinking alcohol and yelling at the top of their voices, "Give us that nigger girl, and she will not kill anyone else." Many of the men were from the coal mines. Others were local citizens that had come to watch the spectacle. Many residents began coming from nearby towns bringing picnic baskets and spreading out blankets on the courthouse lawn to watch the crowd shout its fury. At one point it took on the atmosphere of a carnival as children played with each other and the shouting and drinking of the crowd continued.

As the crowd swelled to about two thousand, the Sheriff decided to move Potter from her cell to a safer place. She was hysterical with fear, along with many other Negro women and men prisoners in the jail. The crowd continued to grow and surged to the fire department, where they took ladders and began breaking through the windows of the courthouse jail.

Many of the men and women prisoners gathered on the roof with Potter and began screaming as the crowd chanted, "The nigger will burn tonight." Then in a mad rush, the men, drunken with rage and hate, crashed through the windows of the jail and headed for the roof. The other prisoners became so filled with fear that they pleaded with the Sheriff to throw Potter off the roof.

The mob rushed up on the roof. The Sheriff was knocked unconscious, and the deputies threw the Potter woman off the building to the crowd below. Some of the other prisoners fell or jumped off the building, breaking their legs and otherwise sustaining severe injuries.

After the Negro woman, Potter, was delivered into the hands of the mob, they roared loudly, almost like a cheer. Someone shouted, "We have her now." Her body bruised and broken was pulled through the crowd and beaten with fists and clubs. She ran screaming and begging for mercy as her clothes were ripped from her body.

Someone with a shotgun then shot her in the stomach. One of the bullets accidentally hit a bystander watching the activities. He was taken to the local hospital for shotgun pellets in the leg. At this time the Potter woman curled herself up into a tight ball moaning in a barely audible state.

Many of the spectators urged everyone not to kill her so fast. She was then bound to the sides of a wooden fence in the flower garden area of the courthouse lawn. A man came out of the mob with a bucket of tar and yelled, "I been waiting all day, girl, to put this on you." He dumped the hot tar over her screaming face; thick lumps scorched her hair and burned off some of her skin. A torch was made with some of the men's torn shirts. When the fire ignited the body of the Negro woman, she leaped up in the air in a howling screech breaking the fence that bound her. She ran for a short distance before falling into a mass of burning flesh. A foul, sickening smell covered the smoking body of the Negro woman as the crackling sound of wood and flesh filled the air with the presence of death.

The mob was not satisfied with her death and began yelling their intent to seek out other niggers in the town that night. The mob turned into a rioting mass of hoodlums breaking into stores and looting. At this point Mayor William Montgomery attempted to plead with the crowd to stop their violent activities, but it was useless. As he was speaking and trying to restore some order, someone threw a rope around his neck and others began hoisting him up a telephone pole. As he hung dangling in midair, an unidentified soldier, who had been observing, climbed up the pole and proceeded to cut him down.

By morning, fourteen people were injured and four were dead from the night of rioting. The Governor issued a court order to bring Tuscaloosa under Marshal Law if the looting and rioting reoccurred this evening. Never in the history of Tuscaloosa, Virginia, has a night of violence occurred like this.

No, I whispered, this cannot be. She can't be dead. Not like this. Oh, God, why did you allow her to die such a horrible death? Why was she born to die in such a miserable state?" And yet, now, no more would she have to suffer under the cruel hands of a hating world. No more would she be fostered out and passed around like a piece of property. I wanted to scream and fume at the heavens for the agony and suffering of my sister, and yet I wanted to weep in thankfulness that her journey of pain was over.

As I read about my sister's brutal death, it seemed as if the aching that had formed in my heart many years ago had burst through the pores of my skin and an unearthly cry erupted from my mouth. How could they kill an eighteen-year-old girl this way? What kind of power does evil have over the minds of men that cause them to move in one destructive group? Anger filled every molecule and cell in my being with hatred. For a moment, I wished I were God, so I would have my revenge over those beings. I would blind all of them in that mob that moved so self-assuredly. I would strike them all in one moment of darkness like Sodom and Gomorrah. Then I would allow stakes to emerge from the ground and they would stumble through them. I would repay each one of them with a plague or sickness that would slowly destroy them. Perhaps I would give each a rare disease that would make pieces of their bodies decay and fall off. But that would be too merciful. I would allow a tornado or a thunderstorm to destroy everything that they owned in one powerful blast. If I were God, I would make people pay for what they had done here on this earth. There would be no waiting process. There would be no layaway sentencing.

As my thoughts began to pierce the heavens, moving over the cornfields and sunlit fields of September quiet, I prayed, Oh, God, make them feel some sense of remorse for what they have done. When there is no one around, when there is no mob cheering their ignorant anger on, when there is no whiskey bottle dominating their actions, when they are alone and the shadows of the evening begin to rest upon their hearts, let a sudden pain fill them with tremendous sorrow. Let the death cry of my sister haunt them in their Sunday school classes or when they are walking with their children along shores of quiet lakes. Let the screams of my sister, as scorching fire burned her flesh, eternally destroy any quiet time that they might seek.

Yet, I would watch those foul creatures that call themselves men return into their world of formality and dignity. And they will wash the blood of my sister from their hands with the white soap of social respectability. They will hide behind their clip-on ties and clean white shirts. They will slink into their world of community service and respectable dignity while the bones of my sister remain smoldering on their streets.

Hatred was filling the shell of my being with its sickening poison. I delighted with the taste of hatred in my mouth. I wanted to see them suffer and die in a violent and brutal way as they made my sister die. I knew that hatred was a terrible friend to converse with: it would fill you with satisfaction, but also make your life a corpse of loneliness. I had seen how hatred turned Mrs. Bradenkins from a loving, gentle woman into a destructive weapon, destroying children's minds. And now I drank the deep water of hatred and I prayed that I lived to see some measure of revenge on those who had killed Ruth in such a barbarous way. I had good reason to hate, I reasoned within myself, but everything that I despised in Mrs. Bradenkins, I would now emulate and eventually become.

11.

I stood trembling in cold silence, staring down at the large, typed headlines haunting my being. My search for Ruth had come to a screeching and bitter end. My face was drenched in tears. I had failed miserably; I helped kill Ruth by letting the state people separate us. I had sworn to Mama that I would take care of Ruth, David, and Sarah, and now Ruth was gone forever, not having even so much as a grave to cover her remains. There would be no investigation into who had killed her. No detectives would ask who had dumped the tar on her body, or who set her body on fire? No arrests would be made, no warrants issued. There was only a pile of bones dumped in a hurriedly dug grave in the Negro section of the cemetery and without even a prayer.

Among the newspaper clippings, I found a letter addressed to me. I held this letter from Ruth in my hands and quietly pressed it against my heart. Slowly and carefully I opened the letter and read her last message to me.

Dear Joseph,

I am writing to you because I know somehow you will read this letter someday. God is directing me to write this letter to you. By the time you have read this letter I will have been long dead. I know that hatred will have already filled your heart when you find out what has happened to me.

Last night as I slept, I talked to Mama and we were walking in a beautiful park with goldfish and rivers and mountains of great beauty. Before I woke up she said that she must go tell Jesus, so that a welcoming committee would meet me. I am ready to die, Joseph. I know that it will be soon, maybe this afternoon or tonight.

All day now a large crowd has been forming on the lawn demanding my death. They're so loud that I can hear them very clearly in my basement cell. May God forgive me, Joseph, for taking a human life. I pray that it will not be used against me in the judgment. I killed Mr. Hector Austerberry, my foster father, Sunday night about 12 midnight. You can't believe what I have gone through in the past few days. In some ways, I will be glad when it is over.

It all started on Sunday. Mr. Austerberry had attended church with his family and I was left at home as always cooking the Sunday meal for the family. When they arrived home from church, everything would be ready for them to eat their dinner. I had everything almost prepared. The table was set with the white porcelain plates that Mrs. Austerberry has me use for Sunday, and crystal glasses with the gold rim were also in place, along with the best silverware. I worked very hard preparing everything for I knew that the family would be home soon from the church service.

However, to my surprise, Mr. Austerberry came home an hour early; he left the rest of the family at church. I remember saying, "Excuse me, Sir, but you are back very early from church. Is there anything wrong?"

He just walked into the living room, picking his teeth, and flopped down on the reupholstered leather chair. He replied, "Nothing wrong, girl, nothing at all. I get tired of listening to that jabbering fool putting on his little song and dance every Sunday morning. Besides there is more important things to do on Sunday morning."

Then he got up, knocking down the living room lamp and smashing it on the floor. Not even noticing what had happened, he walked to the kitchen, demanding to know where the glasses were. I noticed the large whiskey bottle in his coat pocket. Fear rushed through me as he walked by me. I was afraid to be alone in the house when he was drinking. He was quick-tempered and it didn't take much for him to fly off the handle at the slightest thing. When he started drinking, a destructive and hideous creature slithered from within this man. Every time he went on his drinking binges, everyone in the house trembled with fear. Mr. Austerberry would sometimes start his drinking on Saturday night and would not stop until late Sunday night.

We woke up one night about three in the morning to a howling voice in the woods. It was Mr. Austerberry. He had set at least three trees on fire and was running in the woods, laughing drunk. Another morning we awakened to find that the family dog Bruno had his throat cut and had been thrown into a row of bushes in the backyard. Everyone suspected Mr. Austerberry had done it during one of his drinking fits. The violent acts he committed when he was drunk made me feel that anything was possible with him. I believed that he could commit murder when he was drunk. So when I saw the whiskey bottle, I knew that the family was in for a long day and night of drunken madness where he could commit any act of violence.

When he walked by me, the smell of whiskey had a sour aroma. It was only ten in the morning and his legs were already wobbling. As he went into the kitchen, he started screaming that I had hidden the glasses from him. Out of anger, he reached for the pot of chicken dumplings on the stove and threw it, splattering across the walls and cabinets. I dashed to the kitchen and found him a glass. He staggered back into the living room and sat on the chair and spoke to me while pouring whiskey into his glass, spilling most of it on the floor. Suddenly the glass went flying against the wall, shattering in a thousand pieces. He stared at me with eyes glassy and red and with saliva dripping out of his mouth.

Then he charged at me, knocking down the china cabinet and breaking the coffee table in two and yelling it was about time he broke me in. As he threw me on the floor and started to unbutton his pants, he pinned my arms down with his knees. I scratched and hit him but it was to no avail. His body was too heavy for me to push off.

Just then Mirch burst into the room and ran to him, knocking him off of me. He tackled his father and they started fighting and rolling on the floor. All the dishes and silver and glasses crashed to the floor and around the room. When Mirch hit his father in the mouth, he fell into a chair and said that he didn't want to fight anymore.

Mirch is the oldest of the sons and is near the age of nineteen. He shouted at his father, saying, "Everybody knew you was drunk today at church. Everybody in the whole church could smell the liquor on your breath. Why did you even go to church today and embarrass Mama and the rest of us? When I saw you leave in the middle of the service, I knew you were heading home to try to attack Ruth. You are nothing but a miserable dog."

Mirch tried to apologize for his father's actions. He said that as long as he was there he would do his best to protect me. I never did understand how Mr. Austerberry could have such fine sons. None of them emulated their father's destructive ways.

127

We all knew that when Mr. Austerberry started drinking early in the day that it would not end until he would pass out somewhere consumed with his drunken madness. Uneasiness filled the house that night as we all went to bed. We knew he was outside drinking and anything was possible during times like these when he lurked around in the woods. But tonight there was no familiar laughter or any demonic howling in the woods. We thought that perhaps he had passed out already from the whiskey and we had nothing to worry about.

It was about 11:30 that night when I was awakened by a deep hissing voice. When I opened my eyes, Mr. Austerberry stood over me with a knife pointed at my throat. He said if I made any sound that I was a dead girl. My room was a small shed in the back of the house, and even if I cried out now, none of the family could hear me. He made me slowly lead him into the woods away from the house. Then he looked at me and said, "You think you got away from me, don't you, girl? You will never get away from me." Then as he started grabbing at me, trying to kiss me on my neck, tearing open my nightgown, the odor of his body and the reeking of the whiskey made me start to cough and spit up, which also caused him to loosen his grip on me and gave me the opportunity to run.

As I ran through the dark woods, the sound of his howling pierced the air. I ran as fast as I could, but he tracked me from a slight distance. I could see the flickering of the knife in his hand as he chased after me. That's when I saw a large, curved rock by a small pond. I picked it up and threw it with all my might. As the rock landed on his head, I heard a cracking noise and knew that the rock had broken his skull. Then he fell forwards, hitting the ground with a resounding thud and died. Before I realized what was happening, there was a group of men and dogs chasing me through the woods. I tried to tell them that it was an act of self-defense, but they would not believe me. Nobody here will listen to me.

The Austerberry children came down to speak with the Sheriff about their father and how he had tried before to attack me. But the Sheriff would not listen to them. He told them that they should be ashamed for speaking about their father in such an evil manner. And he said they should keep their mouths shut about anything Mr. Austerberry could have done, for the mob that was forming around the jail could possibly hurt them for speaking in such a negative manner.

All the other Colored prisoners are crying and asking to be released. I have decided that if they do break into the jail, I will offer myself up to the mob, hoping they will not attack any of the other colored prisoners.

In the event of my death, I do not want you to feel as if I have been cheated by life. I do not feel cheated, because everything happens for a reason and a purpose. I will never forget the love and the compassion the Austerberry children have shown me. We have played and laughed together. And in some small way, I believe that I have taught them that love is not determined by the color of your skin, that love is a sharing gift. I believe I have taught them that us Colored people are not animals. We are not savages. I believe that love has taught them and me that we are the same. When they left the jail cell today, I knew that I was seeing them for the last time. They were crying so hard and yelling at the Sheriff so loudly, I thought at one time that he was going to put them in handcuffs and arrest them.

I feel as though teaching a small measure of love was my mission for living. I feel like the early Christians waiting to be eaten by the lions. I have been asking God to give me the courage to face death when it comes. I have been praying continually and asking the Lord to forgive me for killing Mr. Austerberry. I have asked Him to meet me on his great throne and forgive me for my sins. If you ever see Sarah or David, tell them that God has a special mission for each of them also.

I now leave you with this gift of living that you may know that death cannot separate us or destroy our love. I now leave you with the power to love, to forgive and to forgive again. I now leave you with a work and a purpose to do. I now leave you all the joys we had as children when we played and laughed together, not questioning the greater purposes of God. I now leave you, Joseph, my brother, only for a little while, for I will be there for you when you need me as you have been there for me in my life when I have needed you.

Love, now and forever,

Ruth

My body was shaking as I put the letter down. Even in the presence of sadness, a sense of pride also filled my being, for Ruth had overcome them all. I felt as if history had been made. Perhaps what my sister did made better people out of all the Austerberry children. And maybe they will strive to help communities build together because of Ruth's small acts of love. I had the kind of feeling that you have after the funeral when you gather at the home to talk and celebrate and remember the life that was. I will remember you, Ruth, I said to myself. And many more will too.

Then I looked down and saw another article. This one appeared very unusual and said:

REPORTS OF SUPERNATURAL OCCURRENCES
AFTER POTTER GIRL'S DEATH

It was reported that many strange and supernatural sightings occurred around the city shortly after four o'clock in the morning on the night the Potter girl was killed. An eyewitness account said that when the body of the Potter girl lay in a pile of burning ashes and wood, there were only a few groups of men gathered around the site. The fire, it is said, intensified almost into brilliance. Then the light shot up into the sky and broke into a shattering array. The lights could be seen as far as Crescent City, fifty miles away. At this point many in the small crowd began screaming and running for cover. One man yelled, "The dead nigger girl has come back to haunt us."

Mr. Bedlow Chasey, a 70-year-old truck driver, had cardiac arrest and was hospitalized after seeing the sight. At one point it seemed as though the light had dived down to earth. There were reports in different parts of the county of the lights being seen by various witnesses.

One report came from the farm of Annabell Jesson. At 4:15 AM they were awakened by a light tumbling through their farm as if it had shape and form. Mr. Jesson tried to fire a shot at it but his shotgun jammed. Later that morning he said he was shocked to find that all his chickens had laid multicolored eggs, some of his sheep had turned a shade of blue, and all the apple trees in his orchard had blossomed.

There was a similar happening on the farm of Mr. Jester Hampton. He reported that he didn't see any lights but all his chickens began laying different colored eggs.

When interviewed, he said that he thought it was a sign from the dead that we should try to get along better. To him, the colored eggs represented the color spectrum of humanity.

Brutha Thompson at Oak Creek, who had been paralyzed since she was a teenager, said that when she saw the light she followed it. Then she realized she was walking for the first time in thirty-four years.

Those who had waited until the very end while Ruth Potter's body burned and the light erupted from the dying fire are claiming that one side of their body had been made darker.

It was also reported that Thomas C. Jones, who was lynched five years ago at the age of fourteen for whistling at Pearly Lee Smith, was seen with the Potter girl about 5:30 AM by Pearly's father. Mr. Smith had to be taken to Immanuel Hospital for hysteria trauma after witnessing the young Jones and the Potter girl playing baseball in his pasture just before dawn.

I sat in the old house devastated by what I had read. In those terrifying moments, I had found and lost my sister, even though she had been dead for more than ten years. That was about the time when I had been discharged from the military and started working for Missouri Life Insurance Company. I had waited all these years only to meet her in the stale embrace of death. I began weeping in a quiet and exhausted moan. It seemed in that moment as if all the good that life held was wiped out of me.

The rumbling of thunder exploded and shook the house as the rain began pouring down. A cold, forceful wind was moving through the fields, and the afternoon sunshine was being swallowed by a purple, misty haze, as I looked out of the cracked and broken window. My journey for Ruth was over. I had found my sister.

In just a few more years all that remained of the house would be gone. Only I would hold the scarred memories of this place, as the slow grinding hand of time would consume the Home of the Good Shepherd into scattering fragments of dust. Perhaps city councilmen would debate and argue over condemning the ancient eyesore or testify to the historical value of it. There would be conversations on how the Home should be preserved as a reminder of a time of grandeur and elegance. In time men would assume that the problems of life were not as difficult as in the present. Perhaps women's organizations would meet with tea and cookies and try to save the Home in their commitment to do some good for humanity. But all of it will be of no avail.

The Home would be overgrown with vegetation. The poppy and ragweed and dandelions would become the orphans. Possums and raccoons would play tag in its corridors and perhaps give birth and raise their offspring in far better harmony than the state people tried to do. There would be other voices crying out in the night then. Crickets and beetle bugs would be singing and reciting their pledges of love and faithfulness to each other. There would be no more brutality in the Home. No more children would be locked in closets, praying unceasingly for the light of dawn. And once again the men would come with their mechanical arms pushing down the walls, tearing holes through the roof, and flattening the grand Victorian casket into broken boards and bricks.

My eyes scanned all the newspaper articles that lay with years of embalmed pain, which my fingers slowly examined again. This part of my life was coming to an end. So many coffins have been made today, I said to myself. The rain was now coming to where I sat at Mrs. Bradenkins' old desk. The room was dripping shamefully with leaks from the tattered roof, and it looked as though the room and I were weeping together in one final cry.

The reality of Ruth's death constantly filled my being with the voices of men shouting, "Kill her. Strip her naked. Shoot her." I knew that from this day forward these voices would speak as my voice, and their hatred would fill my eyes with pain.

As I made one more search through the scattered debris of papers and files, I found one more article buried under all the rest. It described a flood that happened five years after Ruth's death. There was a picture of the flood with faded headlines that read:

587 PEOPLE KILLED AS THE TUSCALOOSA DAM BROKE

The Tuscaloosa Herald, 1945.

A great tragedy happened in the City of Tuscaloosa overnight. The Tuscaloosa River overflowed its banks and raged through the town, hurling mass destruction in its path and leaving 587 people dead in the aftermath. The pounding rains that began almost three weeks ago had caused the river to burst the dam and wildly rush through town.

The heavy rainfall had caused leaks in the dam's structure. City and Federal inspectors reassured everyone that there was nothing to worry about. On Friday, the 14th of April, another inspection was made; it was then discovered that a six-foot crevice had broken through the superstructure. At that time it was reported among a few residents that a band of men vainly worked to fill sandbags to protect the town in case the river broke through the dam.

At approximately 11:30 PM the dam burst in two. Most of the town's residents had no warning. Many of them were swept from their beds and buried under the massive flow of water and debris. Homes were lifted from their foundations like matchboxes. Telephone poles were tossed about like toothpicks and broken in half like pencils.

At one point many people hurried to their roofs, trying to escape the surging flow of water. A great number of bodies floated down river and were crushed by the force of the current. Many floated to safety on makeshift rafts and some clung desperately to tree limbs in the sweeping path of the river.

Never in the 153-year history of Tuscaloosa had anything of this magnitude ever devastated the city. It will be many years before the city recovers from this rampaging destroyer.

The citizens of Tuscaloosa need to commend themselves on their cooperative efforts during this great tragedy. There were many stories of men and women who risked life and limb to save others as the flood swept around them. There were reports of a man who dived into the surging current from a high bank to save a drowning woman and her child. Both survived thanks to this courageous individual. Other stories tell of citizens navigating the twisting water and helping to pull families into their small rowboats. Hearty thanks go out to the nameless men and women who pulled bodies from the flood and helped create make-shift mortuaries. Those who worked diligently to help save their neighbors, friends, and loved ones are the true heroes of Tuscaloosa.

I looked at the article and examined the picture showing a group of men, women, and children standing in line to receive food from the Red Cross. Mud covered their faces, and a worn, pitiful expression filled their eyes. Colored and White men stood together in the same line–grateful to be alive.

Attached to one of the articles was a picture of Ruth walking handcuffed to jail amidst an apparently shouting and avenging mob. Her face reflected an unusual calmness. It was the first time I had seen Ruth since childhood. She had matured into a beautiful, young woman, and resembled a younger version of Mama. I was grateful for this photo of Ruth right before her death.

As I looked at the picture, I thought of one Christmas when we waited impatiently for the sunrise. We could hear Mama and Dad wrapping the presents and putting them under the Christmas tree. It seemed as if the morning would never come. We would whisper to ourselves, "I hope Santa Claus remembers what we want." I wanted a Roy Rogers Rifle. Ruth wanted a baby doll with a layette.

I could remember how we crept down the old creaky stairs, peeking into a world of enchantment. Then we heard our father's voice, saying, "You children get back to bed. Santa won't come until you are entirely asleep." And we would laugh and go bouncing back to our beds, waiting for the magical time. Hopefully these memories will never go away.

But I will not let your death despair me. I will not let depression or self-pity make me withdraw into a dejected, bitter man. I will draw from your strength, as you marched proudly into that mob of killers still maintaining your dignity and self-respect. Not once did you get angry at God. I don't know how I would have stood up against the terrible nightmares that you endured. I pray that such a determination of courage as yours would be mine also.

People like you, Ruth, were born for a mission, a purpose, and a destiny. Yes, it is true, the anger that I have for those who killed you is unbearable. I have searched for you for a very long time. I prayed and pleaded with God that he might open the door to where you were. And now after all these years I found you in this old house in a pile of papers.

I have carried you around in my heart for a long time, wondering how you were surviving each day. Now you have found a greater home. Perhaps by your life and your unwillingness to surrender yourself to Mr. Austerberry, no child will be sold like a piece of property and worked into exhaustion. Through your rebellion against this hurting world, maybe a child will be saved from working in coal mines and in dangerous factories just to earn a daily meal. By taking the life of the drunken devil, Austerberry, perhaps a child will never again be placed in a home where alcoholism and brutality reign.

I understand your life's mission now. You were a path-smoother and have cleared a path for other children to walk without fear and torment. Who will remember you, Ruth, now that you are dead? Will the lying and deceiving state people remember you and how they shuffled us like a deck of playing cards? Will they search for you and discover what happened to your life? Will the town of Tuscaloosa, Virginia, remember? Will they build a sculpture to commemorate your courage and your death? Will the city council and the mayor establish a Ruth Potter Day so that they all might remember how evil can corrupt their dignity and importance?

Will anyone remember how fast you could run? Or how good you could hit a baseball? I will remember how you outran Harold Thomas in the third grade track meet. Harold was bragging to everyone how no one could beat him. On the day of the race Harold was left so far behind that he stopped and cried in front of everyone. You were never afraid to climb to the farthest parts of a tree. I will remember your faith in that which was good and your defiance against evil men. To make a smooth path was your destiny.

The sound of the howling wind outside startled me from my mental photograph book and caused a sudden tremor to move through me. It did not sound like an ordinary wind, but it sounded mournful and scared like the voices of dying men. The wind moved upon the land like a wild, caged beast. I could hear tree limbs breaking and smashing against the old house. Large pieces of the roof were blown away by the force of the wind. The old oak trees that arched over the road leading to the Home of the Good Shepherd were blown down and stacked in piles of twisted and broken shapes.

The road was covered with huge, uprooted trees with their long and twisted roots suspended in midair. I had to climb over limbs and branches as I slowly made my way back to Fayville. The storm had changed the landscape, and I was disoriented and had difficulty trying to find my direction. I kept saying to myself, how could such a destructive storm happen without my being aware of its force? Great pools of water were standing in the fields almost resembling small lakes. Was my mind so consumed with grief for my sister's death that I did not realize what was happening outside?

The sound of thunder still rumbled its threatening voice over the still landscape. And dark hanging clouds blew over the atmosphere filling all things with sadness. As I moved closer to the city, the ground was becoming clotted with debris. There were pieces of plywood, barbed wire fence, window frames, mailboxes, broken pieces of chairs, and a thousand other things blown away in the sudden burst of destruction.

Slowly and methodically, I began to get closer to the city, groping through the massive, tangled pieces of nature, raped and left desolate, waiting for the decay of time to wither its proud roots. As I approached the outskirts of the city, I heard a noise that sounded like a great flock of disoriented birds, flying in aimless circles, trying to find their nesting trees.

When I arrived in the city, I found that the sound I had heard in the distance was that of men and women frantically scratching through the thick, mud-covered streets to find their dead loved ones. The whole city was a mess of broken rubble. In the distance one woman dug feverishly in the mud with her bare hands until she pulled a dead baby from the blackened ground. Her voice poured out in a rage that could be heard far above the rest of the clutter of humanity, shouting, "My baby, my baby, my baby."

The storm had wrecked the proud city like a child that took a stick and stirred up an ant's nest. The bodies of men, women, and children stretched across the ground now void and silent of all that was important in their world. The sounds of hammers and saws filled the air. Black and White men dug through the mud with shovels and spades, trying to salvage any resemblance of life. Their faces were covered with mud so thick and a pain so consuming that once again color was no longer an issue. Survival depended on them working together. Barriers of racism and hate had been broken by grief and loss.

The men searched through the mud pulling up a dead body every once in a while as another family's grief exploded in the cool, saturated air. A morgue was set up on the side of the road near an open field. Poor, wealthy, Black and White, mud-covered men all lay dead in solemn unity. Half-clothed children wandered through the debris, crying as they searched for their dead parents. Wild dogs roamed in packs, barking madly, infected with the disease of loneliness.

A Red Cross truck drove into the city, and immediately a line formed as warm blankets and hot food were dispensed. The rain once again began to fall lightly upon this beaten mass of humanity. I saw many men crying as they stood in the food line. It's funny that when men cry, sometimes there is no noise, only a steady stream of tears.

I approached a man in the food line and asked: "Mister, how could a storm like this crush Fayville so fast?"

He looked at me and said, "Fayville? What are you saying? The Tuscaloosa River broke its dam and the river came straight through the city."

I screamed at him saying, "Where is Fayville?

The sound of raindrops upon the tattered roof woke me from my hazy dream. I was breathing hard and my forehead was covered with sweat. Tuscaloosa flood articles lay before me. I had fallen asleep on the pages of the newspaper articles.

I decided it was time I left the orphanage. With one last look at the room that Mrs. Bradenkins used as her office, I gathered up all the newspaper articles and other information about the rest of the children long gone and forgotten. It was then that I noticed a number written on a piece of paper and decided it might be important, so I copied it.

As I stepped outside this time, I realized that my dream was a message for me to realize that we are truly one. Pains and sorrows affect all of us. And through this process of living, eventually we will all need each other.

12.

"Ruth is dead," were the first words that came out of my mouth as I walked into the room. Claudette looked at me with her piercing, comforting eyes and softly spoke, saying, "Oh, my God." Her hands covered her mouth, and her eyes began to scan my silence, trying to find an open space in my wall of sorrow where she could comfort the hurt, afraid that I might destroy my mind.

Claudette was like that. She would stay awake all night if she knew that one of the patients in the hospital was dying. She would seek new ways to help ease the person into death. Like a sponge she would consume another's sorrow. It was not what she said but the force of her presence that fortified your being with hope.

I walked around the small living room, feeling broken and empty inside. My eyes looked blank and glassy, not wanting to cry anymore. When I was in the orphanage, I had cried everything out of me–no more tears for Ruth would fall from my eyes again. I had to learn how to heal the emptiness in my heart that I felt for her.

I showed Claudette all the old letters, newspaper clippings, and files that I had found in the old orphanage. It was like going into a time warp. One file was filled with the names and pictures of over fifty children with their family histories and where the state people had sent them. "Perhaps someone will come looking for information about their lost brothers or sisters also," she said. Claudette did not say too much; for she knew the process of grief would have to slowly dissipate from my soul, and no amount of words could speed the healing.

When she saw the articles about Ruth's death, her breath began to get heavy and her eyes became wet as she softly said, "She was only a teenager. How could they do that to her?" She buried her head in my neck saying, "My poor Joseph. You wanted so badly to talk to her again and to hold her in your arms and believe you could be a family again. But, I am your family. Do you hear me, Joseph? I am your family."

She truly was my family now. I could not imagine going through this pain alone. She was a force that I could bear my sorrow into. She had been with me through the worse tragedies in my life. When my leg was blown off and I hated everything in life, she stood there helping me to redefine my sense of direction. She became my extra leg to help me walk again. And even this great sadness would not deplete me now. I loved Ruth with everything that I had in me, but it was time to let God deliver judgment. I did all that was humanly possible to find my sister. I was grateful to read these scraps of papers and her last letter to me. And I realized that Ruth did not die alone; she had a family. The Austerberry children became her family, and I believed they mourned her death as I would have. Sometimes we must accept the family that God has given us.

As time passed, Claudette and I tried hard to have children. Each time she became pregnant, somehow it resulted in another miscarriage; and with each lost child, Claudette suffered and cried harder. The doctor discovered she had a blood disease that caused her to be anemic and too weak to give birth. Although we wanted children, this also was denied us.

It was becoming so hard for Claudette to hide the pain of losing each child. I prayed that she would not get so depressed that she would start blaming God for her losing our babies. I thought about Mrs. Bradenkins and how the loss of her children resulted in a twisted personality and broken life. But after her regular shift at the hospital, Claudette began volunteering to care for sick babies and nurse them back to health. It was her way of replacing the children that we had lost. I did not pressure her about having children, because we had each other and that was the only thing that mattered.

Eventually we purchased a small two-story house with a beautiful garden in the backyard. There were two small apple trees with a hammock stretched between them and maple trees lined the street on both sides. Our neighbors were happy and almost proud to have two people so dedicated to fixing up an old house. Claudette helped scrape away the old paint, and we both painted the house and repaired the roof. We replaced the worn shutters on the windows and then built a beautiful white fence in front of the house.

Claudette had been nursing at the hospital for about five years, and I had been a maintenance man at the insurance company for about the same time. But my aspirations went beyond just cleaning floors. I would soon graduate from college with a degree in business and had decided to apply for a job selling insurance and adjusting claims for the company.

Joe Washington was part of the generation that helped kill Ruth. For so many years he helped create an atmosphere of fear and intimidation. In Joe Washington's heyday, his presence would cause the biggest, most muscular men to tremble and submit to his vulgar and demeaning slurs; he moved with a free hand, and no one questioned him. In fact, the institution promoted and sanctioned his racism. They encouraged the Joe Washingtons to put the Coloreds in their place. It was a good time to be a Joe Washington.

But now something was going wrong. Everything was slowly beginning to change. Day by day Joe Washington's raging voice was becoming a trembling whisper. In his domain he caused many men to hide in the janitorial closet, afraid they might be fired for any trivial reason. And now in a strange, paradoxical way, ever so slowly, Joe Washington began to hide and retreat into the safety of the closet, hoping that the other administrators would forget about him, hoping that he would not have to speak about the needs and concerns of his department. Now he was the one who was afraid that someone might discover his ignorance and terminate him.

Word spread like wildfire that I had received my business degree and had applied for a position in the company's sales and claims department. On the day of the interview they asked me

different questions in relationship to the job. I assured them that
I would have no problem selling insurance and handling claims.
Mr. Henderson, the personnel administrator, said that he was
impressed by how dedicated I was to my work while steadfastly
pursuing my goals. Also, my business degree would influence their
decision to hire me. They said they would let me know in a few
days.

Each day I waited nervously for a response to come in
the mail. Everyone thought that I was crazy to think that they
would actually hire me. Every day I ran down the street to meet
the mailman. Almost a week later the response finally came from
Mr. Henderson at the Missouri Life Insurance Company. I excitedly
tore open the envelope and nervously read the letter that said, "We
are pleased to inform you that you have been accepted for the sales
and claim adjuster position. We are happy to be a part of your
success and hope that it will continue with us."

I ran back into the house shouting, "I got it! I got it! I got
the job!" I grabbed Claudette, twirled her around in my arms,
and pretended like we were dancing. She shyly protested, saying,
"Joseph, please stop acting like a lunatic," while laughing with me.

In the following weeks, I studied hard and learned about
the different policies and procedures, premiums, rates, and claim
adjustments. I was trained to present the material to prospective
clients. It was exciting and interesting work that gave me a sense of
purpose and meaning. Mopping floors had not given me the same

feeling of satisfaction; for as hard as I worked cleaning and buffing the floors, the next day they would be just as dirty as the day before. Slowly I began to sell policies and adjust claims. I was consumed in my work and dedicated myself to be the best salesman that I could be.

The company also sent me to different parts of the country to settle insurance claims. I truly loved my work. It gave me a great sense of satisfaction to see the relief on people's faces when I gave them the insurance check that would help them rebuild their fallen lives. It was rewarding work, and I felt that in a small way I was helping humanity.

One morning when I went to my office, to my surprise, there staring at me in silent disbelief was Joe Washington. Wearing a new pinstripe suit and patent leather shoes, I looked like I owned the company as I walked past him. He pretended like he was not looking at me, but my whole appearance struck terror in his small, empty heart. As he walked swiftly away, glancing back at me, he almost ran into a wall. He then disappeared into a closet never to be seen again. Three years ago his presence would have caused me to tremble in a cold sweat, but now the great man was scurrying away like a mouse trying to find a dark and lonely hole.

About a week later, I heard some old friends from maintenance laughing and I asked them what was so amusing. They said Joe Washington had a heart attack in the maintenance closet. When one of the men opened the janitorial closet, Joe Washington fell on the floor like an old tree trunk. The thought of seeing Joe Washington falling out of a closet dead amused me also.

I became the top insurance agent at the company. I was determined to never again allow myself to become inferior just to keep a job. Those long and terrible days were over. For the first time in my life, I bought a new Lincoln Continental with reclining seats and a stereo radio. It was the biggest car I had ever seen in my life. It symbolized my success.

I drove the car home and honked the horn so loud that Claudette came running from the backyard around to the front of the house. "Joseph, where did you get that car?" she asked. "Wherever you got it, you better take it back before you damage something on it."

When I told her I had just bought it, she could not believe it. She protested at first insisting we couldn't afford it and that the old Ford was still running just fine. Finally she went for a ride but warned that we should not get too headstrong with material things. Claudette was a careful woman, not wanting to waste anything. But it was time for us to celebrate in a small way–our dreams were becoming a reality.

For many years I believed that I was inferior and could not develop my mind any further, or that I was born for failure and would never rise above a certain level of employment. However, my income rose dramatically until it was greater than Claudette's for the first time since we were married. We gave away all the old furniture and slowly replaced it with finer furnishings, such as, a dining room set, a new china cabinet filled with elegant porcelain dinnerware, and beautiful Oriental rugs for each room. Our home had become truly beautiful.

Yet all of this did not come without a price. My job was very demanding and required out-of-town travel, sometimes for weeks at a time. I was promoted to assistant coordinator of sales and was responsible for influencing companies to purchase our insurance coverage for their workers. Claudette and I spent very little time together and our relationship deteriorated.

Intently focusing on my job provided an escape–a way to bury all my feelings and hide the pain I felt whenever I thought about Ruth and how she had died. I didn't even want to talk about Ruth anymore, or David, or Sarah for that matter. I'd tried my best to find them. To me that family was now dead, and there was no reason to pursue them any longer.

I wanted so very badly to resist succumbing–to cleanse myself of the cold, reeking smell of the orphanage, from the poverty of my life and the hateful, disturbed people who ruled over me; and to escape from the dirt of 1933 and from the old house of my childhood. Absorbed in my work, I tried to transform my whole being into a new person, void of any past, only believing in myself and my ability.

I will never forget the day Claudette came into my study where I was reviewing some research studies for a prospective company and its insurance needs. Like a little girl, she twirled me around, grabbing my arms, and asking, "Do you want to dance?" Accidentally she knocked over a glass of water onto my report.

"Look what you have done!" I exploded. "You've destroyed my whole day's work. Why don't you leave me alone sometimes?"

With tears flowing down her face, she sobbed, "You don't know, do you? You don't even remember what today is. It's our anniversary. I got all dressed up this evening so that you could take me out to dinner and talk to me again like a human being."

Suddenly I noticed that she was wearing a new dress and had carefully applied make-up to her face–she truly looked beautiful. Her hair was curled and fashioned into a different style.

In a sorrowful voice, she continued, "You have not noticed me for months. What kind of marriage do we have? What has happened to you, Joseph? Has your success made you into a madman? You don't care about me or anything else. You don't even talk to me anymore. We are two strangers living in an ivory tower. You eat your dinner and then run away to your study, and I don't ever see you. You don't even ask me how my day went. What am I to you?–only a maid, someone who just cleans the house and cooks your food? I am your wife. Why have you stopped loving me?" She stormed out of the room, sobbing heavily.

Shaken, I reached out to grab her arm and embrace her, but she pulled away, saying, "Don't you touch me, Joseph. Don't ever touch me again!" The hurt in Claudette's voice caused a deep fear to move through me.

"You used to be so kind and considerate, but now you only care about money. You don't even talk about your brother David or your sister Sarah anymore. Nothing matters to you but your career," she continued.

"Claudette, I'm so sorry. Please forgive me," I pleaded. "I don't know what is wrong with me. Everything is moving so fast now."

Sobbing with a heavy breath, Claudette responded: "I'm leaving you for a few days to rethink our relationship. I'm going to stay with Ethel Wilison, one of the nurses on my station. She has a spare room in her apartment and doesn't mind if I move in for a while."

A few years ago her words would have devastated me, but now I truly believed my work could fill all my needs. Perhaps this separation is what we needed. It would give us time to appreciate each other or realize that our relationship had changed and was beyond repair.

A cold, still, invisible wedge separated us. It was the first time in many years that we didn't want to be near each other. It had become increasingly more apparent that my job was the most important thing to me now. Claudette, I felt, did not see the big picture. After all, I was doing all these things for her. She had a small-town mind and now she wanted me to put my success on hold for a while. If she truly loved me, she would see that I was thinking about taking an early retirement; then perhaps I would buy an RV and travel around the country.

I tried to convince myself that she could not handle success and what it took to reach my goal. Nothing could stagnate my thinking now. Why should I allow my past to depress me? I had dedicated most of my life to finding my brother and sisters, and what had it benefited me? It only brought more pain and frustration. There was nothing I could do to bring them back. I just wanted to bask in the joy of my success. How could Claudette be so selfish and take away my happiness?

The next day Claudette moved out of the house. I resumed my normal work routine. During the day I tried to concentrate on my work and to appear before my co-workers as though nothing was wrong. But I was hurting inside.

Suddenly my world had fallen apart. A deep loneliness began to eat through the external layer of my professionalism. I began making small mistakes, and my work became reckless and disoriented. The pain of losing Claudette hurt me deeply. Nothing worked right for me anymore. Sometimes I went to work with an unshaven face and in a wrinkled suit. I was so consumed with wanting her back that I didn't realize I hadn't ironed my clothes. She had always had my suits cleaned and pressed, and now I looked as if I had robbed the Goodwill store. Everyone in my department began to notice the change in my demeanor. I was constantly drinking coffee, thinking that it would calm my nerves and give me some peace of mind. But I only became angrier with everyone around me.

Two weeks had passed and I had not heard from Claudette. Slowly the house was becoming a shamble. Piles of clothes filled the floor and dirty dishes lined the sink. I sat down in a chair and realized how much I needed her in my life. The next day I worked out an elaborate plan to get her back. First I sent two dozen yellow roses to her at the nurse's station where she worked. Then I began writing her love letters every day and sent them to the apartment house where she was staying. They went something like this:

Dear Claudette,

Last night as I walked in the evening air, I thought about how beautiful the stars were as they descended upon the hills. Yet their beauty is a very small thing compared to yours. Until now, I had never realized how much I needed you in my life. All my work is meaningless without you. The house we worked so hard to build means nothing without your presence in each room. If I could only kiss your sweet lips, touch your soft hands, and see you smile again, I would have a perfect life.

Love,

Your husband, Joseph

After four days there still was no word from Claudette. I had just returned home from work, entered the house without even turning on any lights, and was thinking about what I would do without her. Just then the phone ringing broke through the darkness. I ran towards the phone, gasping for air. It was Claudette. She was weeping and saying that she could not take another day living without me. I cried out to her, "Claudette, don't you ever leave me again."

As I reassessed my commitment to my job, I realized that it was not worth losing Claudette. I continued to work to the best of my ability, but I no longer made it my god. We spent many quiet evenings walking around the lake and holding hands like teenagers, understanding the importance of love.

From that moment on I began to appreciate life again. How I related to Claudette and my co-workers became more important to me. I couldn't run from my past or hope that it would disappear; I had to learn to live with it and try to love and appreciate those parts that I could not change. To keep and maintain the love of my family was my mission in life; I could not throw it all away and pretend that David, Ruth, and Sarah did not exist.

That same week I went into my bedroom closet and examined all the photos, newspaper clippings, and letters that I had kept for so many years. I began to mediate about where Sarah and David might be now or what their life might be like. That was when I found the old telephone number that I had copied from inside Mrs. Bradenkins' old desk. I had never called the number and had totally forgotten all about it. After all these years the number probably had been changed. However, I immediately went to the phone and dialed the number.

A young woman answered. "Excuse me," I said. "I don't mean to disturb you but I found this number among some personal items in a condemned orphanage. You see, I have been trying to find my brother and sisters and haven't had any luck."

"Who is this speaking?" she inquired.

"My name is Joseph Potter. I used to live there when I was a boy many years ago."

"I don't know any Joseph Potter," the girl replied. "And I don't have time to talk to strangers right now."

In the background, I heard a weak voice cry out in the distance: "My Joseph. My Joseph Potter."

"Who is that calling my name," I asked.

"It's my grandmother. She is senile and her mind comes and goes."

Then the voice in the background got stronger. "Joseph Potter. Let me speak to him. I be damned to speak to him right now."

Just then there was a crash. "Excuse me a second," said the girl. "My grandmother is trying to get out of bed and has broken a lamp."

"Bring me the phone," said the old woman. There was a brief struggle, and then I heard an old rasping voice. "Joseph, is that you? Joseph, is that you after all these years?"

"Who is this?" I asked.

"It's me, Betty Van Horn," answered the old woman. "Thank God I found you." She began to cry softly over the phone. "I have been looking for you for so long, but I never lost faith that one day you would show up. I had to use what little strength I have in my body to snatch the phone away from my granddaughter who thinks that I can't do anything anymore. I have been praying that you would call or write one day and here you are. There is so much I have to tell you about your brother and sisters.

"After Mrs. Bradenkins died, we found more letters and information about your family. Your brother David had been writing to you for years, yet Mrs. Bradenkins had been hiding all the letters. I'm so sorry to have to tell you that your sister Ruth was killed by a lynch mob in 1940. There was a big newspaper write-up about it in some devil place called Tuscaloosa, Virginia. I heard your sister Sarah became a woman evangelist somewhere in the Midwest. I was planning to send you all the letters that Mrs. Bradenkins had received over the years; but after you got out of the Army, there was no forwarding address. I prayed that you would call one day.

"There was a terrible fire at the orphanage and it burned down. Oh, that was a most awful day. I received third-degree burns on my legs and became crippled after I tried to run back into the burning house to save some of the children. That was almost ten years ago. I was fifty-six then. I gathered up what few things I could salvage from the house and went to live with my sister and her family in Salina, Kansas.

"I hope, dear boy, these things will help you. You have been searching for so long. I must get off the phone now; it is time for me to take my medication, and make sure all the children are safely tucked into their beds. I am responsible for all the children. Tomorrow, will you help me take the children to church? My God! Somebody put out this fire! Please, call the fire department. Please, call the fire department. They are all dying. All my children are dying."

The young woman got back on the phone. "My grandmother's mind comes and goes. Things that happened long ago have affected her mind. She talks about it often."

I said, "Did you hear what she said? She has information about my brother and sisters. Could you please send them right away?"

The young woman replied: "I will look around in her old chest and see if I can find anything that she was talking about and I'll send it to you. This is the most rational conversation that she has had with anyone in many years. You must call again and talk to her. I believe you can help her regain her memory."

I gave my address and phone number to the young woman. As the new excitement swelled up within me, I felt confident that I was drawing closer to finding my family again.

13.

A large, brown envelope arrived in my mailbox. The return address said Salina, Kansas, Miss Missy Winkleton; but it had to be from Betty Van Horn, I surmised. I had been waiting nearly two months for her to send the information she had on David, Ruth, and Sarah. Who would ever have thought that after all these years she would still have this information for me?

I slowly opened the large envelope, remembering the time when Betty wrote to me after I had been wounded in the war and my leg had been blown off. She had sensed even back then that I was on a mission to find my brother and sisters. Of all the children who were in the orphanage, I was the only one left for her to remember and express some token of love to. Perhaps it was her way to repay all the children who had suffered in that orphanage. She had held on to these letters, waiting a lifetime, knowing deep within her spirit that I would come one day. She must have perceived this mission to which God had set my feet.

Perhaps by finding my family I could locate others from the broken homes and heal some of the hearts that the state people and the housemothers had wounded. I slowly walked towards the backyard, laid my sports jacket in the cool shade of the apple tree, climbed into the swaying hammock, and held the envelope against the descending afternoon sunlight. Salina, Kansas, is not too far from here, I thought to myself. I would like to see Betty Van Horn before she dies and thank her for saving these precious letters for me.

I opened the envelope and pulled out the single, typewritten page that was folded around a small group of letters assembled in a neat little row. They were postmarked from India, Africa, Morocco, and Pakistan–they had to be from David. I could not believe that he had been to all of those places. Whoever would think that of the little runny-nosed kid who could not sleep by himself in the dark? I remember him coming into my bed and rubbing his cold feet against mine. And now he had been to places that I could only imagine. There was another letter from David postmarked New York City and a postcard from Sioux Falls, South Dakota, which was in care of Sarah Potter. Finally I had some piece of information about Sarah.

Tears streaked down my face. I quickly wiped them away. As I held the letters, I thought about how I had buried David and Sarah in the same grave with Ruth. I felt ashamed to even hold their letters in my hands. I gave up on them too quickly. I tried to hide from my past and dismiss them from my mind forever, but once again God would not let me forget them. Somehow he would reveal something of their lives to me. Silently I asked God to forgive me. But a voice spoke to me–not so much in words but in its presence– that forgiveness was not needed. That I was a man who had become exhausted while searching for a hidden past.

I slowly opened the page that had been folded neatly around the small pile of letters and read:

Missy Winkleton

1814 Saratoga Street

Salina, Kansas

Dear Mr. Potter:

I hope everything is going well with you. In relation to the discussion that we had on the telephone, I went through my grandmother's things that she brought when she came to live with her sister in Salina. I was able to locate some of the materials that you requested.

I am my grandmother's caretaker. It is a demanding job. Sometimes it's difficult to understand what she is saying, while at other times she carries on meaningful conversations. Often she does not comprehend anything that I tell her.

Searching through her old trunk that she keeps in her closet, I found this envelope with your name on it. It is amazing that she kept these letters for you all these years.

It must have been a terrible fire that destroyed the orphanage, because sometimes I hear Grandmother crying for no apparent reason while sitting in her chair. She still blames herself and is tormented by the fire. Perhaps if you would come one day, you might help release her from this pain that haunts her soul. Her health is fading quickly. I don't think that it will be very long before she leaves this world.

Every time I speak of you, her face lights up and a smile comes to her lips. She begins to say things like, "They couldn't break him. I knew they could not break him. He was too strong for them."

I don't know all that has happened, but I do feel that you need to come and speak to her before she departs this world. She needs to see your face for some reason that I do not understand. People in her condition pretend that they are living what they are talking about at the moment.

So if you are not too busy, it would do her a world of good to see you. If I find anything else in relation to your brother and sisters, I will send them to you. Good luck on your mission.

Sincerely,

Missy Winkleton

for Betty Van Horn

"God bless you, Betty," I whispered to myself. "God will I will come and see you one last time."

I held a letter from David in my hand. It was worth all the gold in the world just to hear something from him again after all these years. I still kept the first letter he wrote to me in a special box in my closet. I opened the letter, which was postmarked Calcutta, India.

Dear Joseph,

I have been writing to you for quite a long time, and hoping that at least one of my letters would have reached you by now. When I wrote to Mrs. Bradenkins at the Home of the Good Shepherd, she assured me that you would receive my letters. She wrote and told me that you had been adopted by a nice minister and his family. The minister is an evangelist, and he spends a great deal of his time traveling across the country, preaching at various churches.

I just pray that wherever you are, you are as happy as I am. I have been truly blessed to have such kind and considerate foster parents. Even though I am Colored, they treat me as though I am their very own flesh-and-blood son.

Traveling with your minister father, I imagine you have seen a great part of the countryside. All of Mrs. Bradenkins' letters have been very kind, and she seems like a very nice lady. She stated that as soon as you come back in town with your foster parents, she would give you the letters.

Yesterday was my fourteenth birthday. Kahlil, the Indian boy, who lives in the jungle with his father who owns a small herd of elephants, came to the mission with his father and some of their elephants. They had them perform all kinds of tricks in honor of my birthday.

My mother, Marian Mitchell, invited Kahlil and about twenty other children from the closest village to come to my birthday party. Kahlil has a cousin who is a fire-eater. It was incredible to watch him swallow fire sticks and swords–like having my own little circus.

Dr. Mitchell's house was filled with sounds of all my friends playing and enjoying birthday cake. Most of the children who were there had been helped at the mission station. Every time their parents would bring them back, I would make a new friend. Many of them have been near death when they came to the mission, but Dr. Mitchell and the other doctors at the station helped to save their lives. Now it seems strange to see so many laughing children in a land filled with so much sorrow and despair.

Everyone was laughing and playing Pin-the-Tail-on-the-Donkey (it was a real donkey, so Mother Marian made a bow that we could place on the donkey's tail) and eating oatmeal cookies that she had made especially for my party, when Tei Tei brought in his present in a large gunnysack. The sack was bigger than Tei Tei, who is a very small boy. (His mother did not have enough milk for him when he was a baby; so his bones didn't develop right, and he is now bowlegged.) Tei Tei laid his present on the floor and a very large python slithered across the floor and wrapped itself around my mother's feet. She let out the loudest scream that you have ever heard and then took off running hysterically into the house. As she ran through the house, she knocked down the large wooden cage of parakeets that was kept in the dining room. The birds started flying all over the house and the children ran around trying to catch them. It was the wildest and most hilarious scene I had ever seen. One of the birds landed in the middle of my cake and became stuck in the icing. It was the best birthday party I ever had.

The medical mission is run by a team of doctors and nurses. Most of them are here out of a desire to do some kind of Christian service work. The mission is financed by individuals and organizations that want to help others, but fewer and fewer donations are received. Rumors and fear of war in Europe have even spread over here. The mission is about ten miles from Calcutta, where a multitude of people live. If the mission were any closer, we could not help anyone; because we can barely handle the great number that come to us on a daily basis. Sometimes I fear that I might die from one of the diseases that have killed so many here.

As I walk along the horizon of this so different land with its sounds and its people, I remember that not long ago we lived in Mama and Daddy's little house. I didn't know then that only a few years later I would meet such people like Tei Tei and Kahlil. I guess there is a reason for all things.

With much love,

David

Dear Joseph,

I don't know how long we will be able to continue to operate the mission: we are running out of medical supplies daily. Dr. Mitchell is becoming more and more frustrated trying to save this multitude. Sometimes it comes down to deciding who will live and who will die, because everyone cannot be helped. There is not enough vaccine to stop the malaria plague that has claimed so many lives. More people from Calcutta are seeking our help.

This morning when we arrived at the mission there were over two thousand people seeking some kind of medical help. When we tried to enter the building, all of the people grappled to touch us. Some thought our bodies had some healing properties that could save them from their sicknesses. In their attempt to touch us a small riot broke out among the people. One group of men began attacking another group of men. I thought for sure we would be killed. One of the doctors came out with his hunting rifle and began firing shots in the air over the crowd until it became somewhat calm again.

Not only does the mission try to cure their sick bodies, but it also gives loaves of bread and powdered milk to them. Dr. Mitchell sometimes works eighteen hours a day. I used to wonder what kind of a man he was. He never really enjoys life–he is always surrounded by the cries of death and suffering. Often he arrives home late in the evening and is so exhausted that he has even fallen asleep at the dinner table. Mother Marian keeps telling him that he needs more rest and he should take a day off, but he doesn't listen to her.

There's nothing more that Dr. Mitchell would like to do than care for the people that come to him. The other night I went into his study and found him asleep with his head lying on one of the medical books. I got Mother Marian and we carried him to bed–he was so exhausted that he did not even know we were there. The next morning he was gone before I had awakened.

Mother Marian also stays busy during the day. Sometimes she receives large boxes from relief organizations, such as, the Salvation Army and the Red Cross, that are filled with clothes and shoes. After sorting and loading them onto a truck, we often go unescorted into Calcutta to distribute the clothes and shoes to the people living on the streets.

Rahsa, a fisherman who lives near the mission, has become our guide and personal bodyguard. He has warned Mother Marian about going into the city without an escort, but she says that she does not have time to worry like a timid old woman. Occasionally Rahsa has followed us on his rusty old bicycle as the old truck sputters and shoots out clouds of dark smoke and we rumble into the city.

One Saturday morning, Mother Marian and I loaded the truck with clothes and drove into the city. We approached different people who had made their homes on the streets, and she began talking to them and giving out new shirts or pairs of shoes or other pieces of clothing. Some of the people didn't even have clothes, only rags, and children lived naked on the streets. As she started to give a pair of shoes to one man, another man pulled out a knife and threatened to slit our throats if we didn't give the shoes to him. Mother Marian tried to tell him that we had more shoes. Out of desperation and not really believing that people would give away shoes, he pushed her, and with the knife still pointed at us, followed us to the truck. We opened the tarp of the truck. When he saw the clothes and shoes, he started grabbing all that he could carry. Suddenly, he realized that if he killed us, he could just take the whole truck. When he started to come after Mother Marian with the knife, Rahsa appeared out of nowhere and hit the man over the head with a tree branch and knocked him out cold. From that day on Mother Marian never went into the city without Rahsa. However, she still laid two pairs of shoes in the man's hands.

The other day Mother Marian packed a picnic lunch. She said we were going on a picnic with Papa Jacob. I thought she had lost her mind, because the doctor was always too busy working to do anything else. Then she told me to get my baseball glove and bat.

When we arrived at the mission the usual grief and sickness met us. Papa Jacob had just finished giving a young girl a malaria vaccine shot. She was laid on a stretcher that her family had carried for twenty miles through the jungle interior to reach the mission. When Papa Jacob first saw us, he seemed happy, until Mother Marian told him that he was going on a picnic today. In his most dignified voice, he politely told her that he was too busy to go anywhere. Then she almost tore his white jacket as she pulled him with her. Outside, the huge crowd of people began crying for help; they surrounded us until the doctor's hands were freed from Mother Marian. She dashed to the truck, got a broom, and began sweeping the people away from Papa Jacob, saying, "It's my time with him. Do you hear me? It is my time. You have had him long enough. It's my time." The crowd was startled, seeing this crazy woman going through the crowd waving a broom. Finally dropping the broom, she held onto the doctor, sobbing in his arms.

Dr. Peterson told Papa Jacob that he would cover his shift so he could go with his family. It was the first time we had done something enjoyable as a family in a long time. The three of us played baseball until the evening sun began to set on the jungle plains and elephants marched home through the silence obscuring all things.

Love,

Your brother, David

Dear Joseph,

Malaria has caused a great disaster in the land. I was in the city with Mother Marian the other day, and I saw one of the most hideous sights ever. An old wooden cart was being pulled by a donkey and in the cart was a pile of bodies stacked one upon another. Two men would stop the cart every so often to gather up dead bodies and heave them onto the cart. Dr. Mitchell explained that the government was trying to stop the spread of malaria and other diseases. Sometimes the bodies are allowed to lie on the streets for days before someone comes to cremate them. The stink from the rotting bodies makes you want to vomit. It is not uncommon to see a pack of dogs eating the remains of a corpse. Each day there are public cremations somewhere in Calcutta–you can see the smoke from the mission station.

The other day Kahlil and I went over to the village about two miles inside the jungle to see Tei Tei. We wanted to take him with us on our fishing expedition. Often times we take a lunch with us and spend the whole day playing in the jungle. There is a waterfall near his village with water so clear you can see fish swimming in the bottom. Many times we act like pirates on a treasure island. We sword fight each other with broken bamboo sticks. Or we chase monkeys up their trees. The monkeys become so frustrated that they start hitting themselves and each other. They start chattering so loudly that it seems as if every other creature in the jungle can hear their complaints against the human nuisances.

As we walked into Tei Tei's village, we heard the cries of a woman in the distance. It was a horrible, terrifying cry. She was carrying Tei Tei in her arms; his body hung limply like a wet rag. The white parts of his eyes had turned a deep yellow. His body was trembling as if he were cold. Malaria, I whispered to myself: Tei Tei has malaria. By his condition I knew that he didn't have long to live. "Please," she said, "your father can help. Please, take me to him." I could not even speak: I was so filled with shock and despair. I nodded in silence, too consumed to even produce tears.

Tei Tei's mother carefully wrapped his body in an old cloth that was slung around her shoulders, and we began running to the mission station. When we arrived, her crying had become a high-pitched shrill of sorrow. Her voice took on a melodic sound almost like a bird chattering as she spoke: "Dr. Mitchell, help me, please." I grabbed Papa Jacob's jacket, insisting, "You have to do something."

With his stethoscope he listened to Tei Tei's heart and then examined his yellow eyes. Papa Jacob gathered the frail and trembling Tei Tei in his arms and laid him on a cushion in a large room. About a hundred other cushions and mats lay in the room where many more patients struggled for their lives. Papa Jacob took out a long needle and injected chloroquine into Tei Tei; then he wrapped his body in two blankets and slowly began wiping the sweat from his forehead.

As the hours passed, the deep brow began to fold in Papa Jacob's face. I had often seen that expression on his face when he knew death was just a few hours away. Slowly, with his large owl-like head swaying, he spoke solemnly, "Tei Tei is beyond medical help." As Tei Tei's frail little body shivered with fever, he momentarily opened his eyes, and a weak smile erupted. Then he motioned for me to come near and take the flute from his pocket. As I took the flute, his eyes became glassy and blank. His mouth hung open and his tongue–a gray color–fell from his mouth. At that point, Tei Tei's mother took his silent body in her arms and began to weep in that melodic voice.

When Tei Tei gave me his most prized possession, I knew that he was dying. I remembered when I first saw it I asked him where he had bought it. He said, "Man, are you crazy? You Americans think that you have to buy everything.

174

I will teach you how to make one." All day long Tei Tei and I searched in the jungle for the right kind of wood: only teakwood would produce the right sound. Then at long last we found a teakwood tree; and with the bamboo knife that hung from his waist, Tei Tei began to cut a section from the tree. As we sat on a grassy hill, I watched him quickly hollow out a series of holes near the top of the wood. With no more than an ordinary knife an impressive work of beauty was created.

As he worked he explained that his father carves flutes and sells them in the marketplace in the city. Then he showed me the flute that his father had given to him. It was decorated and carved with over a hundred tiny figures depicting every aspect of life. He said his flute had been carved by his great-great-grandfather. Each father added some carving and handed it down to the next generation–someday Tei Tei would pass it on to his son.

After my flute was finished, Tei Tei tested the sound. As we began to play our flutes, Kahlil suggested that we have a parade. Then I proposed that we go back to the mission station and dress up in the clothes Mother Marian gives to the people on the streets. Kahlil said he could get two of his father's elephants, and we could paint designs on them. Then we could invite the kids in the village to parade with us, I added.

When we rode the elephants through Tei Tei's village that day, a crowd of children appeared out of nowhere and followed us as we played our flutes. They laughed at the way we looked, because the clothes we wore were oversized–the pants had to be rolled up, and the jacket sleeves fluttered in the breeze. I found a beat-up, stained hat; Kahlil picked an old top hat with the lining torn out, and Tei Tei got a Dodgers baseball cap. We looked like three deranged penguins that had lost their nests.

As we entered the village on our multicolored elephants, we started to play our flutes. We were the closest thing to a parade that some of these children will ever see. When we reached the middle of the village, the children came out of their bamboo huts, laughing wildly at this ridiculous sight. Then I remembered the small jar of bubbles that I had in my pocket and I started to blow bubbles in the air. A loud cry of oohs and ahs echoed from the children; and before I realized it, everyone in the whole village came out and began to chant and say, "The angel-maker is here." I told Tei Tei that we had better leave; because the crowd was getting unruly, as they began pushing each other and trying to touch the bubbles. That was the best fun that I had ever had!

I remembered the open field where Tei Tei, Kahlil, and I played kick-the-ball. Tall trees and swaying grass had covered the field before Papa Jacob had organized the men in the village to clear it and make an airstrip for cargo planes to land near the mission station. At first planes flew in at least every two weeks to bring food and supplies; now, however, it was a rare sight to see a plane once every two months.

Talk of war constantly fills our days. In fact, some of the doctors are afraid they might be called to report for active duty. Food and supplies are scarce and many of the doctors are preparing to return home. Papa Jacob spends his evenings writing letters requesting more food and medical supplies. He is determined to help the people no matter what happens–I don't think he will ever leave the mission.

Papa Jacob couldn't do anything for Tei Tei now. Only one hope remained for Tei Tei's mother. She took his frail form and went to the Ganges River. (Kahlil and I followed at a distance.) She began to cleanse Tei Tei's body, believing that she could wash away the spirit of death. (The people here consider the Ganges River to be holy–they believe that it can cure disease and bring the dead back to life.) It was past midnight when Kahlil and I left them at the river and headed for home, exhausted and sad.

The next morning I was awakened by the distant sound of drums. Quickly I dressed and ran out of the house. I met Kahlil on the road, and he told me that they were having Tei Tei's funeral in his village. We ran as fast as we could, trying to locate the beating drums. When we arrived at the jungle village, there was a great procession. Men dressed like large multicolored birds danced around Tei Tei's body and leaped in the air while playing tambourines and flutes. Another group of men fanned his body while dancing. Kahlil said that they were fanning away the evil spirits that had plagued Tei Tei's life, so that they would not follow him into his next life.

Tei Tei's body was mounted on a large, decorated, wooden platform covered with all kinds of flowers and pulled by a small donkey. It seemed as though everyone in the village had a flute, filling the air with a high-pitched sound like a thousand birds flying overhead. The drums and the flutes could be heard for miles, perhaps all the way to Calcutta. Behind these groups of dancers, the rest of the village marched and banged on cymbals and chanted in unison, "God is great. God is in all men."

When the large procession had reached the Ganges River, one of the men playing the cymbals stepped forward and cried with a loud voice, "Return." With a large torch they lit the platform of wood and flowers that held Tei Tei's body. It disappeared within a billowing cloud of white, dense smoke as the chanting grew louder, rising to a frantic pace until the smoke and flames had consumed his body, and there was nothing left but a smoldering pile of ashes.

Everyone came forward and gathered small portions of the ashes into cups and bowls and all kinds of pots and containers. Then each one waited by the edge of the river with Tei Tei's ashes. Again one of the men dressed as a bird cried out very loudly, "God is great," and with that everyone lifted their ashes toward the sky and poured them into the Ganges River.

Tei Tei is now part of the river. Every time I go near the river it seems as if I can hear his voice. When no one is around I go deep into the jungle and play the flute that he gave me.

We are all one, Joseph, the sky, the river, the grass, and the dirt. Nothing is destroyed. And nothing is lost.

Love truly,

Your brother, David

14.

Dear Joseph,

This morning as I was preparing to go into Calcutta with Mother Marian to distribute clothes to the homeless on the streets, I heard terrible coughing coming from her room. It sounded as though she could not catch her breath and as if she were on the verge of dying any moment. Ordinarily, I would never have entered her bedroom without permission, but the sound of her coughing frightened me so that I thought she was in serious trouble. When I ran into her room, she was angry at me and told me to please leave her alone and that she didn't need my help. She also reminded me that a gentleman would never enter a lady's room without permission. I tried to explain that I thought something was wrong and I was just trying to help.

Later in the day, we drove to Calcutta to distribute clothes and packets of food, which consisted of a small box of powdered milk, an apple, and a carton of saline crackers. Even though this does not seem like much, to these people it is a feast. The crowd around our rusty little truck was constantly increasing with each minute. We knew it wouldn't take much to start a riot among so many hungry people, so we had them form two lines to bring order to this chaotic scene. We handed out over two thousand small packages, yet there were thousands more who were desperately begging for food.

At one point the crowd started getting out of control. That was when I heard the horrible coughing again and saw Mother Marian holding her throat, desperately gasping for breath. She fainted and disappeared among the swelling sea of bodies pushing around the truck. When the crowd sensed that there was no longer any orderly distribution of food, they began fighting among themselves, fearing they wouldn't get anything to eat. Frantically I sought to find Mother Marian among the sea of bodies. I prayed and hoped that she had not been killed by the crushing and milling feet of the crowd. Rahsa, our personal bodyguard and escort, lifted Mother Marian's limp body from the ground and put her on the truck. Through the grace of God, I managed to climb on top of the truck. Thousands of hands pressed both sides of the truck, reaching and searching for food–for a moment I thought that the whole truck would tip over.

Finally the crowd receded, leaving the truck empty of everything salvageable. Five bodies lay silent on the ground in the aftermath of human destruction, and twenty more men were crying in pain with no one to help them.

Rahsa drove the truck back to the mission as fast as he could, because Mother Marian had a burning fever. When he said the word fever, a cold chill ran through me. Fever could only mean one thing I thought: the demon of malaria had again sunk its fangs into the body of someone I loved. I had seen it all before–the aching, burning body, the trembling coldness, and the lingering, wasting death.

I kept thinking about Tei Tei and how quickly he had died of malaria. I hardly had time to say goodbye, or to tell him how much I enjoyed our times in the jungle, or to thank him for teaching me how to make a flute. And now I knew it would only be a matter of time before Mother Marian–this lovely foster mother of mine, who raised me like her own son–would die too. I moved close to her in the truck; I wanted to let her know how much I loved her. As she drifted from a dazed state, I whispered to her, "Mother Marian, hold on, please. I love you."

When we arrived at the mission, Dr. Shelby, a kind, older friend of Papa Jacob's, came running towards us with an expression of horror on his face. Mother Marian was lying limp in Rahsa's arms. Her skin looked as pale as a ghost with dark circles around her eyes. Normally, Dr. Shelby was a very soft-spoken man; but when he saw Mother Marian, he started shouting to the other doctors to bring a needle with chloroquine.

Finally Papa Jacob came into the room with a frightening sadness in his voice. I can still hear him saying, "Marian, what is wrong with you? You should have told me that you were sick. Something could have been done before now." Then he started to weep uncontrollably. "Don't you know that I used the last batch of vaccine today? It might be weeks before another cargo plane comes with more. Why didn't you come in just five minutes ago? I could have saved the vaccine for you."

I had never seen Papa Jacob so shaken. His fingers trembled as he examined her. Then he began to blame himself for Mother Marian's illness and collapsed into the arms of Dr. Shelby. "My God, why did I use all of the vaccine today? If she dies I don't know what I am going to do." Throughout Papa Jacob's life he had been a very orderly and sophisticated man; now to see him actually crying and revealing humanism was unbelievable. Dr. Shelby tried repeatedly to calm him, but it did little good. Papa Jacob kept saying, "Marian, forgive me, my love, for not thinking. If you die, I don't know what I am going to do."

It's been nearly a week-and-a-half since Mother Marian was brought to the mission. She has improved little and remains in a half-conscious state, barely recognizing anyone. Often I go into her room and try to speak with her. After dozens of times of calling her, she seemed to know me.

She would briefly regain consciousness and look around the room, trying to recognize her surroundings. Slowly lifting her head, she would drink a little water and then try to speak; but her words would only be slurring sounds.

Papa Jacob keeps a constant vigil at Mother Marian's bedside, holding her hands and trying to put life back into her fading body. He talks with her as though she were listening to his every word. It seems very strange that someone–who has watched thousands die and totter between the scales of life and death–now is totally falling apart. Perhaps Mother Marian was his only strength and relief from the burdens of his profession, and now that is fading with every second.

Once when I peeked into her room, I overheard one of his conversations. It was as if he were going back in time, trying to recapture a day when they were innocent and without the demands of the world pressing upon them. "Marian, how are you doing today? I know that you are going to come out of this all right. We have been through worse situations, and what is this little sickness to us?"

He talked about when they were in school. "I still remember when I first met you at Duchesne Academy. You wore a powder-blue dress, black patent leather shoes, and white bobby socks. Because they said I couldn't afford to go to Duchesne Academy and that I had received a scholarship, everyone thought I didn't belong, and no one would accept me but you.

"I remember Maxwell Robinson–the school president, captain of the debate team, and quarterback, who was so popular that every girl wanted to date him–he had his eyes on you. Remember the spring dance when I was talking to you and Maxwell interrupted our conversation? He tried to impress you with his fraternity pin and bragged about how exclusive the fraternity was. We both asked you to dance. But he thought he'd impress you by saying, 'The little rug rats have been allowed to come to our school. This is a private school; if we start letting in the poor White trash, then the niggers will start coming.' You were so angry that you started crying and said that you would be pleased and honored to dance with me.

"And with that dance we built a life together, didn't we Marian? As we danced, we realized how much we had in common and that status had nothing to do with love. Yet, Marian, it was love that helped motivate me to go to school and get my medical degree. It was love that helped me rise to the top of my profession. Our love is too precious to stop now."

I never knew that Papa Jacob–the stern, sober, disciplined man–had so much passion in his soul. Who was this Maxwell Robinson? He would say things like: "Maxwell showered you with flowers and candy, thinking that I couldn't afford to give you those things. He believed that I came from an area in Flatville where broken railroad cars sat idle and the houses were nothing more than dilapidated shacks. He said that you wouldn't have much of a life with me–only a broken down house and rooms full of dirty, runny-nosed kids. But when he found out that my parents had more money than anyone at the Academy, he became a silent, dejected figure; even his physical appearance seemed to shrink from me.

"I will never forget the day I returned home–me, the conquering hero that helped to bring respectability to Flatville–and how everyone called me Dr. Mitchell. No more the poor, smart kid trying to be a doctor. Years later I found Maxwell. He had become an alcoholic, living for the next drink."

Dear Joseph, Mother Marian's sickness is affecting Papa Jacob's mental state. I am frightened for him, as he is beginning to talk to himself all the time.

Love,

Your brother, David

Dear Joseph,

Mother Marian's condition progressively worsens. She remains in an unconscious state and is being fed intravenously. She has lost so much weight that I hardly recognize her. As her life deteriorates, Papa Jacob's life also crumbles away.

All the other doctors now resent and hate him. Before he was the motivating force that kept them working in such primitive conditions. Now he no longer has the desire to practice medicine. Many of his patients are dying, and the additional workload puts a great strain on the other doctors. They have their own problems working with a very small medical supply and trying to save the lives of this great river of humanity that constantly cries out to them. Now all of Papa Jacob's patients have become theirs, and what little time they had for their own personal lives has been consumed.

Before he would constantly supervise the mission, making sure everything ran smoothly. His silent steadfastness, concern for others, and constant dedication inspired hope and strength. Everyone was willing to sacrifice a little bit more for the mission: some of the doctors would go for weeks, eating little other than beans and rice. He persistently wrote letters to relief agencies in the States to get a little more money or supplies for the mission. The mission was his vision, his life work.

But now this great man has changed so much, and the shock has hit us so fast that we haven't had time to absorb how quickly he has deteriorated. It seems as if the seeds of hope he planted have blown away. Nothing remains but the mobs of hungry, sick, and dying people and only this small group of doctors, living in fear and waiting for the next ship or plane to take them away from this God-forbidden place. War is escalating every day in Europe and Nazi forces are infiltrating the Pakistan borders. It will be just a matter of time before they reach the mission.

A cargo plane finally arrived the other day. Papa Jacob's face lit up like a Christmas tree as he ran to the landing strip like a wild man, yelling at the pilot for any vaccine. To his disappointment there was nothing on the plane but some boxes of powdered milk and eggs. I thought right then that he might die of despair. What made matters even worse was that before the plane took off, the remaining doctors boarded the plane and left for the States.

The mission is now dark and deserted, but people still come every day with their dying children seeking life. Dr. Shelby is the only doctor who didn't leave; he is too old to really practice medicine anymore. He came to India to help the unfortunate in his last years of life; he still takes out his little black bag and does what he can for the most serious cases. However, most of his time is spent giving out candy to the vast hordes of children that follow him. I believe that his pockets are an eternal candy store–he has a piece of candy for every child in India. I wish I could do something for the people other than watch Dr. Shelby give out candy. I still mix up the boxes of powdered milk and eggs in the large vat by the side of the mission; the people line up, as I pour a little milk into their tin cups.

Through all of this, Papa Jacob walks around the mission looking like a Zombie. He has grown a ragged beard, and his white doctor's clothes are soiled and black. It has been weeks since he has taken a bath or washed his face. Most of his time is spent having conversations with Mother Marian that she cannot hear.

The other afternoon I happened to look in Mother Marian's room and saw Papa Jacob having his usual conversation with her. Suddenly I noticed that her skin had turned gray and her eyelids were black. I ran in and touched her face and arms–I knew she was dead. I cried out to Papa Jacob but he acted as though he could not hear me. I didn't know how long she had been like this but her body was hard and rigid. I was crying and telling Papa Jacob that we must do something, but he kept rubbing his head and saying that she will be all right.

I ran out of the room. I had to find Dr. Shelby. I found him near the landing strip passing out candy. From a distance I screamed at him: "Mother Marian is dead." All the children became quiet and stillness filled the air. We went back to her room. Dr. Shelby tried to convince Papa Jacob that we had to bury her body, but Papa Jacob kept telling him that she would be all right in time. Dr. Shelby grabbed Papa Jacob and gave him a bear hug saying, "You listen to me. It is over. She is gone. But you still have your son who loves you and doesn't want you to die too." Papa Jacob collapsed in his arms, crying, "I'm sorry for acting the way I have." That was the first time in weeks that I saw him in his right mind.

The next morning men from the village dug a grave beside the mission. Large crowds of people from the surrounding villages came. The children from Mother Marian's Sunday school class sang Amazing Grace. Dr. Shelby read the eulogy over Mother Marian while I held Papa Jacob's hand. As her body was slowly lowered into the ground, a man from the crowd yelled, "God is great." And the vast crowd chanted back, "God is great," as the voices of thousands began to weep for their dear mother. Then each one placed a handful of dirt on the grave till eventually Mother Marian's body that was wrapped in white linen was covered up to be seen no more. Everyone knew that the mission was now officially closed.

When the crowd began walking back to their village homes and their beds on the streets, one man came back crying very loudly, "She gave me not one, but two pairs of shoes.

Love,

Your brother, David

Dear Joseph,

It was about 1:30 in the morning when I was awakened by the sound of men breaking through the front and back doors of the mission. They were running through the mission taking anything that wasn't nailed down. In the darkness they had become men without faces, almost like demons in a dream flooding this small sanctuary, which they knew was deserted and would never be open again. The large band of thieves began ripping rugs from the floor, pulling wood paneling off the walls and fighting to the death over the furniture. I heard men crying out in terrible anguish, their bodies hitting the floor in eerie thuds.

Dr. Shelby told Papa Jacob that we must leave the mission at once. I had witnessed before what a mob could do in a manner of minutes and how quickly people could be crushed and trampled when fear moved through them. In the excitement of trying to leave my bedroom, I accidentally knocked over a kerosene lamp. Fire spread through the room, shooting up the curtains and engulfing the room with intense heat. I fought the flames until I was exhausted, trying to put out this spreading dragon's tongue that was devouring the only home that I had ever known. The fire seemed to be possessed as it hopped across the room in a leapfrog manner. It looked as if I saw faces in the fire laughing and telling me that I was going to die.

I was ready to dash out of the burning mission, hoping that I would be able to save myself before the room became a scorching infernal; but I remembered that Papa Jacob was still somewhere in the house. I saw him standing in a daze in the middle of the infernal. Running toward him, I screamed as loud as I could, "Papa Jacob, get out of here, please. Why are you just standing here? Don't you realize that we could die?" He didn't say a word but just looked into the fire as if ready to accept this fiery death. As I grabbed him and pushed him through a wall of fire, we both tumbled through the front door onto the soft, cool dirt.

The thieves seemed unconcerned with the fact that the house was burning. They continued to rip through boxes of powdered milk and eggs. Some of their faces were covered with the powdery substance as they violently fell to their deaths. The screams of the men permeated the darkness. It was hard to tell if they were dying from the flames or from the brutal blows of insanity that enveloped the room. All around me there were gleams of knives and clubs swinging frantically through the shadows of the darkness.

As we stood watching the incineration of Papa Jacob's dream, I looked through the dense cloud of the mission and in a brief instant saw our faithful guide, Rahsa, fighting with another man over a box of powdered milk. The white powdery substance covered his face: he looked like a possessed ghost that had just escaped from the abyss. He looked at me in a strange way, almost transmitting a feeling of anger toward me and saying, "You know it always comes down to this. You foreigners watching us fight over crumbs of bread as you pack up your bags and run in fear. In all that you do, you really don't know us."

As the smoke poured out of the small white frame structure, quietness streaked across Papa Jacob's eyes–at that moment he also died. And he died hard. It wasn't an easy death. For the rest of the night we huddled around an old teak tree finding a little comfort in being together. I was so frightened that night that I thought the men would come and kill us. Somehow we were spared and that night we fell asleep under the tree.

The next morning we were aroused by the whirring of a plane engine. It was not one of the cargo planes bringing supplies, but a small plane that I couldn't identify. As it landed, the propellers began forming clouds of dust. I ran toward the plane until I could see a great star on the side of it. It was a war plane.

That was the first time the reality of war became fixed in my being. We had lived to a certain degree in our own little world that very few wanted to enter. I had heard about the prevailing war in Europe that had now escalated to the point of global disaster. In some ways, I could understand Papa Jacob's emptiness. What could Hitler do to us? We had witnessed death in so many forms that we had become depleted of its terror. And by some insane reasoning, a quick death with a bullet on a noble battlefield seemed more merciful than starving from malnutrition and depression in utter loneliness.

The pilot told us that he was on a reconnaissance mission when he saw the smoke rising from the burning building and decided to investigate. The latest reports stated that the Nazis might be trying to push toward the Pakistan border, and it would be best for all foreigners to leave the country until the situation could be assessed.

I was more than ready to leave this land forever. I did not feel that we were failures–we had accomplished that great purpose of making known the power of love. Love does not fail. Love rises and cools the burning sun into a river of hope. Love can make a dying child smile after seeing your smile. Love breaks the backbone of loneliness and gathers that which is discarded and plants a field.

Joseph, please forgive me for being so poetic, but this journal has been a form of cleansing, of pouring strength into my weary spirit. My journal is my family, a record that cannot be destroyed by the state people, by Father's drunken fits, or the cancer that destroyed Mama's body. It is my record to you, to let you know that I did exist, that we were a family. And that can never be destroyed. These letters that I write are my daily conversations, my prayer.

A great toll has been exacted upon both of my families. My adopted mother Marian sleeps in the brown dust of India. And I believe that dust falls upon the lips and faces of this people and is breathed in the air. Sometimes I hear Mother Marian's laughter in the voices of the children. My father, Dr. Mitchell Jacob, the traditional pillar of common sense, now cannot understand the reality of losing that which he thought was so indestructible. I read somewhere in the scriptures that if you hold onto something you will lose it. And if you let go, that is when you have gained. I now know that it is not important if our footsteps are petrified in the sand. What is important is that we have made the sand sacred for others to walk on. We come to this life to separate. We come, my brother, to love only for a little while, to pour ourselves into the wind, to help another child breathe easier.

I do not know how to bring my Father back; he is living in another time when he and Mother Marian were young and in love and wanted to change the world. That's why they wanted to adopt me. They wanted to be the forerunners of change and break this bondage of prejudice and hatred that created the dead generations before them.

At the last minute, Dr. Shelby abruptly changed his mind about leaving saying that he only had a few more years to live anyway; and if the Nazis killed him, it wouldn't make much difference. Besides he still had a few more pieces of candy to hand out. As the plane slowly ascended from the soft dust of the landing strip heading for home, I looked out my cabin window; and in one brief instant, I saw Dr. Shelby walking unconcerned, passing out candy to a pack of children. He was no longer worried about where his next meal was coming from or where he would sleep during the night. All that mattered was the love that he could give and receive in this fleeting dust of time.

This is my last letter from India. As we move through the thick white clouds flying over a thousand memories and a thousand dreams, I remember the flute that Tei Tei gave me, and something about passing the flute down to the next generation. And I believe that's why we are here, Joseph–to pass down the best of ourselves to someone else, to make a few more faces happy while there's time.

God bless, David

Napa Valley, California

Dear Joseph,

Our trip home to California was long, exhausting, dangerous, and very sobering. My spirit felt cleansed and liberated: I had overcome most of my fears, passed through the worrisome period of childhood, and somehow through it all I had become a man. A new strength emerged within me–a determination that could overcome any test of life.

As we crossed the majestic Pacific Ocean, I sensed that my soul could travel through time and space to the dusty streets of India. In an instant I was there in every drop of medicine that they desperately fought for and in the small packets of food distributed by the Red Cross. Somehow I knew that once again God would send another servant to wade through the desperation of human hurt, and another Papa Jacob would have just enough strength to pour out for a season. That God would take another David from the cold slums of Kansas to ride elephants with a Tei Tei in a happy rain forest. There is a medicine that is not confined to a pill nor reduced to a vaccine. When you give of yourself, you are the power that heals and can cure all diseases: you are the force for the mind to believe.

When the funding for the mission was ending, and the rest of the doctors had fled for their lives, a group of young doctors collected donations and formed a rescue party; because they felt that the legendary Dr. Jacob was too important to be forgotten. They had learned about Papa Jacob's plight from a pictorial spread in Life magazine. There were basic shots of him and Marian holding sick babies in their arms while concerned mothers looked on. And there was a picture of me mixing bowls of oatmeal and powdered milk. Somehow his work had not been forgotten. When I showed it to Papa Jacob, he hardly even glanced at it but humped his shoulders and slumped back down in his seat.

The cargo plane was a bulky contraption that shook violently as we passed through cumulus clouds. It was sponsored by relief agencies and carried food to starving people throughout the world. But now there are no more relief planes for the war is in full force.

Before the flight the doctors had taken precautions; they painted the iron cross over the stars-and-stripes symbol. Once a German plane descended from the clouds and flew by just to look us over. It was a tense moment. I was told to duck while everyone else waved at him. Speaking in German, one of the doctors told the enemy pilot that we were carrying supplies for the troops at the Italian and Pakistan borders and had gotten off course. The German pilot uttered something about our being stupid and then flew off. It was a dangerous trip: we could have been shot down at any time.

It had been many years since Papa Jacob had adopted me and began his work in India. I had thought I would surely die and fall into some great pit. Now I knew how the slaves felt when they were torn away from their family, homeland, and everything they had known, and why they would rather face death than be taken into captivity. Once while crossing the sea, I hid in a closet for a whole day. Everyone thought that I had jumped overboard. I prayed that I would open my eyes and be at home on Christmas morning and that brief period of happiness would be preserved and played again and again.

Now we both looked like refugees. Dirt covered Papa Jacob in heavy layers so you couldn't distinguish his skin. He had mutated into a farm hand. His boots were worn and cracked and somehow they looked five sizes too big for him. My body was growing at an unbelievable rate, and I was always outgrowing shoes, shirts, and pants. I think I weighed as much as a wet fly. Papa Jacob started calling me Macaroni, because when I walked I resembled a long piece of macaroni.

Ultimately I had become Papa Jacob's son and only heir. Skin color was of little importance to him–his enemies were polio, malaria, and malnutrition. I was rescued from the orphanage because he wanted to cheat death; to alter a human life and change prearranged events; and to save life, struggling life, crying life, believing in hope. At age twelve I grew up fast having endured riots, malaria, and the embrace of death in every form. But now I had to survive. I had to continue. I had to see what was over the horizon.

Your brother, David

Dear Joseph,

Because I was taken so quickly to the mission field, my memory of Papa Jacob's estate had long vanished. Never did I realize the extent of the beauty and wealth of his land. As our taxi weaved up the dusty road to the main house, we passed by fields of grapes that stretched over the horizon as far as you could see. The harvest was in full operation. Large trucks lined the road as men, women, and children carried bundles of grapes and stacked them neatly in boxes.

When they saw Papa Jacob, they cheered: Papa Jacob is home, Papa Jacob is back! A mob of men, women, and children surrounded the car, reaching out to touch him with their grape-stained fingers. They held up their grapes–their life's work, their pride, their honor–for him to see. These migrant workers were not unknown faces struggling in the fields of obscurity; they, too, were his family. He rolled the window down and called out some of the workers' names. A smile erupted from Papa Jacob's dirt-baked face; he even grinned. His mind was not so impaired that he couldn't muster the strength to ask: How is the harvest? Who had the new babies? Was the company renting out his lands treating them right? A new vitality seemed to flow through him. I looked in amazement and fear at him. But then as quickly as it came, he slowly fell back into the seat exhausted, as if he had swallowed the last remnants of life and the hard, evil shell began to cover him again. His little hollow body sat down, and tears filled his eyes.

Your brother, David

Dear Joseph,

As a boy, Papa Jacob had lived on his father's estate. He always said the grapes were sacred; they were the legacy of his people: for the grapes always produced; they were always there to rescue him. Houses come and go, furniture breaks and is discarded, but the grapes would always be there to give him meaning and purpose again. I wondered whether the grapes could restore his life this time.

Later I learned that Papa Jacob had used most of his inheritance to fund his mission dream: pay doctors, buy medicines, and maintain equipment. He emptied all of his bank accounts, sold stocks and bonds, until there was nothing left but the grape fields. Once again they rescued him from financial disaster–paid off the taxes, kept the lights on, and put food on our plates. Through seasons of drought, hail, and plagues the grapes come back; they do not perish. We are like the grapes. We cannot be destroyed; we cannot be killed; we cannot die until all has been fulfilled. We are servants of God, Joseph, to be used by the earth. We have been plucked up, trampled upon, and scattered across the earth, but we keep coming back with stronger vitality and spirit.

The main house with two white pillars in the front resembled Greek architecture and had more than thirty rooms. The furniture had been covered in gray tarp for a number of years. Pigeons had nested in the ceiling, and some of the books that lined the shelves had fallen into heaps on the floor. Large, gold-framed paintings that looked expensive hung in every room. Even though rumors persisted for years that Jacob had died from malnutrition at the mission, the house had never been broken into or looted. The migrant workers kept a vigil on Papa Jacob's property and made sure no robbers took his possessions.

Papa Jacob walked around the place like a ghost. Everything in the house reminded him of Marian and had to remain in the same place to preserve her memory. Nothing could be moved except for cleaning. In the following weeks I cleaned the chandeliers, dusted and polished the bronze staircase, and washed the marble floors until their glory slowly surfaced. With each cleaning the rooms began to come alive. One day as Papa Jacob walked in the front entrance, he mumbled something about the house being the showcase of the community at one time, and having parties and other social foolishness.

The mahogany furniture and the marble floor reminded me of the train station where Father used to be a porter. I have come full circle; I am waiting now for the porter to call me to a new destiny.

Papa Jacob often told me how his father came to this country from Romania in the early 1900s with only one coat and the clothes he had on his back. There was much sickness and disease in the small immigrant community. Everyone knew of his natural ability to mix different herbs to make medicines; he cured many people of pneumonia, whooping cough, and diarrhea. To earn enough money to pay for medical school, he worked in a laundry and cleaned chimneys. However, he ranked so high in his class that he received a scholarship.

When he graduated, he returned to that small community of immigrants and set up his medical practice. After years of helping the poor, he bought these grape fields and retired to this valley, where he began his winemaking business. There's a wine cellar in the house that's filled with bottles of wine from different years. Eventually he became too old to practice medicine, so he passed his skill on to his son. And once again another Jacob began to set up his medical practice among the poor.

Caring, I believe, is the true medicine; it is the giving of your heart that redeems and restores others. There were times when we ran out of food and medicine at the mission, and we had nothing to give some sick person who had traveled many miles. I learned that there is healing in a touch or just holding someone's hands that can strengthen the soul. Through just a prayer, I have seen life return to dark, dead bodies, and food appear from nowhere, so we could feed the hungry.

Then again there is a sickness that knows no healing. Even when you appear well, there may be a scar of bitterness and hate deep within you. I believe that Papa Jacob's hatred is with God. He is like a tree with dead bark around his soul. But with just the right touch, life will come back, dreams will be restored, abilities will be repaired and a soul will burst with light.

Every day since Papa Jacob took me from the orphanage, I was under his tutelage. He showed me how to treat patients, taught me what diseases did to the body, and how to diagnose tumors, cancers, gangrene, and pneumonia. My destiny was already decided. I received the gift that Mama somehow knew I would: to be a healer.

For untold years Papa Jacob and his father helped the migrant workers; but for the first time during the thirties, the grapes did not produce; for five years the fields lay dormant. The grapes would grow to a certain height and die. Everything in the country was reduced to dust and wind. The migrant workers moved on trying to find work. That's when Papa Jacob heard a voice that told him to start a mission in India.

Once I asked him whether he still heard voices, and he said, only the wrong kind.

Your brother, David

Dear Joseph,

I have taken control of Papa Jacob's business affairs. While sorting through his records, I discovered that he had accumulated almost $100,000 from rent income in one account. I used that money to hire a staff of nurses and caregivers, because I was afraid he might die; and it was becoming more difficult for me to care for him. He needed something more than I had to give. Also, I hired people to paint, plaster, and rebuild the falling staircases.

Everything was returning to what it had been– everything, except Papa Jacob, who would just sit in his wheelchair like a dead man without any expression on his face. Although I prayed and tried to encourage him daily, it did not help. He would not eat the dinners prepared for him and was becoming a bag of bones. The nurses tried to feed him and help him into bed. One of the nurses said that he was developing bed sores on his body from not moving. So each day they would help him into a wheelchair and push his little slumped body around the house, trying to stimulate him. He was being given pills to get up in the morning and pills for falling asleep at night. One night I found him lying in bed trembling, and asking for a certain pill. Once I gave it to him, he slumped down like a beaten rag and fell asleep. A hissing, rattling noise came from his body, and I knew that he would die soon if I didn't get some help for him. As I stared at him he suddenly awoke, saying, David, "Please, help me, please." Then he drifted off again into a rattling sleep.

I remember the old trains and how they would come screeching into the station with their old, rusty parts, clattering and rattling as they tried to stop. Ancient old wheels grinding down into petrified rusty silence never to run again. He had only a few weeks left before he would die.

The nurses were trying to heal Papa Jacob's body, but it was his soul that was sick, rusty, and petrified. He needed a healer, and I was not qualified. Maybe I was too close to him to comfort him, I don't know. All my prayers seemed to bounce off the ceiling and crumble in the air. I placed an ad in the newspaper for another caregiver that read: "Need a caregiver to help my ill father. Must be a life teacher and a spiritual healer."

None of the dozen women I interviewed were right for the task. All during the interviews, Papa Jacob sat still without any emotion. Then one lady came in with a long résumé of her qualifications and demanded to see the resident's caregiver. "Surely a Colored boy like you has nothing to do with supervising a house like this." And she kept saying, "If you don't show me the caregiver I will get you fired." I tried to tell her that my father owned the house and I was acting on his behalf.

Then she snapped, "Don't you talk to me like that, you little overgrown raisin." Suddenly Papa Jacob sat up in his chair and laughed like a hyena. Blood began rushing into his head, and a hooting sound came from him. Arching his back like a lion that had found some old piece of meat in his teeth, he grinned with a crazy looking expression like a dead man that had just awakened in the middle of his own funeral. For the first time in months I heard him speak. "David, my son, why are you wasting our time on that old bag? That cow doesn't need to be working for us but on a farm." Then he let out another loud laugh. I stood looking amazed at him.

"And don't you talk about my son, you old pale face cracker."

With that the woman almost ran out of the room, while Papa Jacob began laughing and grinning like a child who had just shot his pea shooter at the teacher.

"Who's next? Bring them in. I have not had this much fun in years."

I looked totally bewildered at him now. Papa Jacob was grinning like a cat that had fallen out of a window and landed on his feet. He seemed to be monitoring me to see what I would do next. I felt exhausted. There was no use in interviewing anyone else now. At least, I said to myself, he is laughing and showing signs of life. However, I didn't know whether that was good or bad. He was down right amused at me now, and even asked me if there were anymore applicants coming today. I told him that I would discontinue the interviews; it was a bad idea to find a counselor. He shot back at me. "I don't need any darn counselor, motivator, life teacher, or whatever the heck you put in the paper."

The word "paper" poured through my veins like cold water. I didn't even know that the old coot still kept up with what was going on in the world. He had me believing that he had died and went to some unreachable level in hell. I was completely ready to end the interviews. I was frustrated, annoyed, and elated by Papa Jacob's activity.

Nevertheless one of the caregivers said another woman was waiting to be interviewed. Papa Jacob sat up in his chair with a stupid, wild-looking grin on his face: he was ready for round two.

Mama Flo was a huge, dark-skinned, Black woman. What struck me was the fact that she wore dainty, little white gloves and looked as though she was ready for a Sunday school meeting. Her voile dress trimmed in lace appeared as if it was made out of tissue paper. She had solid upper arms that bulged with muscles–the kind that did not come from washing clothes or lifting babies, but from lifting rocks to build a bridge or hauling dirt from a ditch.

She sat motionless with her little gloves folded so gracefully in her lap, skillfully sipping her tea like a debutante on prom night. She wiped her mouth ever so carefully and proceeded to fold her napkin so perfectly that a battalion of soldiers could not fold it with anymore precision.

"I had a dream of a very lonely man sitting in a wheelchair, who was holding something in his hands. When I asked him what he was holding, he said it was his heart; but when I touched it, it turned into a bird and flew out of his hands. I knew by this that the Lord was speaking to me, but I did not know then where he wanted me to go until I read the ad in the newspaper for a spiritual healer. A cold, happy chill went through my body, and I knew I had to come here."

At that moment Papa Jacob, who had been hiding in the background, wheeled forward. The woman, with tears in her eyes, whispered, "You are the one."

The stupid grin returned to his face, and he sneered at her like a wild animal, sensing some danger that only he knew. He cried out like a madman. "Who let her in the door? You're not going to interview another one, are you?"

Papa Jacob was a wreck. He would sit in his wheelchair making strange noises as the caregiver tried to comb his hair and wash his face. I caught one poor woman before she fled saying that I needed a priest rather than a caregiver for him.

I always felt like Papa Jacob was putting on an act during these times. Yet there were times that I wasn't sure. He smiled again, perhaps believing that he had another victim to torment.

While I tried to continue the interview, Papa Jacob started laughing loudly; it almost frightened me, for this was the most noise I had heard him make in months. The hyena was out–he had another victim to frighten and chase away.

As I began the interview again, Papa Jacob kept interrupting me. "Why are you dressed in white? Where are you going, sister? To church? You're going to need a really big church and pew, sister: I know it takes a lot of room for you to praise the Lord."

I didn't know how to handle the situation. I smiled stupidly and explained that he had been sick and was not in his right mind.

"Who are you calling not in their right mind? I taught you everything you know," he quickly responded. Then his laughter took on another tone, like stored up evil inside of him. "There's a moose loose in the house. There's a moose loose in the house. Somebody bring out the big guns; a moose is loose."

While Papa Jacob was laughing so hard that he almost gagged on his words, Mama Flo sat very calmly, drinking her tea and carefully eating her cookies. "I see your father really does need help. He's the person I saw in my dream. How long has he been in this condition?"

"For almost six months," I replied.

"For six months you let him run around here without taking a bath! I am surprised that you haven't died from his stench."

At that remark Papa Jacob became furious and started shaking his bony finger at her, saying, "Who is this woman in my house, David? You get rid of her right now."

"I am surprised, Mr. David, that your father's smell didn't make all the grapes in the fields fall off their branches and wither away. His odor would even make the birds fall from the sky."

Papa Jacob became so infuriated that he stood up and started shaking his finger, saying, "The last time I saw a balloon that big was at the 1929 World's Fair." He felt like he was in control again; the stupid smile appeared on his face as if he had won a great war. He started dancing and imitating a revivalist preacher. "Brothers and sisters, what shall we do with this moose that has come to give her testimony? I think that we need to take this moose out of the house."

Waving and fluttering his hands in the air, he continued: "There was a time when the moose ran free and were allowed to go wherever they wanted. They were everywhere. But the Lord said the moose shall not rule the land. Now, brothers and sisters, the moose has to go. I wonder who is going to help this moose with this big caboose?"

He was having a good time until Mama Flo said, "I bet a piece of soap would slide off of you, hit the ground, fossilize, shrivel up, and beg for mercy. You stink so bad that if the skunks had a convention, they would elect you as Grand Potentate Emeritus."

"David, you get this woman out of my house, right now. Do you hear me?"

In sheer wonderment, I cried, "Look, you're walking again. The doctors said that you might not ever walk again. But look you're walking and jumping up and down! They said that you would never leave that wheelchair."

Papa Jacob looked at himself as he almost lost his balance. He slowly limped back to the wheelchair, as if every joint in his body was aching. Putting on the most sorrowful expression, he almost spoke with the sincerity of God himself. "David, my son, please, if you care for me, get this woman out of our house. I feel that nothing but bad things can come from her. Please, I am begging you."

Just as quickly as his sickness came upon him, it left again. The hyena was out, and the stupid grin appeared on his face as he began singing a song about how he saw an elephant with a dress.

Mama Flo asked to be excused from the interview for a minute. In a graceful motion with one arm, she knocked Papa Jacob and his wheelchair over on its side. He was shocked and quickly jumped up, his eyes bugging out of his head with every vein in his face exposed, yelling, "There's a mad woman in the house," as he pushed his wheelchair hurriedly down the hall.

I didn't know what to say to her at this point, except "You're hired"; for I had not seen Papa Jacob move that fast in months. I feel like things are really going to change now.

Your brother,

David

Dear Joseph,

The next day Mama Flo knocked loudly on the door of the mansion, waking up everyone in the house. With broom in hand she came through the door like a whirlwind descending upon some abandoned island. I asked if she was going to do some housework before helping Papa Jacob.

In a voice that sounded older than that which spoke to Moses at the burning bush, she said, "I've come to clean house today." As she proceeded upstairs, I heard Papa Jacob screaming at the top of his lungs as broken glass and pills hit the floor. "Help me, Lord. Help me, Jesus. My pills–don't destroy my bottles of pills."

"You devils are trying to kill him with all those pills you're putting down his throat," she yelled while swinging her broom. Nurses and aides rolled down the stairs like tumbleweeds. One nurse glided across the floor as if her butt was covered with wax. It was amazing to see the strength of a Samson in one person. If I had the jawbone of an ass, I would have given it to her.

When I ran upstairs, I saw Papa Jacob crawling on the floor, trying to retrieve the scattered pills. "David," he screamed at me, "how can you allow this crazy woman in our house? She is trying to kill me. Can't you see it? Pleeese, help meeee! My God, this is the end of the world!"

Quickly he got up from the floor and started running for his life. Two more nurses were knocked down the stairs. As Mama Flo passed by me with her broom raised high in the air, she said that had she not accepted God, she would put these nurses in a full Nelson and break their skinny little backbones. The sound of glass breaking and people running continued for a while.

Every so often Papa Jacob gave me a disgusted look as he ran away from the flying broom, saying that he was going to disinherit me and send me back to India. He was cursing so much that his false teeth fell out several times; and his words became slurred, until only he could understand them.

I have never seen him that mad or have that much energy. It was refreshing to see him move so fast. For so long I had watched him stagger around, unable to lift himself up; now he was sprinting around the house as if he were running in a track meet.

As the last nurse ran out of the house, I yelled, "Do you want your paycheck?" She answered, "If you can't mail it, you can keep it."

Papa Jacob was on his knees, moaning, as he gathered the last pills and started to put them in his robe. Just then Mama Flo came by with her broom and knocked them all out of his hands. In one swift motion she dumped them into the trash.

In a high-pitched voice, he pleaded: "Why doesn't anyone hear me? Save me from this woman. Please, somebody."

Mama Flo was singing a gospel song as she began running water in the bathtub. Rising and looking puzzled, Papa Jacob asked what she was doing, but she would not answer him. She just hummed and sang her song while checking the water temperature and adding a little soap that created a cloud of suds.

"Is that for me?" Papa Jacob inquired. "Are you going to make me take a bath? You must be out of your mind if you think I'm going to take a bath." Laughing, he said, "You've really lost your mind, lady, if you think I'm going in there. I'm a grown man and you're not going to put me in no bubble bath. I will take a bath if I want to and I don't need a crazy Colored woman to make me."

Mama Flo got quiet again. "Look Dr. Mitchell, I'm here to help you. We can do this the easy way or the hard way. You have not had a bath for months. You stink, and I mean you really stink. When I came into the house and applied for this job, I thought something was burning. Then I found out it was you."

There was a loud crash as Papa Jacob plopped in the water. Quietness filled the house.

I ran down the hallway to the bathroom. I didn't know what had happened. Maybe he had lost his mind and killed her. Maybe he had pushed her out the window. Or maybe Mama Flo had put him into a headlock and suffocated him.

It was the clash of the Titans. I regretted having put them together. Lord, please forgive me, I uttered under my breath as I peeked into the bathroom. Papa Jacob was sitting in the bathtub fully clothed with a head full of suds while Mama Flo was slowly shampooing his hair and singing, "Wade in the water. Wade in the water, children."

The water was more of a baptism than a bath. The dirt on his skin seemed to be connected to his spirit and to his past. Once the dirt came off, a new man slowly emerged. As she continued to wash him, I thought I saw tears in his eyes. He spoke to her in a dignified voice. "Thank you, Madam, for helping me take a bath. I am now capable of finishing my bath; so if you don't mind, I need some privacy."

"Yes, I know how you feel. We all need some privacy sometimes." She gathered her broom and started cleaning up the debris left from her arrival.

When the door closed, I thought I could hear Papa Jacob singing.

Your brother, David

Dear Joseph,

Since leaving India, I've been recording my experiences, and some day I'll send my journal to you. Finally I'm on my way to medical school. I have ten white shirts that Mama Flo washed and ironed to perfection, and a picnic basket that she prepared with enough food to feed an army.

I'm the only Colored passenger on the train besides the white-coat men who quietly and precisely make sure the coffee cups are filled and cream is on the table. They are like invisible men working without a personality or a name. Passengers call out, "George, fill my cup. George, can you get me some milk? George, can you get me some sugar?" How could so many men have the same name? I wonder.

The war is on everyone's mind, but the silence of the train offers a brief pause in the heartbeat, a way to forget that the world is in chaos. The tapping of the train wheels has become a comforting melody causing me to drift in and out of sleep. I had a disturbing dream about a group of people that were kidnapped by an evil beast. The beast was devouring them one at a time before I could heal them. Moreover, every time I would heal someone, the beast would tear them apart and fling their mangled bodies back at me laughing. Then the beast ripped my medical bag from my hands, tore holes in my chest, and left me standing there bleeding against a wall of bodies.

The voice of the conductor calling out "Nyack, New York," woke me. I had arrived at the International School of Medicine and Science.

Before I left for medical school, Papa Jacob gave me his father's old, black, beat-up, medical bag. It still contained some of his old equipment. In one of the compartments I found a pair of wire-rimmed glasses exactly like the ones I wear. (I started wearing glasses right after coming from India. The mission did not have adequate lighting and most of the time we had to use candlelight to see and read by.) Papa Jacob has passed these ancient tools on to me to fight an ancient enemy, to change the atmosphere, to cure disease, and to meet death.

Your brother, David

Dear Joseph,

My experience in India was the training ground, a living classroom, and a contributing factor in my decision to follow in Papa Jacob's footsteps. I remember one time when I had first started living with Papa Jacob. There was a Black boy named Steven who also was about twelve years old. We discovered a bee hole buried in the ground. Steven found a large stick lying nearby and stuck it in the hole to see how deep it was. It didn't occur to either of us that the bees would not like it.

With ink pen in hand, I asked, "How deep is it? I want to record how deep it is."

"Maybe six inches so far," he said, with a calm and reassuring voice.

Then like a cloud of rage funneling up from the earth, looking for the intruders that disturbed their earthly world, the bees shot up Steven's nose and down his back. In horror I watched as the bees attacked his legs and arms. Suddenly they circled around my head, and I screamed in pain.

We both took off running down the street calling for help; we tripped and fell on each other. The bees delighted in our sudden misfortune and began attacking our buttocks and back. I ran wildly towards home. With dead bees falling from his back and buttocks, Steven ran for home crying, "No more observations for today."

Now here I am years later trying to examine this hole full of bees again. Would I be able to stand against their stinging attacks, or would I fold my black bag and run for home again?

Your brother, David

Dear Joseph,

I stood in many lines to get textbooks. As I was walking upstairs looking for my anatomy class, the books fell down the stairs in a noisy heap, creating quite a scene. A young African man named Hakim Wajakas tried to help me. He began stacking my books in a leaning, wobbling tower. Some of the young men gathered around us started laughing at me as I struggled with my books. Hakim shouted at the group. "Surely you have somebody to operate on." That brought them back to reality and caused them to shudder; for none of us were doctors yet, and some would eventually return home with their black bags in hand.

Through this embarrassing incident I got to know Hakim. He is an exchange student from an African country called Rwanda. His country is engaged in a civil war and desperately needs doctors. Because he had a high grade point average and desired to study science, a missionary group gave him a scholarship to medical school.

The day he was to leave for America, one of the bloodiest wars broke out between two of the largest warlord factions. In one last desperate attempt to restore honor and dignity to their people, the tribal men donned their traditional war robes, painted their faces, and armed themselves with spears and drums to fight the warlords and their army of men with machine guns and grenades.

His brothers decided to join the fight to regain the city in one major blood bath. Hakim was ready to fight, also, but they forced him onto an airplane, tied him down, and gave him one of the missionary doctor's bags. His family would not have him be a part of any of the fighting. Instead they insisted that he should study medicine to learn to help their people on another level. Hakim took the last flight out of the country before the airport was destroyed.

The newspaper reported the death toll as unknown–thousands of mass graves were being dug hurriedly to control the spread of disease. Many of his cousins and uncles were killed in the fighting until most of the men no longer existed. And one of his brothers was missing and was presumed dead–killed in one of the grenade attacks launched by the warlord's men.

He says, "I am ashamed of myself, because I did not stay to fight the devils that have corrupted our land. I should have fought them to the death along with my family members. I should have worn my warrior robe and faced death unafraid. Now my medical bag is my spear and my medicines will be my shield. I will return to my people and heal their bodies after the warlords have killed each other and their bones are but dust upon my shoes."

Living in the city has become too dangerous for everyone. The warlords expelled all the students, closed the universities, and killed the teachers and professors. They control the food, water, and medicines going into the city. The outskirts of the city are covered with mines that have claimed hundreds of lives; the survivors hobble around on crutches and walking sticks. Thousands of people have lost their feet, legs, and arms. The warlords are like parasites: they leave nothing but fear and bodies in roadside ditches.

The refugees are living from day to day in a mud pit. The camp where his family lives is a tent city with no clean water or food for the people to eat. In order to survive they fight over the handful of grain and rice that is distributed to them. Children walk the streets like living skeletons.

Sometimes he receives letters from his family about who has been killed or lost a limb, but he hasn't heard from them in over two months and doesn't know whether they are alive or have died of starvation in the refugee camp. Mass graves are dug every day; people are dying because of the war, and still others who escape the war die from malnutrition.

One day he asked me where I came from and what my family was like. I told him that my White adopted father is possessed and just recently had a wrestling match with his Colored nanny and lost. He looked at me and laughed and said, "I thought I had problems."

I told him how we came from India, how Papa Jacob and Mother Marian ran a missionary there for many years, how the mission burned down, and how we barely managed to escape with our lives. I recounted how I had lost my family years ago when the state people separated us forever.

Looking at me strangely, he said, "You have not lost your family: you have inherited my family, and you have many more families to meet. You are truly chosen, like the elders say in my country, to change the atmosphere."

Your brother, David

Dear Joseph,

As the weeks passed, Hakim helped me with my classes. He has a brilliant mind (scoring the highest on the daily exams) and explained how I could develop my study habits and retain what I read. He showed me where the city bus routes went and how to get around. Hakim is the most resourceful person that I have ever met. He could hold on to five dollars for two weeks–a loaf of bread in his country would be a feast to him.

I have never seen anyone so dedicated to his studies; he lives with his books, soaking in every bit of information. "On the path of destiny, sacrifice is the road map," he says. He can hardly wait to get back to his own country and set up a clinic where he can stop thousands from dying and bleeding.

Sometimes I've gone to his room and found him crying–his paper wet with tears, and he would say that his people are faced with death and destruction every day, while he is surrounded with so much food and peace. Anytime he feels that he is wasting time, he stands in front of the mirror and hits himself with a ruler saying, "Wake up body. Wake up mind. I didn't come this far to fail. I didn't come this far to lie down. I didn't come this far to lay down my weapons of warfare. I am anointed to be a healer. I will dig up this hard ground and blossom where I am at."

Every day he encourages me to stop wasting time, and tells me that I should study as if my life depended on it. "David, there are people waiting for you. These people will die if you give up. You need to visualize your purpose and see yourself helping them in their mud huts. You need to see yourself helping mothers deliver their babies. You need to envision yourself as more than just carrying a black bag."

Hakim's skin color is so black it looks like shimmering velvet; it is perfectly smooth except for the tribal markings and scars artistically drawn on his face that look like lightning bolts. Sometimes he wears beautiful robes on campus. Each robe represents a day of offering and repentance: one robe is for giving to others, another robe represents sacrifice, and another robe signifies service. He said that when I have achieved the state of readiness he will give me a robe.

Your brother, David

Dear Joseph,

We are like fish caught in a great net, drawn from all over the world, carrying the hopes, dreams, and spirit of our families. No one is considered strange or odd, for we are all different. You have to be strange to enter this difficult field. Throughout all time healers have always been considered peculiar. We grow up examining ant hills, looking at the veins of leaves, and carrying notebooks to record observations when we have found some dead animal along the road.

There are no prejudices here. When diseases attack our loved ones, we do not care if the hand is black as midnight or white like snow. We are the ready instruments of life, standing against plagues that have staggered like drunkards falling against the frail bodies of humanity. However, I fear that somebody will die after I have given my very best. I feel like a human aspirin that is broken apart and given out in bits of hope. Medicine is not the only cure here; my soul is also taken and used like manna. Joseph, I fear that there will be nothing left of me.

We have examinations every day; the pace of the studying is overwhelming at times. I am constantly studying, reading and rereading, until the words become blurred images on the page. We write journals on cells and molecule construction. One young doctor is trying to develop a vaccine to eradicate polio; of course, no one believes that he will succeed.

Our classes on anatomy are eight hours long. At night I go to my little room, drained, and often sleep in my clothes. Sleep is the most precious gift that we all seek.

Every time we start dissecting cadavers and lifting various organs from them, some of the young geniuses pass out, leave the room shaking, and some hurriedly pack their clothes and never return. The remains of people who could not afford funerals are used for our instruction. Many died in barroom brawls or their bodies were smashed in farm accidents. Some were found dead along the roadside with knife wounds or gunshots that have torn their bodies in half. I often find them fascinating to work on, wondering how their lives had been and how they ended in this final state.

Slowly my grades have improved. Grades are posted daily on the Earned Board. Mine are in the middle of the list, far behind Hakim who stays at the top of the grade chart. Sometimes I've wanted to quit, and have even thrown my doctor's bag down and cursed Papa Jacob. "Why did he send me here? I can't fulfill some old man's dream. I am just a Colored boy from the sticks. Papa Jacob, do you hear me, old man? What have you done to me?"

Then Hakim reminds me that a generation of people is waiting for me to succeed. Speaking in his broken English and African dialect, he tells me that I need to be submissive to my calling. "You are still trying to do things your way. Every doctor knows that his life is not his own."

Your brother, David

Dear Joseph,

Today Hakim received a letter from his family in Rwanda. He was so excited when he ran into my small room behind the library. It had been months since he had received any news from them. He began dancing and singing a song of victory in his tribal language. Then he sat down exhausted and began reading the letter.

Dear Hakim,

It is raining in the refugee camp; it has been raining for days. It seems as if the skies are forever dark and the atmosphere is thick with smoke. I do not know if the smoke is from the dust or from the bombs exploding within the city. There are over ten thousand people living in this mud and filth-infested tent city. If there is such a place as hell on earth, it is here.

We wash in a river that is filled with parasites and leeches. Clean water is the most precious item in the camp, and many people are killed over a pot of water. The rain provides water, but it turns the ground into a mud pit; when the rainy season stops, the ground hardens and becomes crusted; then our lips blister from the heat. We are then forced to drink the water from the river. Although we boil the water, many people still get sick and die from the parasites. The spread of disease is everywhere in the camp. Every day hundreds of graves are dug; sometimes bodies are thrown together in mass graves, in an effort to quell the spread of disease. They are buried in the same clothes they died in–there is no time for a sermon. Someone may utter a little prayer over their bodies, but there is nothing else we can do for them.

Rwanda was once a beautiful land. Do you remember when we were children and how we used to go into the forest and play tag and eat the delicious fruit from the trees? Do you remember how we used to fall asleep under the shade trees? The warlords have divided the forest, and whole areas have been burned down, while other parts of the forest have been logged and stripped. The lumber is sold to neighboring countries to finance the warlords' armies and pay for weapons.

Do you remember when the only conflict in the country was the soccer games? We used to go into the stadium and wear our favorite team's colors. Now the colors that the warlords wear represent death for our people.

ZsaZsa-Baba, the cruelest of the young warlords, first came as a benefactor, bringing bread and milk to poor people in the cities. But this was only a ploy to recruit young men into his army. Those that refused were taken from their families and forced to fight or were hung in the forest. Then he began to corrupt the police by paying them off. They became legal assassins, terrifying anyone that defied ZsaZsa-Baba and his thugs.

Those police and community leaders who appeared to be honest and spoke out against his death squads had bombs thrown into their homes. Or they were kidnapped and executed or ambushed in their cars. Death can come at any time. A bomb killed dozens of people while they were enjoying a delicious meal in a restaurant.

The city is now overrun with packs of teenage boys, who are high on crude dope that they chew like tobacco. They drive through the streets sitting on top of jeeps mounted with machine guns ready to kill and rape any moving being. That is why everyone has left the city.

But outside the city walls death is just slower and crueler. Sometimes for fun soldiers position themselves on the hillsides overlooking

231

the refugee camp and kill people in the middle of their conversations and mothers who are rocking their children to sleep. When this happens, crowds panic and many people are crushed to death trying to escape the sniper's bullets. There is no reason why the soldiers should do this. The other day one of your brothers was almost killed when a bullet grazed his temple.

My prayers are forever with you,

Mother Mayla

There was more than one letter in the envelope, which he continued to read aloud in a weak voice, pausing from time to time. Consuming the words, his eyes appeared wet, but he continued.

Dear Hakim,

The other day two men almost fought to the death over a sack of cornmeal. The women have no milk for their children to drink, not even in their breasts; for their babies have long since sucked it all from their mothers. Now they suck hopelessly on air, holding onto their mothers in a dreamless stare.

It seems as if God has forgotten all about us. The other night a miracle occurred. The stars were exceptionally bright on the plains, everything became quiet and still and in one sudden prayer as we looked up in this crystal night, and one by one everyone started singing. A huge sound like waves of harmony flooded the ground and spread through the air. It was maybe our last song of praise. The last sound of beauty that we could give. The last sound to drown out this pain in our bodies.

Your mother, Mayla

It is the season of change, the time of fulfillment, where dreams take form and move in our bodies or become black holes in our soul where we can no longer hear our happiness. Now it would take force, strong hands to hold onto the rudder.

After ten years of study, I am finally going to be a doctor. It was a slow process that matured me beyond my years. I would often take the train back home to see Papa Jacob. He had come so far with his healing with Mama Flo's help that he is considering being a doctor again.

The last time I was home, Papa Jacob was running around in the vineyard playing tag with the migrant children. He has made a total recovery in less than a year. I received a letter from Papa Jacob about two weeks ago in which he said that the mission field is his own backyard. He is determined to help the migrant workers. With Mama Flo's help, he goes into the fields every day with his medical bag, giving everyone free medical examinations and paying for any medicines they need.

One of his great concerns is that so many of the children have asthma. All the time he lived in the mansion and walked in the fields, he never heard the coughing and wheezing of the migrant children. "I am ashamed," he said, "for having waited so long to help these people. I don't know why I had to go to India when I had a mission in my own backyard."

He feels more alive and excited about life than he has in twenty years. His purpose has returned, and the healing properties in Mama Flo's chicken have resurrected the dead. That day when Mama Flo made him take a bath, self-pity and humiliation washed off of him.

"Once again I began to talk to God," Papa Jacob wrote. "I had stopped talking to him after Marian had died." He felt that he had betrayed those trusted in his dreams, those who believed that his medical bag was anointed. "I am back and not in my physical body. The mind can be wrecked, clogged up, the wheels of creative thought and life can rust, and years can go by lying in a bed or hiding in a locked room. I wanted the world to know what I was doing. Now I feel most blessed if I can help someone to use the bathroom.

"We are given an assignment in our life and every day we must take a test. Mama Flo told me that she was praying for her next assignment when she had a vision of an old man crumbled up in a wheelchair hating life. I am her assignment for healing.

"She told me that once she had owned a house of prostitution and that a John came in one night to use her services. One of her new recruits, a young, seventeen-year-old girl, who had just run away from home, was servicing the John, when Mama Flo heard a terrified scream coming from one of the rooms. One of the prostitutes came running downstairs crying out, 'He is killing her.' Mama Flo ran upstairs into the room and saw the flash of the knife in the darkness as he plunged it into the girl's chest. Managing to clutch the John's neck, she choked him to death right before the knife came down again.

"The young girl survived the attack, but Mama Flo was sentenced to fifteen years at hard labor for killing a prominent White man. There in that prison camp, on the dark floor away from the glamour and the money, is when she began to hear from God again. She said that she would work for others and build another house to help women get off the street.

"One night when she was praying, she saw my face in a vision. And she saw me doubled up in pain, and she could feel my sorrow. Instantly she knew I was the one when she applied for the job in the newspaper."

Your brother, David

Dear Joseph,

Sometimes I would study all night until the sun came up. Hakim would come into my room and say, "The future is closer than we realize. Thousands of people will die if you don't complete your classes. All that is learned in life is for this moment. Don't take the easy path; don't become a cry baby; don't go back home." Grasping my hands and looking at them, he would say, "Do you see it?"

"See what?"

"It is there. You do not see it?"

"I see nothing."

"That is why you want to fail; for you see nothing. But I see somebody operating, visiting his patients, holding his own destiny. Each finger stands for your journey: Preparation, Patience, Production, Prayer, and Purpose. Never say you have nothing in your hands," he used to tell me.

Dear Joseph,

After graduation I interned in a small hospital in Hutchinson, Kansas, where I was treated with respect by my coworkers, as the care of the sick from this middleclass town became my assignment.

The war is over; Hitler was killed in a final blast–the dreams of a madman were destroyed as a huddled coward was burned to ashes in a bunker in Berlin. I was prepared to join the military and become a doctor on the front line. It was my desire to help the soldiers on the battlefield, to operate in a makeshift tent, and to treat those who would not survive being transported a long distance. I knew that my destiny would be like Papa Jacob's: I would go to the mission field.

I have received an invitation from a missionary group in Rwanda that was looking for doctors to help treat children with parasites growing in their bodies. I jumped at the chance to go to Hakim's country. I had not seen him since graduation. Somehow the letters from him had stopped coming and those I sent were never answered.

I could have helped Papa Jacob at the mansion, but that was truly his backyard now. I had to find my own backyard.

I believe that it was not an accident that Hakim had entered my life. My mind had become a field where Hakim had planted the seeds of hope and healing. I would go to Africa; I would put on my robes of purpose and destiny.

Your brother, David

Rawanda, Africa

Dear Joseph,

Can you imagine this: I am in Africa! Rwanda is a very beautiful country; the trees are the deepest green that I have ever seen. Big orange and red flowers hang from the trees where the monkeys chatter to each other and play tag at the tops of the branches. The coastal waters are crystal clear, and huge waves beat against the shore. Large flocks of white birds search for schools of fish and then dive suddenly into the ocean.

The plane ride was smooth until we approached Rwanda: the wind shook the plane so hard that I almost fell out of my seat. Now I have returned to my homeland. So many centuries ago my forefathers were stolen from this land. As the plane flew over the ocean, I wondered how many slaves were still chained together on the ocean floor. I could almost hear their voices calling out to me from under the waters.

The missionary organization offered me free rent and board for a five-year stay and a large sum of money after my tenure. My special interests are diseases: malaria, measles, and chicken pox. I was working on developing cures for tropical diseases and believed that I could help stop the spread of these diseases in Rwanda. Maybe I could help develop a vaccine to isolate these terrors.

The missionary team is a collection of humanitarians from many different countries. There are interns and seasoned veterans, Blacks from other African countries, and Blacks and Whites from America and Europe. Pakistanis and Asians all work together here. They arrived with only the possessions they could carry in their hands, and they live in makeshift tents near the villages. We all heard the same inner voice calling us here to help. That voice would not give them any rest through all their years of study.

When I first came, I found the land was almost devastated by the tribal wars. Starving children sit lifeless along the roadside. Relatives often bring their dead bodies to the mission. Many of the children have big gashes in their heads–soldiers from the Hutu tribe tried to exterminate all of the Tutsi tribe–and others have no ears. Men with machetes have crippled an entire generation by cutting off their noses, eyes, arms, and hands. They would appear in the night wearing camouflage clothing and kill people while they slept. It is said that the rivers have turned into blood for over a month.

The tribal wars have ended. ZsaZsa-Baba has killed the tribal leaders and has made himself president of the country. He lives in a secure mansion with unbelievable wealth. A surplus tax is assessed on everything that the peasants have. When they cannot pay the tax, his men take whatever they can use. Sometimes homes are looted and young women are taken to his mansion to serve as concubines.

Your brother, David

Dear Joseph,

The people of Rwanda are such a beautiful people; they are like the migrant workers at Papa Jacob's estate. Most of them are farmers and make a living by planting potatoes and corn in the fields. They rise in the morning singing and beating their drums. Their music can be heard for miles around. When telephone lines are broken, they communicate with each other through the drums. It is a conversation in sound, giving praises to God for the ability to work and possess another day.

It has been ten years since the warlords ruled the land, and the ground is still littered with mines. While making medical rounds in the villages, Dr. McNeal–an intern from Iowa–found an orphaned, three-year-old boy named Popeye lying in the dirt. He saw a little hand moving out of the trash bin and realized that there was life buried under it. He cleaned up the boy and brought him to the mission. One of the elders said that his family had been murdered one night because they refused to give up their sack of grain.

One day I saw Popeye carrying Dr. McNeal's medical bag and listening to him as he treated others in the nearby village. I had a flashback of myself with Papa Jacob. Once again a divine hand had put people together from different backgrounds.

He was named Popeye because one of his eyes had been cut out. When he first came to the mission, he didn't trust anyone. Sometimes he would hide his food from dinner, thinking that there would be no more. When ZsaZsa-Baba's men drove by in their trucks, he would hold onto my pants in fear.

For the first year, we thought he had a speech impediment because he wouldn't talk. I believed that speaking would bring him back into the world again. Slowly I began to teach him the alphabet and sounds by drawing pictures of forest animals. The trauma that had devastated his mind left not only physical damage but a deep hurt that could take years to release. (I don't know if I have truly released my hurt over what happened to our family. I have been going through the motion, but I have never cried out. Maybe I could finally cry out in this place.)

When Popeye wasn't helping Dr. McNeal, he was traveling with me as I vaccinated children in the villages. I formed a little baseball team with the children around the mission. All of the doctors pooled their money to order uniforms for the children. We cleared a field and cut the weeds with hand sickles.

I remember the day the uniforms arrived from the airport. Before we could hand them out, soldiers in a truck pointed their guns at us and demanded to know what was in our truck. They picked up the uniforms and started to pull out the baseball gloves. To the amazement of all of us, they began laughing. Then they all jumped into their truck and drove away.

For an instant I thought we would be gunned down over baseball uniforms. However, the children seemed to quickly forget the danger and were laughing and digging through the uniforms like on Christmas morning. Perhaps I should be like Popeye and learn how to forget and live for the day I am given.

Your brother, David

Dear Joseph,

As we were giving vaccinations near the capital city, I saw bright, colorful flowers growing among tall weeds and twisting vines in a clearing in the jungle. I left the group of doctors I was with to investigate. I noticed a woman picking the flowers and tying them into a bouquet. She wore the most beautiful robe and looked like a princess in a garden of flowers. I asked her what her name was and she said that it was Zear.

As we continued talking, I learned that she had completed her nursing degree in America and had returned to Rwanda to help her parents and her village. She and other native doctors were trying to reopen the city hospital that had been closed for years because of the wars. ZsaZsa-Baba had given them permission to reopen it, giving them first access to the military and governmental branches. Although she receives a small stipend from the hospital, most of her work is voluntary. She had heard about the mission that was started in the countryside and wants to help us also.

We had heard that the hospital lines were long, there were few medical supplies, and only one or two doctors for thousands. The refugees that once lived on the plains had returned to their homes in the city. Although the mission had more medical supplies and doctors for the tribal peoples in the countryside, many who lived in the city lacked transportation to travel two hundred miles to the mission. Moreover, those who walked were often killed by bandits and thieves living in the forest.

When I had some free time, I would drive along the dangerous road to the city to see her. I began volunteering to help those in the city. Zear began following me back to the mission, and together we would go through the countryside in the old medical jeep giving out vaccines for whooping cough and malaria.

Before long soldiers started coming to the mission and taking all the medical supplies. We heard they were selling them on the Black Market in the city to once again fatten ZsaZsa-BaBa's bank account. To hide the medical supplies, we dug holes in the ground and covered them with brush. Once when we heard they were coming into the villages, we put on surgical masks, gloves, and gowns and declared that there was a raging plague affecting the bowels of anyone exposed to it. The soldiers quickly ran back to their trucks, tripping and falling over each other.

ZsaZsa-Baba has proclaimed that he is going to make the roads safe by killing any small factions of warlords' armies hiding in the forest. What that means is that he is going to kill anyone that he doesn't like. Death squads are going into the bush. It has been rumored that at least a hundred people have been blindfolded and executed in mass killings. Also he fears the new disease that we discovered (that destroys the immune system of its victims) is slowly spreading, and we do not know enough about it to help anyone. The village doctors right now are considered servants of the state.

Your brother, David

Dear Joseph,

The other day we received an official letter from the Potentate Exalted Ruler inviting us to come to dinner at his palace on September 3, at 3:30 PM. All the doctors in the mission believed that he wanted to use it as a publicity photo for the foreign press that were always trying to find some information about what was going on in the country. This would be a good opportunity for him to show how stable the country had become under his rule.

The first time I went to ZsaZsa-Baba's palace, I noticed that the stones leading to his driveway were made out of an unusual substance. It seemed like the ground cracked as we walked up to the mansion. I asked the driver what the stones were made out of. He said they were made out of the bones of his enemies. ZsaZsa-Baba had them crushed in a tree grinder and spread out on his driveway. Then the driver started laughing and said, "Do you believe everything that you hear?"

When we first arrived ZsaZsa-Baba was standing on his patio, wearing a military uniform decorated with gold leaves and medallions on his shoulders. His complexion was like coal and seemed to glisten in the sunlight. The whites of his eyes were like snow, and his eyes were black circles that could not be read.

He spoke with a marvelous, charming, perfect English-British accent. While the flashing light of the photographers' cameras snapped pictures of him, he spoke to us on how beneficial we were to the country and how he was committed to our protection and success. He then told the reporters that before his rule the country was in great disorder, and the warlords kept the country divided. There was no health care and the people lived in fear. Almost as if scripted, some children came forward with flowers and presented them to him. He went on saying, "These little ones now have a world where they can grow up and live in peace."

Next soldiers led us into a dark hall where the lights were turned off and a movie was started, showing ZsaZsa-Baba entering a village where all the people were coming out and singing to him. His men were climbing out of their trucks and giving crates of food to the people. The movie ended with an old lady kissing his hands and washing them with her tears.

After the movie ended one of the doctors spoke up, saying that the village in the movie no longer existed. Everyone had been killed by one of Zsa-Zsa's death squads; the areas were graded over, and the people were dumped into a mass grave.

At that point ZsaZsa-Baba raised his calm and controlled voice to one like a madman, spitting saliva out of his mouth and yelling, "You negative devils can't see what I have done. You foreigners come into the country just looking, never contributing anything. You are the plague of this country; you are the rottenness in our bones." He started hitting the small platform, almost breaking it.

The reporters looked at him and started snapping more pictures. I heard the clicking of his soldiers' guns around us. A small, uniformed man approached ZsaZsa-Baba and whispered something in his ear, after which he smiled at us and then left in a hurry. The small man was his press secretary. He spoke in a calming manner and said that the Potentate had to leave on important business but wished to express his concern and love for everyone.

We were then escorted to a banquet hall where dinner had been prepared for us. The table was filled with everything imaginable to eat. But it was a silent, rushed dinner. ZsaZsa-Baba's soldiers kept close vigil over us with their guns strapped to their sides. After dinner we were rushed to our cars and the reporters' cameras were confiscated. There were some scuffles with the reporters not wanting to give up their cameras. They were pushed into their cars and driven off by ZsaZsa-Baba's men–perhaps to the airport; I don't know.

The next day I drove into the bush land to see the village depicted in the movie. The land had been graded over; there was nothing left. I saw an old woman sobbing over this great pile of dirt, and I asked her why she was crying.

"This is the only thing that remains of my people. The whole tribe was killed in one mass execution one night. ZsaZsa-Baba demanded that all the children between the ages of eight and thirteen serve in his army. The mothers and fathers refused to give up their children and banded together to fight him. He killed everyone, burned their bodies, and knocked down their homes until there was nothing left.

"And the sad thing about this is that no one else knows this happened but me. I hid in the bush while the killing went on. Men, women, and children were blindfolded; with their hands tied together, they were shot one at a time in the head. I survived because I ran under a mass of fallen trees in the jungle."

I left the woman on her dirt pile with ZsaZsa-Baba's food still in my stomach, churning like cold death within me. All of his enemies are dead, and he is king of the criminals. The land is at peace.

Perhaps he started off wanting to do good things. In the beginning the death squad was called the People's Hope. They helped to cultivate the land and start schools; they gave free milk to the children. ZsaZsa-Baba's fame grew and the people gave him godlike qualities.

After each new territory was taken, his soldiers of Hope became a band of locusts, an army of hoodlums that controlled every moment in his people's lives. Now his is the only form of government; his death squads seem to be everywhere reporting back to him.

Our mission has been in operation for over three years, and our medical supplies have been stolen more than ten times. The doctors working here are becoming more frightened. One day ZsaZsa-Baba's soldiers came and took the last serum for malaria out of our supply truck. When Dr. Michael Morland, who is from a small town in the Midwest, returned from the city and found that the serum was gone, he became so angry that he jumped in the medical truck and went to ZsaZsa-Baba's palace. We tried to stop him, but he drove off in a rage.

The only other vehicle we had was an old supply truck. That day the battery was down. When we finally got the old truck working, we drove to the palace. As we approached, the guards came out with their guns drawn. They clicked their triggers, and I thought for sure we would be killed in an instant. ZsaZsa-Baba came out smiling and somewhat laughing, saying that there would be no need for violence because our doctor was not there. His men had reported seeing someone on the main road with a flat tire. He said we should check it out.

We searched the road and located the doctor's truck, which was filled with blood as if he had been attacked by an animal. We found his bloodied shirt and pants ripped up in a clearing in the forest. By all reason it appeared that he had stopped and a lion had dragged him away. Days later some tribal warriors found pieces of his body, sure signs that he had been eaten by an animal.

We knew that ZsaZsa-Baba had something to do with it, but there was no proof to indict him. He came into the camp with a carload of flowers the day the doctor's body was being shipped back to America. Behind him was another truck full of medical supplies. Before he left he yelled out of his car at the doctors. "If you ask in a polite manner, you will receive polite manner." We took his flowers and poured gasoline on them and vowed to avenge Dr. Michael's death.

There is a war that we shall fight, and it is with ZsaZsa-Baba, the last of the warlords. I shall not rest until his body lies under the ground and becomes a playground for children.

Your brother, David

Dear Joseph,

The other day when I was at the hospital in the city, I showed the doctors some sterilization procedures while Zear translated everything I said–she speaks five languages. We were becoming an inseparable team. Although she earned a medical degree, she did not pursue an internship: she wanted to make sure that her father and mother were still safe in their village. As I struggled with the different cultures of the people, Zear helped me to understand what makes the patients more comfortable during my examinations.

Dr. Mallrafee, the head physician, had worked on new serums for tropical diseases and had published his findings in a few medical journals. However, recently he began to write about a new disease created by a monkey bite that could destroy the immune system of its victims. He said that he was working on a new vaccine for this disease; but he had been ridiculed by the medical community, and his findings were ignored. The experimental vaccine he had created and all of his findings were destroyed during the war between the warlords. Half of the hospital had been burned and looted; only a dark frame remained.

The city was a collection of dark, burned-out shells. Every once in a while as I traveled through the city, I would see the most depressed look on the faces of people searching through the rubble of one of the buildings, kicking through the ashes, overturning boards, or just standing as if remembering a time that had passed away.

Sometimes Zear would visit me at the mission. On one of the few days that I had off, she came and pulled me out of bed, tickling my feet and saying, "You say you are a doctor of compassion and hope. The only hope I see here is that you hope you don't wake up today." Then we would start our day visiting the local tribes, giving out vaccines, and telling mothers what foods to give their babies. Sometimes we would find homeless children walking alone in the woods. Zear would call out to them, give them a box of cereal and milk, and hold them in her arms and rock them to sleep. There were thousands of children like this; some would survive in the forest, and others would die.

Small groups of warlords are banding together again in the jungle and attacking anyone they can find. When Zear came looking for me at the mission the other day, she was in a horrible panic. Her mother had barely escaped death while walking through the jungle to fill her water pot. A hatchet man had jumped out from the bushes and swung his blade at her mother, missing her arm by inches before she was able to run back to the village for safety.

As I held Zear in my arms, I knew that we would spend the rest of our lives together and in time she would become my wife. Zear's father insisted that we marry in the village in the traditional way.

Your brother, David

Rwanda, Africa

Dear Joseph,

The people in the village have an ancient custom called "Running of the Groom." I was told to spend the night away from Zear in a village hut by myself. Early in the morning, about fifty or sixty young men came to my hut to wake me, beating drums and yelling. They were tall and dark-skinned, like beautiful trees carved out of mahogany, with white tribal markings that looked like lightning bolts. They wore beautiful robes–like none I had ever seen before–robes with birds and peacocks and eagles; some had feathers in their hair. They danced and leaped around me in unison, singing in their language that this is the day of preparation, the day of power and purpose.

Prior to my wedding day, one of them draped a purple robe around me and gave me a spear. The stick looked as though thousands had carried it before me. There were names, perhaps hundreds of them, carved on it. Then from out of nowhere an old man, whose skin looked as wrinkled as an elephant's hide, appeared. His eyes were like black wells that had no bottom. I was afraid to look at him.

He touched me and examined my face; then he started painting my face with lightning bolts and cloud shapes, and explained: "The lightning bolts and the clouds represent the atmosphere and the spirit of the living God has made you more than dust. And this God of the atmosphere shall lift you, shall cause you to compass the heavens; and the seeds of your children shall drop down from the skies and spring forth and walk upon the land. You must accept this change; all things shall be different now. Nothing shall be as it was. Do you accept your role as a husband and as a man?"

I nodded my head and the young men began clapping and singing once again even louder. "Praise God, Praise God! This is the day of change."

And then the old man raised his hand and slowly lowered it. The young men became quiet, almost motionless, striking the pose of the animal depicted on the robes they wore. In one hurried motion, I was grabbed by one of the young men and we began running in the dark jungle.

The morning sun was slowly breaking over the trees; orange and red hues began to softly paint the sky. As we ran through the villages, I could hear their voices on either side of me, shouting in the twilight: "The Bridegroom Cometh, the Bridegroom Cometh."

At times I felt I would faint, but the young men would push me back on my feet. I ran through Zear's village and caught a quick glimpse of her smiling at me in amazement and silently laughing to herself. An old woman placed a broom in her hands and was showing her the proper way to clean a house. I also laughed at her as I sped by not even having time to wave my hand. I pleaded with the young men to let me rest just for a few seconds.

Shortly I was taken to a hidden waterfall in an underwater cave in the forest. I was pushed into the turquoise-colored water by the riverbank and was told to follow the swimmers under the water until we came up to the filtered light of the cave. Sunlight poured through the cracks of a mountain and flooded the place with glowing light. It was a place few knew existed. And then all the young men got quiet as we stood on the soft, sandy shore. I thought they wanted me to pray. Then they looked at me and all of them picked me up, laughing and threw me into the sparkling waterfall. We spent hours wrestling and throwing each other into the underwater amusement park. I never had so much fun in all my life!

As the sun was setting in the twilight skies, they told me to swim underwater again until I came up on the banks of the river. Next I must climb a tree. It was a tangled, dark, twisted tree with thousands of branches that shot up towards the sky. The tree must have been two hundred years old or more. When I reached the top of the tree, I was to eat a certain kind of fruit that only grows at the very top. The young men called the tree the "Giving Tree."

Pleading with them, I repeated that I had no more strength, as I fell exhausted to the earth. In unison they replied that a weak man cannot take a wife. A weak man cannot complete this test. "Are you sure," they asked, "that you love Zear? Your ancestors are calling to you to climb the 'Giving Tree' before the light of day is gone. You must do this now or you will not see what you are supposed to see."

So I gathered the last fragments of my strength and began to scale this massive tree. Amazingly my strength returned as I touched the tree. The young men began to sing again as I ascended to the top. They sang a new song about how out of a round womb we are born, out of round eyes we see, and out of a round mouth we breathe, and return to the round earth of God's embrace.

At the top of the tree, I saw what appeared to be pears. I gathered one and started eating it; it was sweet like honey. Then I ate another. One of the young men shouted: "David, do you not know that this fruit grew especially for you? All summer long it ripened, for it knew that you were coming. So it ripened until you were ready to eat it."

And then as if nature were listening in the evening twilight, thousands of butterflies appeared from under the leaves. Their florescent wings reflected the descending sunlight. These glowing specks of light bounced around me. From my position, I could see the sun going down behind the mountains, and in one brief moment the twilight illuminated a rock formation on a distant mountain. It appeared as if hands were reaching towards the skies. I felt as if the mountains were speaking to me and I was speaking to them.

Then one of the young men said, "David, lift both of your hands into the skies and repeat after me. 'Lord, I am your servant. Give me your Grace, give me your Mercy. Make me a Giving Tree to give to all that come to me. Make me a Giving Tree, enduring with silent, confident strength, until the time comes to make my fruit ready. I will wait until my change comes.'"

Darkness fell upon the treetops and the sky painting was gone. One of the young men took his knife, cut down some tall, slender branches, tied vines around old dry tree leaves, and set them on fire to provide light while I climbed down from the tree. Again we began running towards a large hill overlooking the forest. I pleaded with them. "I cannot run any longer. I am about to faint; I am about to fall dead. Do you hear me?" I was ready to fight them if they did not let me go. I stopped and looked at them, saying, "Leave me alone, now. I have done enough. Do you hear me? I have done enough."

"It is almost over," they answered.

"I have run all day. I cannot take another step. Do you hear me?" I shouted.

One of them said: "You must now climb this last hill to see what you should see. If you climb this hill before the day has ended, you will be the groom that God has chosen to marry within our tribe. If not, we will shun you; we will not accept you. You will come to our village, and we will not talk to you. We will see you in the marketplace and we will look away."

I stared at them in silence and started running up the mountain with every muscle in my body aching. I thought I would pass out from hunger and lack of sleep. My leg muscles bugled with pain and strength as I began to run again. I cried out: "God, help me. Lord, help me to make it. Help me, Lord. Help me, Lord. LORD, HELP MEEEEE."

They shouted back at me: "Run, man of God, run. RUNN MANNNN OF GOD. RUNN MANNNN OF GODDDD. Use everything in you now. You must make it to the top of the hill. Speak to your God and ask for help now."

Although I didn't feel alive anymore, somehow I began to speed up. I made my way up the soft, grassy hill and collapsed in the cool, windy clearing. I lay almost like a dead man that was alive but barely breathing. And now other men came up the mountain hill; they brought pots of water and washed my body. They carried me into a small tent filled with tables of food and water–roasted fish and lamb, warm, baked bread, grapes and oranges that I hungrily devoured.

I rested on a small cot. Before falling asleep, I felt soft, warm blankets being draped over me. I slept for hours; it was still night when I awakened and looked at my watch: it was four AM.

The young men came into the tent with more fruit and bread. They rubbed my arms and legs with scented oil and cocoa butter. I have never been so exhausted. Every muscle and bone in my body was hurting, but sleep and food were slowly restoring my strength. Underneath the pain and soreness, I felt good. It was a goodness that transcended the pain. I felt as if I had touched God in this running, and he reached out and helped me to run. Somehow I grasped what this day of testing meant. There is a power that we must rely on which is greater than our physical being. When our own physical strength is gone, there is a power that replenishes, restores, and causes us to repent for our lack of trying.

The young men built a fire on top of the mountain and ministered to my every need. It was a brilliant night, and from this mountain I could see the whole horizon. Every star was out and shining on the forest. I had made it through the ritual that thousands before me had done. Had I known what I had to go through, I doubt whether I would have even married Zear, I laughed to myself. I was connected with these people now and forever.

As the cool wind of the evening blew gently, the young men sat around the fire, singing softly again. The old man, whose skin looked like elephant hide, was carried up the mountain by a group of men from Zear's village. I came out of my tent and sat with the young men as the old man stepped off the makeshift cart. The young men put out the fire. Everything became quiet, and I could only hear the wind blowing through the trees below.

The old man started to paint my face again and said, "You are a man of destiny. You have been born with an earth suit; today you have been given a suit of the spirit. You cannot be killed, and you cannot die; you are eternal."

With the soft wind blowing across the mountain and moving through the trees, the first beams of sunlight blessed the earth. The young men began beating the drums again. I knew I could not run or swim or climb another mountain. But now they came with the marriage robe, an embroidered cloth with stars and writings on it. The robe bore the names of generations of men that had integrity and honor and had kept their commitment and vows.

While I was sleeping, the young men had made banners and flags out of papier-mâché, proclaiming faith and prosperity to the marriage and the generations to come. With blue and gold paint, they decorated their foreheads and cheeks with lightning bolts and clouds. They wore brilliant robes of many colors and fabrics–tweeds, silks, and cotton–painstakingly sewed together to form the wings of birds, eagles, hawks, and doves. The designs looked like moons, planets, and suns exploding and descending. Some robes had scriptures from the Bible and the proverbs of their people inscribed on them. Names of families of men and women and deeds that would only be remembered on these special days adorned other robes. It reminded me of a parade I had once seen as a child in California. And now young boys wearing gold-colored capes came up the mountain with drums.

Then the old man uttered a prayer (as it was interpreted to me). "Strengthen the young man about to take a wife. May his seed endure forever."

With that we began to march down the mountain toward the village as the light of the sun rose above the trees. The drumbeat changed and it sounded like a caddish steadily tapping, like the sound of a train turning its great wheel against the sky. The march was a ritual of manhood called "the power of life." In a sense it resembled an old-fashioned cakewalk where one leg was lifted high in the air, then came down, and everyone shook their shoulders in rhythm to the music and the drums. As we marched back to the village, the young men sang a new song (as it was interpreted for me). "I am my Beloved, and my Beloved is mine." I had conquered the waterfall, the Giving Tree, and the mountains. I felt good.

When we arrived, everyone was waiting for us, greeting us with streamers and banners and dancing. As we approached a flower-covered hut, Zear peeked out, smiling at me. First the older woman opened the hut cover, and then Zear slowly appeared, wearing a white lace dress covered with gold trim and lilies. I tell you, Joseph, I almost lost my breath; I could not believe that she would be mine.

The men and women sang in waves of choruses–when one voice ended another would start chanting the same line in harmony and with prayer. Then everything became quiet as we were led to the center of the village where the old man awaited. (I do not know how he made it back to the village before me, but he did.)

After taking my hand and placing it in Zear's hands, he said, "David Potter, repeat after me. 'I am my Beloved and my Beloved is mine. Where I will sleep is where she will sleep. Where I will go, she will go. Where I will eat, she will eat. She is my Beloved and my Beloved is mine. No storms, no heat, no cold, no water, no fire, no flood shall stop me from providing, from praying, from preparing, from proclaiming, or perfecting my love for her.'

"Let angels dance between you now; let the clouds become your shoes; let this day become your atmosphere and breathe in each other's dreams for now and forever."

Then with all his might he shouted: "God is great and God is good." And everyone repeated the words after him.

He tied our hands together with a cord. A special booth had been built for us and everyone brought us gifts–

handmade robes, sandals, blankets, pies, and cakes. That day we danced with everyone in the village until we fell asleep in each other's arms.

Can you believe this? Today I have run with warriors, swam under waters, climbed a tree, and scaled a mountain! I now know that neither the Depression, or the state people, or sickness, nor death can stop me. And it cannot stop you,

Joseph. I will tell you now what they told me: RUN, MAN OF GOD, RUNNNNN.

Love,

Your brother, David

Dear Joseph,

We have been waiting for over two months for a shipment of vaccine to arrive. The doctors are in a panic because there is an epidemic of smallpox and malaria that is spreading through the villages. For the last three years it has barely rained, and we are running out of food and water. Every day people are dying, and we are powerless to do anything about it. It appears that I am reliving the same thing all over again. This mission is crowded with sick people, and we can only watch them suffer and die. I have written countless letters to the World Relief agencies, and they have informed me that the vaccine and medical supplies were sent months ago.

The other day a mother came to the mission with a dead baby cradled against her breast. She was delirious with grief–no one had the heart to tell her that her baby was already dead. I pray every day that the supplies will arrive before more die.

Today a little boy informed me that he had seen some food trucks come to the village, but ZsaZsa had intercepted them and had stockpiled them at his palace. He saw men selling boxes of care relief food and medicines to those that could afford them. Upon hearing that, two other doctors and I jumped in our jeep and drove twenty miles to the palace to confirm the report. I was so angry that I didn't notice the security guards and sped past the entrance without stopping. The guards shouted at us to stop and fired warning shots in the air. I knew that we would be in serious trouble with ZsaZsa, but it was too late to undo the damage now. If it was true that he had taken the food and medical supplies, I would pour my wrath on him today.

When we arrived at the palace, ZsaZsa's security army surrounded our jeep with their machine guns drawn. One man said, "Please, do not move or we will be forced to kill you where you stand." Another guard pointed a gun at Dr. Wilderbee (a man in his late sixties), forced him out of the jeep, ordered him to drop to his knees, and folded his arms behind his neck. Then they did the same with all of us.

Suddenly ZsaZsa's voice interrupted our kneeling session. "What is the meaning of this commotion?"

"These men drove through the checkpoint and headed towards the palace. We stopped them before they got to you," the man replied.

Everything was quiet once again like the rumblings of a storm cloud and the rushing force of evil moving on the plains. To our surprise, ZsaZsa said: "How dare you threaten these men like this; they are doctors trying to help our people. How dare you treat these guests in our country in that manner! Get those guns away from them right this minute. For this I will kill you myself."

We all looked at each other dumbfounded. I thought for sure that he would reward his guards for acting so swiftly against us. After all the stories I had heard about his cruelty and lack of compassion, I did not know what to think now. Were they all lies created by other warlords just to destroy him? Perhaps this was the only weapon ZsaZsa's enemies could hurl at him to destroy his reputation. Maybe I was misled by those who did not want to restore order to this land of devastation and despair.

ZsaZsa was in a rage, looking like a heathen and screaming at his men about embarrassing him. Every vein in his face looked as if it would explode. Then he approached us, brushing the dust off of our clothes, saying, "Please accept my apologies for the stupidity of my men. They don't seem to know my guests from my enemies. They will be severely reprimanded for this behavior."

Once again ZsaZsa began dusting the dirt from our pants and continued speaking. "You must understand the land is still teeming with renegade warlords. I have made quite a few enemies by restoring prosperity and order to the land. So you can understand our rash behavior at times. We must take certain precautions in these dangerous times, so I have given my soldiers orders to shoot to kill anyone who comes into this area without my permission. The very fact that you have been seen with me at my dinner parties should have been reason enough for them to withdraw their guns. You see they have failed their mission because you are still alive," he said laughing somewhat. "Once again I extend my apologies to you, for I realize the great work you are doing in the villages and in the jungle. I would like to help with your effort more, but I am very busy running the country."

With that ZsaZsa's smile returned–brighter than a Christmas tree at midnight. Listening to him I had almost forgotten why we were there; his voice and manner seemed to consume everyone's thought. Finally I mustered the courage to speak out for the group; all the others were so terrified by the guns that they just wanted to leave in one piece.

"It has been brought to our attention that you have been seizing our supplies and boxes of food and medicines sent by the relief agencies and selling them in the markets," I stated.

The kind face of the beloved benefactor became twisted as he yelled out insults. "Lies. Lies. Disgusted lies created by my enemies. I would never commit such dastardly acts; I am a man of integrity, a man of honor, a man of God. Do not come to my palace and insult me like this. Let me lose all that I have if I speak not the truth."

I don't know if somebody was listening in the skies. Maybe mama sent one of the angels to intervene, but at that moment a can of compressed corn fell out of one soldier's knapsack and rolled in front of ZsaZsa's feet. Everyone looked stunned to see the can stamped with Care Relief on its side.

ZsaZsa tried to speak but nothing came out of his mouth. He began choking on his words, making some unintelligible sounds. In one sweeping blow he backhanded the soldier so hard that I thought I heard teeth breaking. The man pleaded with ZsaZsa for mercy and said he had only taken a little for himself. Before he could finish his next sentence, ZsaZsa knocked him to the ground as his men pointed their guns to his head, ready to kill him at ZsaZsa's command. They ripped off his shirt, and other food items fell out. The man tried to stand up and say something about following orders, but there was too much blood in his mouth for anyone to understand him.

Then another blow hit him in the face. He was on the verge of becoming unconscious as he pointed with a weak hand towards the area near the palace with thick rubber tree leaves and bamboo stalks. The soldiers dragged him to his feet towards the hidden crates.

ZsaZsa assured us that his men would bring all the supplies back to our camp in less than an hour. With more apologies, he escorted us to our jeep. As we drove away we heard gunfire–the man was probably killed for his thievery and making ZsaZsa look like a liar. We were just happy to be safely away from the palace.

Your brother, David

Dear Joseph,

I do not know what to believe about ZsaZsa. The villagers are always talking about his crimes and the people that he has kidnapped or killed. Today he delivered the stolen crates of food and medicines himself. When the people saw the five trucks, they ran yelling and screaming, "The Almighty has delivered us again."

ZsaZsa sat on grain sacks on top of one truck, smiling and laughing as the people grappled for food in a panic. Apparently no one noticed him in the rush to obtain food. Suddenly he jumped down from the truck into the middle of the crowd. The clamor of the crowd abruptly halted and only the wind could be heard blowing through the trees in the distance. Everyone stood motionless, petrified with fear, not even wanting to put food into their mouths.

Then ZsaZsa exploded, saying, "I saved you from certain death. I saved you this day, and you cannot even say thank you."

He grabbed an old man and forcefully poured a box of meal into his mouth. The frail old man stood there coughing and choking, his face covered with the powdery substance but too afraid to move. Maybe this was a way they could hold onto their last fragments of dignity. They refused to honor him through their starvation.

Throwing the man down, ZsaZsa spoke again in that dignified voice. "Apparently my people are not as hungry as we were led to believe. They do not care about their own lives. Why should I? Yet I will have mercy on them; for mercy is why I have come to save them." He commanded his men to throw all the food and medicines off the trucks, and then they drove away in a cloud of dust.

Immediately the crowd converged on the food in a desperate panic. The power of prayer, the nourishment of food, and the application of medicines were the hands of God, wrestling death temporarily into dust. Once again children slept against the milk-filled breasts of their mothers and singing was heard in the fields as grain was planted for a future harvest. Everyone believed that all the warlords were dead and the land would never again be devastated. After so many years of lying dormant, yellow stalks of wheat began to sprout like lost children returning home.

Joseph, I never heard again from Hakim after medical school. I asked many of the villagers if they knew his family or had heard of his people, but no one knew him. He was my trainer and mentor, preparing me for what I would face here. I believe I have been passing my test, but I wish he were here to grade me. He knew that I would have to be strong to face this challenge.

Somewhere in this camp I became Dr. Potter–no longer just a kid carrying Papa Jacob's bag. Three of the doctors are brothers, who attended medical school together and graduated a year apart. Each one has specialized in different areas of medicines. Bob, Brad, and Brooks–the "B" brothers–sometimes go into the most dangerous places of the jungle looking for villagers that need help. They have been warned of bandits and thieves that kill stranded travelers with clubs. Often they find orphans in the jungles and have started their own orphan community. They have cleared an area of the jungle, built a stadium out of crates and pieces of boards, and organized Sunday baseball games.

The brothers want to secretly observe ZsaZsa's palace to learn what he is really doing. I warned them that spying on him was foolish, because we had come close to death the last time. However, I mentioned that when I climbed to the top of a tree, I heard a voice say that I was eternal and I could not die.

Your brother, David

Dear Joseph,

Drums have been beating for almost two weeks. A tribal war between the Hutus and Tutsis is festering. A message came from a neighboring village last night describing the massacre that occurred when the Hutus invaded the Tutsis villages. Every man, woman, and child was hacked to death by men carrying machetes. The Hutus are like a band of locusts; they will not be content until everyone is killed. The stink of death fills the air for miles; no one could go into the village and bury the bodies, because of the surprise attacks by the Hutus. Great fear has now consumed the country; people are collecting guns in great number.

I am confused, Joseph, because the Hutus look like the Tutsis; they are both tall and dark-skinned, except the Tutsis are taller. Now once again great masses of people are leaving the country and refugees are living on the plain on the outskirts of the city. Every day we hear reports about neighboring villages where people are being hacked to death in just minutes.

It was just a matter of time before they would come for us. So we gathered all the food and water we could carry and any weapons we could find to protect ourselves and fortified the mission. We built trenches around the mission and cut down trees, hoping that it would stop any vehicles from penetrating our defenses. However, often one of the Hutus would drive through the village in a jeep with a man sitting on the back with a mounted machine gun spewing bullets everywhere. And the tribal warriors would come in hacking to death any survivors.

I didn't know whether we could hold out against the tribal warriors that were a day away from us. That night all the men formed a line surrounding the mission. We were determined to fight to the death if necessary. There was nothing else we could do now but fight.

During the night a young boy, who had escaped the slaughter of his village, staggered into the mission bleeding. The Hutus had cut his face and head with a machete.

Somehow he managed to walk five miles to warn us that they were coming. We bandaged his face and wrapped his head as best we could, but he died from loss of blood.

Zear is pregnant with our second child. My son Jacob has learned to shoot a rifle. I have always believed in peace, but I don't know what to think anymore. I didn't want to see my son and wife killed like the boy who came to our mission. God, why did I stay in Africa? I could have moved my wife and son out of here years ago. But trying to carry out the tradition of Papa Jacob...who did I think I was to put my family in this situation? I said to myself many times.

Now we all waited, listening for any signs of life coming from the jungle. There was nothing else to do. All the work we had done in the past hours had taken its toll on me, and I fell asleep in one of the trenches with a gun in my hand. I felt ashamed–I had come here to heal people, not to destroy them.

Suddenly I was awakened by the sound of machine gunfire maybe five miles away and people screaming. Maybe the Hutus had killed the refugees on the plains. I didn't know what to think, but I knew that people were pleading for their lives and dying. My God, I asked myself, what is going on? I thought I must have been out of my mind to come here. I could have stayed at Papa Jacob's vineyard; at least I would have been safe there. The killing went on for hours until the light of day began to appear over the top of the trees.

Then a man ran out of the jungle yelling that he was a messenger. "The Ordained of God has put an end to the death and the warfare in the land. He has executed all the enemies of the government. Peace has returned to the land again. The Ordained of God has killed them all. Only a few more are facing death, and then this nightmare will be over."

"Who is the Ordained of God?" I asked.

He yelled back, "ZsaZsa-Baba. He killed them all."

Dr. Wilderbee, the "B" brothers, and I decided to go where we had seen pillars of smoke rising. When we arrived at a large clearing on the plains, we saw about three hundred men stripped naked on their knees with their hands behind their necks. As ZsaZsa's men walked by each one shooting them in the head, their bodies were kicked into a huge trench behind them. Hutus and Tutsi warriors were now lying together.

I could not believe so many people were being gunned down! I ran towards ZsaZsa crying out and pleading with him. "Why must you kill them now? You have already defeated them."

He looked at me amazed and then started laughing. "Are you some kind of fool? You and your whole village would have been hacked to death if I did not stop this madness last night. These men were killers and they deserved a quick death."

Then he grabbed my collar and dragged me to another pit where the corpses of men, women, and children lay. Their bodies were already starting to stink as the morning sun started to shine on the ground. His men poured large buckets of gasoline onto the pile of bodies and set them on fire.

"What would happen to your precious medical center? It would not exist right now if it were not for me," ZsaZsa continued.

Standing over me and sneering, he said, "You are too weak to survive here. You would have to let your own people die. You don't deserve to live." He smiled at me with teeth stained with the blood of the people that he had killed. And then he hit me in the face and broke one of my front teeth. Next he motioned to his men to strip my clothes off. Laughing, he said, "It is time that you started a mission somewhere else."

When the doctors saw from a distance that I was being prepared to be executed, they ran off.

"Leave them alone," ZsaZsa told his men. "We have one coward today; we do not need to kill anymore."

With my clothes torn off, I was led towards the trench where they were going to shoot me and let my body fall into the Tutsi and Hutu grave behind me. They wrapped the torn strips from my shirt around my head until I could no longer see.

I could not believe I would be facing death so quickly; I did not have time to say goodbye to Zear or little Jacob. I would never see my unborn baby. God have mercy on me, I whispered to myself.

Next I heard ZsaZsa saying, "Gentlemen on the count of three you know what to do. One–two–three." The sound of guns exploded in my head as I fell to the earth and urinated on myself. I heard his men laughing at me. Slowly I removed the rag from my eyes and saw all of them jumping into their trucks, and ZsaZsa calling out, "I cannot kill you. You are a doctor; we need doctors in this country." They drove away in a procession of trucks and jeeps, leaving me alone on the dusty plain with a pile of bodies burning behind me.

Your brother, David

Dear Joseph,

The fighting is over; there is no more killing. It seems as if the land has once again survived this season of drought. Dust has covered the young sprouts that are struggling to survive. The sprouts have been squashed by boots, burned with fire, and cut down beyond recognition; yet they are peeking through the soil, laughing in the morning dew. The dust of war has covered the graves but it does not record where they were buried, what their dreams were, nor praise the dead. Sometimes the dust can last up to three months, until nothing can live in this environment. Even the animals go into hiding as these winds reclaim the plains. Zebras and antelopes find refuge from the devastating elements by hiding in the tall brush and along the hillsides. Death has even conquered the dust like a band member who has marched proudly in the streets unhindered or broken in his stride. But the dust has come too late. There is nothing here but bodies to be claimed by the earth and time. Yet there is something here that even death or nature could not overcome. Only a certain species of bird can live in this environment and survive.

ZsaZsa-Baba is like a parasite that always survives by feeding sumptuously on the bones of others when there is nothing else to eat. He has emerged once again as a hero, because he stopped the fighting between the Tutsis and Hutus. He filled more graves than both groups could do together. It appears that he had become bored with running the country and the warfare gave him reason to justify his position.

Yet the people did not cheer for him, nor did they give him a parade for what he did. ZsaZsa did not stop with killing the Tutsis and Hutus; instead he lined up his enemies and executed them one at a time. He staged a victory celebration for himself and a parade and threatened the villagers if they did not attend and cheer for him–only at gunpoint did they comply.

He invited the foreign press to the palace for his victory party. In a letter to us he apologized for what had happened to us on the plains at the end of the tribal wars. He said that I should forgive him for his rude display of cruelty. After all, when he arrived, he was in the spirit of the battle and I should understand that the only thing that mattered was the survival of his people. It was a sickening attempt to cover his back, before the international community arrived; for he did not know who I would tell about the war and the number of people that he had killed and burned that day.

Days after the killings his men came through the mission and seized all the cameras, hoping to destroy any evidence as to what had happened on the plains.

Your brother, David

Dear Joseph,

All I have now to send to you are these letters. You may never see them, but I have placed them in God's hands. I may never see you, Joseph, but I will never forget the short time we shared together even after Mama died–you kept us together and made sure she had a decent funeral. I wish you were here so that I might have a decent funeral. I do not know when ZsaZsa's men will come for me and destroy the mission. I have left instructions with Papa Jacob to keep all my letters. This is my last request that these letters survive.

Papa Jacob wrote that we should leave here while there is time. However, I cannot abandon the mission or the doctors who have fought so hard to keep it. Perhaps this is my last swan song. I have sent Zear and my child Jacob out of the mission. They are traveling with some young men towards the airport on their way to Papa Jacob's vineyards.

One of ZsaZsa's men defected the other day. In the middle of the night he came to the mission crying and saying that ZsaZsa was going to kill him. He was so afraid that he would hardly say his name out loud. ZsaZsa had taken on some godlike quality, and the people believe that just saying his name out loud would cause him to come to their home and execute them. They are consumed with fear and superstition. Young girls, they say, are offered to him in a ritual to pacify his wrath.

The defector said that ZsaZsa had started the tribal wars between the Tutsis and Hutus. He was the one who burned down the villages of the Tutsis and then left their tribal markings and shields on the ground. Whole groups were executed so fast that ZsaZsa did not take the time to make sure they were dead before burying them. Sometimes you could hear the muffled sound under the dirt of them begging for mercy. He said that he felt unclean and had tried washing his hands but nothing had worked.

Moreover he had told the whole story to a reporter and somehow ZsaZsa found out about it. Hearing drums beating in the distance, he thought it was ZsaZsa's men looking for him. In a panic he ran into the bush. A few days later we heard that they found someone in the wilderness with his tongue cut out. The wrath of ZsaZsa had detected him–he was a spirit that could see in the dark, take the form of a bird, or become the vines in the jungle and choke you to death.

Something unpredictable happened the other day. A truck rumbled into the mission with soldiers calling out to the doctors, "The anointed of God is about to die; you must save him." In one sudden motion, they laid ZsaZsa on a cot before me. He could not talk; it was as if he was choking to death. We were all shocked beyond belief. I asked what was wrong and they said that a poisonous snake had crawled into the palace and had bitten him. They brought the dead snake: it was a baby, so its venom wasn't enough to kill a man, only paralyze him temporarily.

My enemy lay before me, delivered on a silver tray. I felt like David standing before Saul. Maybe I should overdose him with a shot of morphine–that would be a quick way to annihilate him. But I am still a doctor and I cannot do this even to him. I decided that I would have some fun and cried out saying, "Furglia disease has taken hold of him. It will be only a matter of time before he swells up and his organs burst within him." ZsaZsa could not do anything but moan. The soldiers cried out in fear.

"Yes, it acts very quickly," I said as I closed my bag. "Take him away; there is nothing I can do for him."

Just then guns were pressed against my head and someone said, "Do something now or die."

I cleaned and stitched the wound. The toxin was wearing off. As he started coming to, he looked at me with anger in his eyes, "We will meet again, Potter." There was no mercy in his eyes, no forgiveness. As quickly as they came, they loaded him in the truck and disappeared in the darkness.

The other day I received a *National Geographic* in the mail with a picture on the cover of Papa Jacob holding one of the migrant worker's babies in his arms, listening with a stethoscope to the child's heartbeat. The caption read: "A Mission Field Is His Backyard." Papa Jacob had somehow made his peace with God and found a new mission field just outside his door. God in his own time gave him a new purpose and a new assignment.

I wonder how long I can keep my family in this land where death is all around. Surely I can find a job at some community hospital where I would not endanger my life. But Zear would not have it any other way. When the young men tried to drive her to the airport, she fought to come back to me. Now we are waiting for ZsaZsa to return. Everyone is afraid to leave the area. We are running out of food and medical supplies, and our water is almost gone. Yet we are still here.

Your brother, David

Dear Joseph,

Can you believe this good news! Today I received a letter from Papa Jacob. Missy Winkleton had written to him about my brother. She said he was a boy at the Good Shepherd Home in the thirties, whom she had been searching for. I picked the letter up in my hands with tears streaming from my eyes–I could not believe that after all these years there was some information about my family, my history, my life. I cried out loud, running through the camp.

Zear and the other doctors thought that I had been attacked. She ran to me, checking me over from head to foot. Clasping the old letter in my hands, I told her I was all right. "I don't know how Missy Winkleton found me," I said, "but she knows where Joseph is." What a marvelous day! The paper felt as if it had been sitting on someone's office desk for a long time. I began to read it.

Dear David Potter,

I am the caretaker and niece of Betty Van Horn. I was reading an article in the *National Geographic* about Papa Jacob. It mentioned that he had a son David, who was Colored and was working as a doctor in Africa. I would not have thought much about it, except he said that your name before you were adopted was Potter. When I read that, I asked my aunt if she remembered you. She said that she remembered a Joseph Potter had a brother named David and two sisters named Ruth and Sarah.

I am sending these letters to you because she died last week. I hope you are the brother that Joseph and Betty Van Horn have been searching for, for so many years.

The letter went something like this.

It is raining here in Salina, Kansas. A horrible storm is raging outside, as if something needed to be resolved, or something in the atmosphere needed to be set free.

Betty took me in when my mother and father died in a car accident when I was very young. She said that she worked at a place called the Home of the Good Shepard, which was an orphanage in the thirties. She has been kind to me over the years, yet there has been some haunting pain in her eyes that I cannot explain. Ever since I can remember she has talked about a horrible demonic woman named Bradenkins.

"We helped her beat the children," she said, "and locked them in dark closets. Sometimes in life you can be a follower to the point of stupidity.

"I remember when she told me to beat Joseph. The other housemothers and I dragged him into the basement, where we had taken other children before to receive their beatings. But somehow when we took him into the basement, everything went completely black. We could not see anything. It was as though the basement was a portal; we could not feel the floor or any walls. I heard the other housemother screaming as we somehow were transported to the front yard, looking at the evening stars.

"Something about this Joseph scared all of us. I could not speak about this for many years. Something protected Joseph, but something grabbed us and took us outside in one motion. It was as if God were saying enough is enough.

"The night that Joseph finally ran away, everyone was afraid to go after him. From that time on, I could not hit another child. I felt so far away from God that I realized it was time to change, and I began to really care for the children. I washed their clothes and tried to cook real meals for them. Mrs. Bradenkins still believed that we were feeding them wheat paste, but we were now feeding them a new meal, one made from our heart."

My dear Mr. Potter, I am sending these letters to you in care of Dr. Mitchell, your Papa Jacob. I pray they might benefit you.

I examined these letters from her niece. Could this be my brother? I wondered.

These are the last words Betty Van Horn dictated to me, she wrote: "I have never seen a storm last so long. For four days now it has raged against the skies. Betty is the sweetest woman I have ever known. She was almost seventy when she took me in. A tireless worker for so many children's causes, she has spent most of her life feeding the homeless in the soup kitchen that she started in the city.

She has always talked about Joseph and what happened to her that night. Her face was burned on one side–something weird happened to all in the home when it burned down. She said it was a sign from God that he would mark all of those who needed to change. After Mrs. Bradenkins' death, the Home of the Good Shepherd became a different place.

In the basement she found file after file about long forgotten children that entered the orphanage. "I don't know how the fire started," Betty said, "but there comes a time when certain things must come to an end. I was awakened out of my sleep on July 27, 1937, when black smoke came pouring out of the room that Mrs. Bradenkins used to stay in. The fire moved through the house like it was trying to attack the children. Briefly I thought I saw Mrs. Bradenkins inside the fire running and laughing. However, I knew she had died a month ago and she could not be here. But I tell you, Joseph, I could smell her. She was in that house, evil was there, and now she came back. I called out to the children: 'Mrs. Bradenkins is back in the house again. Run for your lives.'

"She had come to reap revenge on the children one last time. The flames smelled like a mixture of salt and sweat, as if hell had opened a door. I tell you I could hear her hissing and screaming from the fire. I was frightened out of my mind, but I ran faster than the fire. I wrapped children under my coat and led them out of the screaming, hissing flames.

"I tell you something. I spoke to that fire: 'You devil woman Bradenkins, I command you to go back to hell, to the wretched place from which you came.' I was able to lead fourteen children out of the house before it developed into a screaming blaze. Yet seven other children were killed that night–somehow she got to them first. I tried to go back in but the other housemothers held me back; but I broke loose, and in a last desperate attempt, I ran through the burning house. I saw the staircase collapse and chairs and tables flying through the air. Then I saw two more children hiding in a corner crying out. The fire was almost on them. I wrapped them in my coat and ran toward the front window and we all fell out together. We all heard Mrs. Bradenkins laughing as the house fell in a blaze of rubble."

I will be writing to you again to confirm my findings about your brother.

Sincerely,

Missy Winkleton

Dear Joseph,

Laughing and playing kick-the-ball in the field with a group of children, I had completely forgotten about the possibility that ZsaZsa's soldiers could come and destroy the mission at any moment. It seemed that God had made this happy time for me to laugh.

However, as I grabbed the ball and started running with it, I was tackled to the ground by the children. Just then a young man ran towards me, breathlessly urging me, "Dr. Potter, you must come immediately. Please come, now! Your Papa Jacob is on the phone. Something has happened; you must come!"

The urgent tone of his voice sent fear through my veins. I prayed silently. "Lord, I need your help. I cannot take any more bad news." Once again I was thrust back into the reality of the mission and my surroundings. I dusted myself off and ran back to the mission with the young man.

"Papa Jacob is on the phone, David. You need to speak with him," Zear said as she handed me the phone.

I heard Papa Jacob's garbled voice in the distance, saying, "David, what took you so long to answer this phone? There is so much static on this line that it sounds like a chicken scratching in a hen house. Are you ready for this, David? Missy Winkleton called me and gave me what I think is the phone number of your brother Joseph."

I became quiet; my breath was taken away, and tears began welling up in my eyes. I could hear him saying, "Son, are you still there? Are you still on the line?"

"Yes Papa," I said, "I am still here."

"She called me and left a number for you to call if you want to reach your brother."

I heard Mama Flo's voice in the background saying, "Have you been eating all right? I am going to send you some of my chicken."

"Son, when are you coming home? I am worried about you."

I hurriedly wrote down the number as the phone went dead. Over and over again, I called the number but only received static. It was not unusual for the phone to go dead for days and then operate again without notice.

Zear looked at me and said, "David, don't give up now."

I dialed the number again and a woman answered.

"I am David Potter, Dr. David Potter, and I'm calling from Africa. I received a letter from Missy Winkleton, who believes that Joseph Potter is my brother," I said.

Rwanda, Africa

Dear Joseph,

I will never forget the day I called you. The woman who answered the phone said, "I am Claudette Potter. Yes, my husband's name is Joseph. My God, my God, yes, he had a brother named David and also two sisters named Ruth and Sarah. Yes, pleassse stay on the phone; I will get him right away."

In the background I could hear some screaming and laughter. "Joseph, there's a man on the phone and he's calling from Africa. I think it is your brother."

The next breathless voice I heard was yours. "Yes, yes, I am Joseph Potter. Who are you?"

"I think I am your brother David."

You began crying out, "HOLIEEEEE MOLLLLIE! It is really you!"

We were sobbing, laughing, and saying, "THE HOLIEEE MOLLLIES ARE BACK AGAIN. WATCH OUT WORLD! WE'RE BACK AGAIN."

We talked about everything that had happened to us over the last twenty years–about our foster homes, how you had lost your leg in the Army, about my wife, son Jacob, and new baby on the way.

Then you got quiet and said, "I have to tell you about Ruth. She was killed in the South. It was a horrible death, but before she died she saw Mama. My spirit is at peace with her now; because I know that she is all right, David. I can just feel it within me. She is all right, David."

I asked, "What about Sarah? What about our little sister Sarah?"

"All I know is that she is something like a healer in the Midwest. That's all I know."

We talked for over an hour as the phone became increasingly more static. We made plans to spend Christmas day together in America opening presents.

Just then the static filled the phone and it went dead. With hands held high towards the sky, I whispered, "Thank you."

Your brother,

David

15.

Filled with excitement and walking around with a stupid grin on my face for days, I began planning for my brother's arrival in December. I heard from that little, skinny runt! And he had become a doctor working in Africa–imagine that! I could not wait to see him again.

The skies of late October were now turning into sudden transitions of sunlight and wind. It was a time when nature was struggling within itself. Huge white clouds would appear floating freely in the skies unhindered, unstoppable and unbroken, only to be torn apart minutes later, punctured by sunlight and intense winds.

Our house was a beautiful expression of love and hard work. We had scraped, painted, and plastered the house, repaired the roof, built a new picket fence, and replaced old windows. We cultivated the ground and planted a beautiful garden that produced pumpkins and watermelons and squash. The early autumn harvest was now under way, and Claudette was busy in the backyard collecting squash and melons in an old gunny sack.

Sitting on the front porch I thought about how David must look now. I imagined him coming through the train station carrying his bags and briefcase, looking very dignified with his small spectacles resting on his nose, wearing a dark fedora and long, black trench coat. His wife Zear would be walking with him, moving through the crowd and holding little Jacob's hand. Then in the middle of the huge crowd he would see me in the distance, drop his bags and briefcase, and run toward me with his spectacles flying off his nose and trench coat flapping in the wind. No longer looking like David the doctor, but looking like David the little brother that I remembered. We would hug each other in the train station, falling on the floor, laughing and tumbling while everyone walked by gawking.

Now the train station was gone, and we were children again rolling down a midnight hillside, watching the stars twinkling in the night. The wind began picking up; leaves began to swirl in small circular motions.

Then I heard something that sounded like a scream, and the neighbor's dogs began barking wildly. The wind descended in a fury; dormant leaves now became a storm blowing through the yard. The force of the wind and dust suddenly disrupted the warm and peaceful afternoon and caused me to cover my face with my hands.

Something was not right–I could feel it. The atmosphere was cold and lonely. I heard thunder in the skies and saw flashes of lightning. There were no reports of this storm on the news. Why didn't they warn us of this sudden storm earlier? I called out to Claudette. "Claudette, there's a storm coming. You need to take cover. Claudette, do you hear me? There's a storm coming and you need to take cover now."

When she didn't answer, I ran to the backyard where I found her lying on the ground in the garden. Her eyes were still and clear; they did not move as she looked up towards the sky. I shook her and pleaded with her to wake up, but she did not move. "Oh, my God, what has happened?" I cried out. But the rushing of the leaves around me muffled my pleadings towards the heavens.

16.

Standing amid the autumn leaves and holding her in my arms, I cried out for anyone to help me. In one brief moment she was gone. Surely I should've had time to just say goodbye. I should've had time to let her know how she had redeemed me during the war when I was ready to let my life be tossed on the junk pile.

"Claudette, you polished me, poured new wine into this old vessel, and allowed me to shine again," I lamented as I shook her and pleaded with her to wake up. But nothing happened. The soft brown eyes just stared at me, unaware of my pleading and crying. Frantically I ran to the house to call the emergency operator for help. Then I ran back to her shouting, "Not now, Claudette. Don't you leave, not just yet, not just yet! I want you to meet my brother David. You will like him. We are going to spend Christmas together. Don't you leave, not just yet! You have to come back to me; I can't make it by myself. Claudette, wake up. Don't you leave me! Dear God, please don't let her leave me, not just now." I fell upon her tiny body, sobbing uncontrollably.

When the paramedics arrived, a small crowd of neighbors came out of their houses to see what had happened. I heard them whispering, "Something has happened to Claudette. Oh God, I hope she is all right. She is not moving. Oh, dear God!"

The paramedics pulled me away so they could check her vital signs, but there was no response. I could tell from the frightened look on their faces that the situation was critical. They quickly placed her on a stretcher and almost ran towards the ambulance as I followed close behind, reaching out to her, trying to hold her one last time. One of them said, "Please, Mr. Potter, you have to let us do our job."

At the hospital I knew that she had died when I saw the doctors walking towards me with their eyes still and motionless. They said that she had died quickly of an aneurysm. A vein in her head had ruptured not allowing blood and oxygen to flow through her.

My wife of thirty-one years had passed as quickly as the wind that sweeps over the leaves, lifts them in the air, and scatters them to unknown destinations. I wept again, falling weakly into the arms of the doctor. "Surely you can do something. Take your black bags and do something," I yelled. "Please, have mercy."

"We're sorry, Mr. Potter, but she died long before arriving at the hospital." They assured me that they had done all they could but death came quickly. It ripped her from my arms cruelly, hurtfully, without mercy.

I came home alone, still looking for her to call me in to eat dinner or ask me when I was coming inside. "You've been raking those leaves long enough. You don't want to catch a cold," I could hear her saying. I walked from room to room trying to see her again.

All her clothes still hung in the closet, because I could not move or rearrange anything; everything had to stay the same. I was not ready to let Claudette go or allow her sweetness to evaporate into the heavens.

Anger flooded through me like water overflowing a lake, knocking down trees, overtaking roads, and destroying houses. Alone in the darkened house, I cried out to God. "Why must you take everyone that I love? Everything that I wanted to hold on to, you allowed it to be taken from my arms. What am I supposed to do now?"

I called all her relatives and informed everyone that she knew and worked with about the funeral arrangements. Ladies from the church came to the house with dinners and fruit baskets and freshly baked bread. The day of the funeral the minister at the church spoke of her sacrifice of service, her subtle, gentle, but powerful compassion in helping others. The church was filled to capacity, and an overflow of people stood outside. People from the surrounding neighborhoods came to our house. Claudette's relatives were going through the house asking when I was going to remove her clothes. Some of them began helping themselves to her belongings–one of her aunts had five dresses crumpled in her arms saying, "She was a sweet child, but she won't need these anymore."

In a rage I yelled at everyone. "You leave Claudette's things alone. How dare you move her stuff! You have no right to go through her things!" I told them that the funeral was over and they should leave the house. I could not take this flock of vultures anymore.

All during the week people came to tell me how she had helped them in the hospital when they were so afraid of being alone and didn't know whether they were going to make it. Young mothers related how she watched their children so they could run their errands. In autumn she took our homegrown vegetables to feed the homeless. She was always canning, sewing, and patching, or holding someone's hand. Claudette was a jar of God's honey; she was sweeter than a strawberry sundae on a hot summer's day.

The very next day I awakened to the sound of a tree falling in the backyard. Another storm had arisen and the morning was dark and cold; the sound of thunder shook the house. Rain was pounding on the house as if it were falling in buckets. What was happening in the heavens? I was frightened and wanted to hide in the closet until the storm was gone.

My grief for Claudette was so overwhelming that I did not even want to dress myself or wash my face. I wanted to hide in the closet until the darkness was gone, until the storm was over, until I could hear her voice in the house again.

Unexpectedly I heard someone knocking on the front door. At first I thought it was the rain or hail pounding against the door. But the knocking was urgent and relentless. Slowly I put on my robe and found my house shoes in the dark. Who could be knocking on my door in the middle of this storm? I opened the door and peeked outside. A young man from a delivery service was standing there. "Are you Mr. Joseph Potter?"

"Yes."

"I have an international letter that I need you to sign for."

I signed for the letter and tore open the important-looking envelope that read:

To Mr. Potter on behalf of the International Community and the United Nations.

> I regret to inform you that a mass execution has occurred in Rwanda, Africa. Chancellor ZsaZsa-Baba has executed fifty-four doctors, one of whom is your brother, Dr. David Potter. A survivor said that Dr. Potter valiantly went into the forest and fought ZsaZsa's soldiers when a group of children had been taken from a neighboring village to be sold into slavery.

> An army of peacekeepers and freedom fighters have arrived in the country to airlift any survivors out of the region. The international community will not tolerate this injustice from the Rwandan government. Plans are being made by allied countries to fight until human and civil rights are restored to the citizens of that nation.

> Foreign Ambassador of the United States
> Dr. Henry McMillian

Once again I fell to my knees crying and asking God to send one of the big locomotives to me–like the ones I remember when

T. S. Eure

I was a child and my father was a porter. I can still hear his voice in the station. "Now boarding to Milwaukee, St. Louis, Chicago. All aboard. Now loading." Oh come for me, mighty train. Lift your wheels through this hail and rain. Take me, for my bags are packed.

17.

I have discovered that a porch swing can become a time machine. For ten years I did nothing but sit and watch the decay of my home and the ruin of my mind. The paint slowly started to peel away; the manicured lawn became a sprawling thicket with wild hedges sprouting everywhere. Dust covered the shelves and filled the cupboards. The gutters began to fall off the house in a sloping manner. And newspapers began filling the porch and yard.

Comfortable in my time machine I rocked back and forth, not caring for anyone and no one caring for me. I had enough money from my retirement to live the rest of my days inside my house. I paid all my bills by mail and had groceries delivered to the house. Eventually going out on the porch took too much effort, so I retreated into the darkness of the house to be seen by no one again.

Every so often I could hear the neighborhood children talking about me as they walked past the house, saying, "That is crazy, old man Potter's house. His wife died a few years ago and he still keeps her body in his room." They always ran by the house daring each other to go in and see my wife's dead body.

The neighbors constantly complained about my yard and how it looked like a jungle. I received citation after citation from the city demanding that I cut the grass, trim the hedges, and repair my house. But I ignored their letters.

When Claudette was alive, I used to like looking at the trees–their beautiful branches and leaves were a welcome relief from the summer's heat. But something happened to the trees. Perhaps they did not hear laughter anymore. Perhaps the trees could not hear Claudette and me playfully wrestling on the lawn in the twilight hours. Perhaps they could not hear the neighbors coming by telling stories and laughing under them. Now nothing would grow right. The trees resembled dead hands reaching out. Only a few leaves would branch out in the spring and then wither into brown twigs by August. Twisted branches graced the lawn and green, thick moss began covering the dark brown bark. Maybe the trees needed someone to whisper to them or to pray under their branches. But I did not feel like talking to them.

Weeds growing in the lawn had sharp, sticky thorns that assaulted any visitors. A thorny vine had started growing in front of the house threatening anyone coming near. Ten years had passed since I last cut my hair, and twisted white locks had erupted from my head in tangled strands. The house was cluttered with old bottles and stacks of papers and broken dishes. One room was filled with piles of books lying on the floor creating a dusty library. Over the years I had taken the prescription of depression and relaxed with my feet up in this cozy recliner of self-pity. I considered taking my life, but that also would require too much effort. I had lived for years in my tattered pajamas; my house shoes were so old they looked like balls of dust on my feet.

Autumn was coming once again. The wind was stirring up the dead things that sought to dig themselves into the earth, and some creatures had wrapped themselves up into a tight ball in their den, content not to see the sunlight for another season.

But today when I looked out the window, I saw something causing the apple tree to sway from side to side. It was the only tree that had survived the disease-eaten lawn and moss-covered landscape. It would fight each year to push out a fair amount of apples in this thicket of despair. I saw children stealing apples. A little skinny kid was shaking the branches while a fat one was shimmering across a limb. I heard the little skinny kid say, "Hurry up, you fool. Can't you move any faster? If you wake up Crazy Old Man Potter, our goose will really be cooked."

The fat kid answered. "Will you be quiet down there? I am almost to the good ones."

The skinny kid started shaking the tree violently with a rattling sound. Anger swelled up within me, starting in my toes and slowly moving through my joints and bones, causing me to shake and tremble. I screamed out, weakly at first, my voice cracking and rumbling. "How dare you come on my property and steal my apples. I could have made a pie or apple fritters out of those apples. I could have canned me some sliced apples and had them during the winter. I could have made some apple butter or apple bread."

I could not allow this injustice to continue. I found an old stick in the yard and raised it over my head, yelling at the kids: "You get out of my yard or I'll beat you with this stick. Do you hear me? I will beat you with my last ounce of strength. I will beat you until I break this stick over your heads."

Somehow I connected with the tree–it was the only source of life in the yard. Claudette had planted the tree the very first year we moved into the house. Now they were not stealing apples, they were stealing the last fragments of my soul.

The kids looked terrified and screamed at the top of their voices. "Crazy Old Man Potter is out of the house and he's going to kill us. Run for your lives."

The small skinny kid took off like a flash running to the fence and squeezing through a hole where they had bent back a board. I could not catch him for he sped by me so fast that I almost stumbled. The fat kid was now high on a tree limb. He cried out almost moaning and saying, "Ohhhhhh, Ohhhhhh, Pleassse, someone help me!" Then all at once the limb broke and he came crashing through the tree, breaking limb after limb until he hit the ground like a sack of potatoes.

He quickly sprang to his feet, dodging me in a shifting motion. He almost succeeded as he ran towards the hole in the fence, but somehow in the final moment before his escape to freedom, his jeans caught on the rough board. I was ready to beat this kid senseless. I was ready to beat him for causing Claudette to die and leaving me alone in this house. I was ready to beat him for not allowing me to have Christmas with David again, and for allowing the state people to separate me from Ruth and Sarah. I was going to beat him until I felt good about myself again.

But something began to happen. Pain paralyzed me and caused me to fall backward, staggering in the yard. I could not catch my breath. "I cannot breathe," I said to myself. "Somebody, help me. I cannot breathe. Help me, please, someone."

18.

I couldn't see anything–the yard, the apple tree, the children–everything was gone. But I heard the howling wind moving across the small shelter in which I was confined. I was afraid but I felt for the door latch above me and stumbled out of the darkness into the bright light of a Midwestern plain. White, soft clouds floated silently across the sky and depleted cornfields spread out in front of me.

Something like this had happened before when the housemothers tried to beat me in the basement of the orphanage. One moment they were with me and the next moment they had vanished. I could not explain the strange things that occurred. But now it was happening again. Apparently I had climbed out of a storm cellar of a condemned farmhouse. Old, broken down farm equipment lay rusting all about. The roof of the house was torn off as if a storm had come through and destroyed it in one motion.

While standing in my bed pajamas and old house shoes, I saw a little boy riding an old bicycle. He stopped in front of me and said, "Mister, are you all right? Do you need a doctor?" I assured him that I was fine. But I knew that I needed to change my clothes. I found a suitcase by the cellar door with neatly folded clothes–a pair of overalls, a flannel shirt, a pair of old boots, and a sun-baked hat atop a pitchfork. I put on the clothes and began walking down the dusty road.

Looking at my new surroundings, I felt a sense of relief. The memories of the house and my years of hiding seemed so distant now.

There is little vegetation here, as if a major drought had devoured the land. Dust blows everywhere. I can even taste it in my mouth as it falls on my lips. Faded, yellow, dead cornstalks poke out of the cracked and broken soil. Erosion has caused trees to be uprooted, creating a feast for termites and beetle bugs to enjoy. Skeletons of dead rabbits and squirrels lay scattered upon the ground. Without warning the dust rolls down a hillside creating a temporary daytime fog.

In the distance I see homes that are partly covered with dust. These ancient ruins have now surrendered as the dust blows into the windows of abandoned farmhouses. The dust has buried old farm machinery that stands like useless skeletons in forgotten fields. Nothing is green here; not a single leaf or twig shows any signs of life.

As I walk through the clapboard neighborhoods, I see women wrapping their children's faces with holy quilts, believing they will be preserved against these merciless elements. Men wander through the fields looking lost; their skin is cracked and bleached like the fields. The dust has settled between their teeth and filled their ears. There is no need to dress up anymore or put on a Sunday shirt.

I see a weather-beaten sign that says Welcome to Kansas. I need water; I can hardly breathe. A little fat kid is selling apples near a broken-down shack. To my surprise he asks, "Do you still want your apples?"

"Apples?"

"Yes," he says, "from the apple tree."

Then I remember this is the same kid that I chased in my front yard. "What are you doing here?"

"I get around," the kid replies.

Then I see a farmhouse and about twelve Model T cars assembled around an old house.

"What's going on over there," I asked the boy.

"They're having a sale."

I walked up to the yard where the sale was taking place. A solemn procession of men and women were standing in front of the small, wood-framed house. The men were dressed in blue jeans, and patched-up, thread-bare overalls. The auctioneer's voice sounded like the whistling howl of a flute out of tune, like the rattling, throaty sound that men make when their dreams suffocate in the atmosphere.

The auctioneer hollers, "What do I hear for this fine tilling hoe; it is still as sharp as the day it was made."

A weak hand rises in the air. "I'll give you five dollars for it.

An old, termite-eaten lawn chair with weak hinges was brought up next. Someone bought it for fifteen dollars. Old, cracked jars and vases were sold for a dollar each. Tractor parts and combines were the last items sold.

Then a man, his wife, and five children appeared. They loaded everything they had into an old, beat-up, open-seated truck. Crates and gunny sacks were all tied down. One by one the neighbors brought them gifts and said their last goodbyes. One old guy came hobbling with a cane, holding up a huge jar of pennies, dimes and quarters. He said, "I have been saving these coins for more years than I have lived. I really don't have enough life left to spend it all. I pray that they will bless you in your new home in California."

The man in the truck protested, saying that he could not take it. The old man reached in and grabbed the man's arms, saying, "Those children of yours have to eat. I am going to be covered with this dust. At least something good will branch out and grow elsewhere." Then he walked away.

Next a large woman came to the truck saying, "I saved these preserves for many years. Do you remember fifteen years ago when we had that harvest dance, and we had so much produce that year that our bins could not hold them all? Do you remember when we had the dance over at the McGinnis barn, and the tables were filled with so many pies that we ran out of table space for them? I saved and canned those apples from that year. We took our shoes off and danced until the roosters crowed in the morning. When you eat these apples, I want you to think of that time." With that the old lady stepped back and cried in the arms of another woman.

Another old woman stepped forward quietly saying, "I sewed all of our names on this blanket so you will never forget us when we're all gone, and the land has redeemed itself, and your grandchildren come back to find our graves and bless the land."

Then the man in the truck came out and took off his hat. He looked like a piece of driftwood, the dark circles around his eyes and his sun-baked face bore testimony to the fight with nature that he had endured. Sounding like a Civil War general leaving his troops for the last time, he said, "You have done some good things for my family. I am not good at making speeches, but I understand what it means to be a neighbor. It's not just a word; it's a way of living. I now know that nothing can destroy us. This dust cannot destroy us; the banks cannot destroy us, not even the termites, as long as we are able to share what we have. The bank may be able to foreclose on our home, but they will not be able to overcome our strength to endure and fight and survive; for we will return to bless you as you have blessed us." With that he loaded his wife and children on the truck and drove down the road with the engine backfiring in a cloud of smoke.

As I looked around I wondered how anyone could live in this environment. Then I spoke up. "Why don't you people just leave? You need to get out of here. I am going to find the way out of here too. Why would you stay in such a place?"

Suddenly I heard a clap of thunder and saw lightning flash in the darkened skies. Someone cried out, "My God, it's going to rain!" Then another clap of thunder sounded and a bolt of lightning knocked down an old tree in the distance. All at once as if some heavenly switch was turned on, a deluge of water poured down. People were laughing and taking their shoes off and dancing as the water poured into the cracks and crevices of the earth. Quickly pools of mud formed on the once dry ground. An old man sat down in the mud laughing and crying at the same time; his friends were trying to get him to go home and take cover. The rain turned into blowing, bucket-size raindrops that splattered the faces of the rain dancers. An old fence was picked up and blown into fragments. Roofs were being torn off of homes and shingles were twirling through the air.

When I looked around, I found that everyone had left the area to take shelter in their homes. The wind was now picking up with unbelievable force, and the rain and darkness were so thick that I could no longer see anything. I crawled on the ground looking for somewhere to take cover; maybe if I could find an old shack or broken crate I could crawl inside. Then I felt something on the ground; it was the latch of the storm cellar. I do not know how it appeared here, but I was grateful for it. As I crawled into the dark cellar and closed the door, I heard the wind howling over my head; I curled up in a fetal position and fell asleep.

Once again the wind is moving over the storm cellar. Perhaps this is what death is like–moving through time trying to find people and regain memories. Then all at once everything was quiet. I did not know what to think. I was afraid to open the cellar door, not knowing what I would see. Would I be home again? Would I be in my bed or just walking around in my darkened house? I wanted to open the cellar door and find Claudette in the kitchen baking pies or reading a book and sipping tea. Oh God, please take me back there, I pleaded in my silent prayer.

I knew there was something else for me to see, so I slowly opened the cellar door and found myself coming up from the sewer of a cobblestone street. Looking up I saw the little shops of a European-looking village with names written on the windows. Once again I found a suitcase with clothes neatly folded: a wool-blended business suit with cuffed pants and a jacket with a big yellow star on the sleeve. I quickly put the perfectly fitted outfit on and walked down the street.

Inside one shop I saw an elderly man with a white fluffy beard working on a table filled with clocks. In another shop a man was tapping with a little hammer on the back of shoes. I went in and asked him what he was doing. Looking at me strangely he said, "Obviously, I am fixing shoes." I asked him where I was, and he answered, "You must be a stranger around here. This is Danzig. If you are hungry there is a shop down the street that sells the best Danish rolls. You should give it a try." After wishing me the best day, he returned to finish his work, as customers would come in shortly wanting their shoes.

A window display of handmade furniture with beautifully shaped coffee tables and dining room tables, some with gold embossed edges caught my attention. Wrinkle-faced men grinning and pointing to their works said, "Nice looking isn't it?" I stood nodding my approval of their work.

China shops exhibited beautiful plates used for special occasions and ceremonies. In another shop silver spoons and forks were polished to perfection and engraved with scriptures proclaiming the greatness of God.

The architecture of the city was amazing–huge cathedrals and synagogues with ascending arches reached towards the sky. I heard laughter in the parks where children were playing tag and eating ice cream, while someone else was telling them to be still so they could take their picture. Women were walking their babies in strollers and stopping periodically to smile at them and talk to them.

Danzig. The name began to run through my mind over and over. Do I know this place? I am sure I've heard of it before. Then I remembered when I was in the military and we went through Poland and the City of Danzig. It was all burned down and every shop window was broken out. The Nazis did something horrible here. Could this possibly be the same place? It is so beautiful, so peaceful and happy. But I remembered when we went through the city there were pieces of glass everywhere. As we crawled around trying to take cover, pieces of glass would sometimes get caught in my boot, and I would have to take my knife to remove them.

The sergeant said that the Nazis had something that they called the "Night of the Broken Glass." One night they came in and destroyed every Jewish shop and burned down all the synagogues in the city. Who would now believe this place was so beautiful? I had to warn these people. I had to let them know what was going to happen.

I had come now before the disaster, before it was all gone. Maybe that was the reason why I was here–to help them to organize and recruit volunteers to defend the city.

When I looked again, I noticed everyone wore the bright yellow stars. Young girls walked past me with sporty sweaters, laughing and giggling and wearing their yellow stars, almost like a fashion statement. Businessmen and professors wore yellow stars on the lapels of their tweed and plaid suits. I stopped one of them and said, "Excuse me, sir. What does the star mean?" He looked at me amazed and walked away.

Finally I sat down on a park bench next to an old man, who was feeding the pigeons and stroking his long, white beard–he resembled a human form of God. I said, "Sir, can you tell me why so many people are wearing stars on their clothing? I am new to the city and I cannot understand why."

He looked at me and said, "This is the way for them to identify us. Unlike you, our skin is not dark; they have marked us with this star. The Star of David is our symbol, which the Nazis try to use against us, but we wear it as a sign of strength. They cannot take our sacred symbol and destroy us with it.

"At first we protested against it and would not wear it. Then we realized that in time this would pass; and seeing that it posed no physical threat, we submitted to it."

"Listen," I pleaded with the man, "you must leave here now or join others and fight, for they are coming to burn down Danzig. Every shop, everything, all of it will be no more."

He laughed at me saying, "Surely you do not observe our rules of being drunk in public. Perhaps you have been at the tavern too long today."

"Please, sir, you must leave now while you can. I beg you." Then I ran through the park trying to talk to the young mothers, telling them they needed to leave the city because the Nazis were coming. They too thought I had lost my mind; and grabbing their babies, they swiftly walked away.

I interrupted businessmen eating their lunch in the park, saying, "Sirs, you must leave here. Please, hear me. I have been here before and they are coming; the Nazis will destroy it all." They excused themselves, folded their newspaper neatly under their arms, and walked away.

Tired of excuses, I returned to the shoe shop to talk to the old shoemaker. "You must believe me. All of this is going to be destroyed, everything, even your shop. I have come from another time, and I have walked through the city when it was burned down."

The old man said, "Son, you must calm yourself. Yes, we have heard reports of people in other parts of the country being killed by the Germans, but that will never happen here. Just look at our community–the commerce, the trade, and the products we produce. Our factories are helping others, and even Germans come here to eat our bread and buy our shoes. Why would they destroy something that is helping them?" As he locked his shop, he said, "Go home and rest your mind. Things will be better tomorrow."

As the sun began to set, soft shadows fell over the shops and homes. White picket fences and storybook-looking homes were slowly being overtaken by the twilight. I could hear mothers calling their children to come home. What a quiet and peaceful place I thought as I walked down the street hearing only an occasional dog barking.

After walking around the city all day, my legs ached and I needed to rest. I found an old oak tree in the park and lay at its base to rest. The tree had large green leaves and holes in its trunk where owls and bats were probably resting for the night.

All at once I heard glass breaking, like something heavy crashing through a window. I sprang to my feet and looked at the shops. The Nazis were throwing bricks through the windows. It is happening! Oh, God, I said. I heard the sound of boots marching in the streets, guns going off, and women screaming, "Please, don't kill my children." There was so much glass breaking that it sounded like a rainstorm.

Soldiers quickly stormed homes, kicked down doors, and threw beautiful tables and chairs out the open windows. They stacked a large pile of furniture on the street and set it on fire. Homes were ransacked and valuable items were loaded onto large trucks. Other soldiers ran through the homes setting curtains on fire.

With guns pointed at them, men, women, and children were paraded through the street. I noticed that some were dressed as if they were going on a vacation. Women walked out of their homes wearing makeup, furs, and jewels. Men carried their briefcases and wore business suits. Some women held on tightly to their china sets and silverware. But it was all quickly taken away and loaded onto trucks and carted away.

Now their shoes were removed and piled in the streets. When some of the men started to fight back, guns were fired and dead bodies began to litter the ground. I walked through the crowd of people almost invisible, just observing the insanity.

I saw a group of boys throwing rocks at a Nazis truck. Soldiers jumped out of the truck and lined the boys up. I heard the click of guns as I ran towards them shouting, "What in God's name are you doing? These are children, you devils." I was hit in the face with a rifle butt and forced to march with the children in a large human line towards a train station near the edge of the city. Glass lay everywhere in the street, and all the beautiful shops were burning.

One soldier stood in front of a synagogue and shot out the circular stained glass window. As other soldiers ran with cans of gasoline to torch the beautiful synagogue, people began weeping. When one man fell to the ground weeping, a soldier kicked him in the face.

A small boy in the crowd was crying because he could not find his mommy. Someone whispered that his mother had been thrown out of a window and broke her neck. Someone else asked: Is it true that they are sending us to the death camps where they sent the rest of the Jews?

Then I remembered that I was already dead. What more could they do to me? Even in this place I could still feel pain in my jaw, so if I died it could be a way to return to my time again. I held the child's hand and assured him that everything was going to be all right. I am here for a reason that I don't know yet.

Just then there was a commotion far back in the line. A group of men rushed the soldiers knocking one of them down and taking his gun. Everyone in the line fell to the ground as we heard gunfire. All the soldiers who were watching us rushed towards the back of the line.

We were standing by the park when I noticed the tree that I had sat by earlier. I remembered the hole in the tree that was camouflaged by bushes and branches–nature's perfect hiding place! It was big enough for me to hide in for days without being detected. But then I realized that this hiding place was not for me but for the child. I whispered to the boy, "When I say run, I want you to run towards the tree and go inside one of the holes. Do not come out until everyone is gone. Then after that God will tell you what to do."

When I told the child to go, he broke loose from the line and started running towards the tree. A soldier ran after me, firing shots after I ran from the line. It did not matter now if I died because I was already dead. A group of soldiers then started chasing after me, forgetting about the people standing in the line. I turned around briefly and in the distance I saw the child make it to the tree and disappear in the hedges.

I started laughing out loud while running. A bullet grazed my leg and I tumbled onto the street. A soldier kicked me in the face. But I kept laughing so loudly that it startled them. Then it dawned on me, when I was back home all I had was one leg. "Guess what, I have been shot two times in the same leg. Can you believe this?" They marched me back to the line of people, as I limped and hopped towards the train station. One of the guards said, "Why didn't you just shoot him and get him out of our way?" He replied that I was too stupid to be shot. He called me a drunken fool and walked away.

We finally arrived at the large train station where boxcars were waiting for us. Like cattle and livestock, we were herded into the cars. I heard the boxcar doors slamming shut all around me. They pushed the group of people that I was in line with into a darkened boxcar. Bodies began falling upon each other as the train jerked into motion. In the darkness I heard the rumbling of the train; the huge engine began to chug and we were moving. I started laughing again saying, "You can't kill me. I cannot die. You can't kill me."

As the train took a sharp turn, bodies fell upon bodies and people began screaming, praying, and holding onto anything that did not move. Then gaining a deeper strength from this confinement, everyone began saying softly, "I refuse to die no matter what you do to me. I refuse to die no matter how you try." It almost became a chant, sounding like a choir in this darkness. There is something about praying in the darkness–you can feel your prayers leaving your body, moving upward and unhindered by your surroundings. You can feel your prayers rising into God's consciousness. All of us were strangers when we went into the boxcar and now we were a family. Our minds became one; instantly we created an invisible photo book that the survivors would show to their children forever. The chanting of this boxcar choir had now slowed to a whisper. There was nothing now to do but sit and wait.

I thought about the child in the tree and prayed that God would have mercy on him. Then I realized that I hadn't had compassion for anyone for years. I selfishly stayed in my house, cursing the world and anyone that entered mine. I felt ashamed as I looked back at the last seconds of my life when I was chasing kids out of my yard because they were stealing apples. In the flashback I did not notice the holes in the kids' jeans nor the beat-up tennis shoes that they wore. I did not see how they were eating the apples as if it were their only meal. I did not see the tattered jackets they wore.

I quietly asked God to forgive me. I blamed everyone for the death of Claudette. When was the last time I really cared? I still had a sister out there, Sarah, that now I did not care to find. I did not care when there was a need in my community or when I heard about a neighbor who had lost a loved one. I did not care when someone had lost his home and everything was taken away. I didn't care but stayed in my room peeking out of my blinds and cursing all who walked past my house.

Finally the train stopped after many hours and we were unloaded. Once again we went through a humiliating inspection: they looked at our hair and teeth, and divided the men and women and passed out striped prison-looking clothes.

Why hadn't I done something worthwhile rather than sitting in my house and feeling sorry for myself? There was an orphanage and a group home in town where I could have volunteered my time and services or mentored a fatherless child. I could have sent my extra money to the relief agencies around the world to help children in remote villages. I could have gone and met Papa Jacob in California and learned more about my brother David.

I didn't care then, but now I realized that it was time to care again.

We stepped out of the boxcar into an old, dilapidated factory yard. The tracks curved into a semi-circle where the trains would come, unload their human cargo, and go back out. Old train parts were scattered about; sparks from welders and the sound of hammers pounding could be heard all around. Groups of men were inspecting large diesel wheels, while other men were connecting engine parts.

Then another door opened leading outside where people were being loaded onto trucks. I heard someone in the line say, "They're taking us to the death camps."

Next I saw a basement storm cellar with the same kind of latch design as the one I came out of in Danzig. Could this be my portal back or just an ordinary basement door? I did not know for sure. Perhaps this cellar was not my portal but just a tool shed, or a place where they stored potatoes or food items. A group of street signs needing repair lay cluttered near the entrance of the cellar door. Some of the signs read: "Yield. Danger. Turn Left. Turn Right. Pedestrian Walkway." But the sign that caught my eye from all the rest leaning right on the cellar door read: "This Way" with an arrow pointing down.

This was my last opportunity to return to my world. I knew I wanted to get back and redeem the hollow part of my past existence. The time had come for me to gather the last fragments of my strength and make a run for the cellar door. In one of David's letters he said something about running with his last strength to survive when he ran up a mountain tired and exhausted. He said that he felt good after he ran one last time with all of his might.

If I were to die again, I would feel good this day. I broke loose from the line yelling, "I feel good!" I ran limping, hopping, and sprinting away. The soldiers aimed their weapons at me again. Miraculously one of the soldiers dropped his weapon; and as it fell to the floor, it went off and shot another soldier in the foot. Other soldiers also aimed their guns at me, but their guns jammed. I heard them clicking the triggers as they desperately tried to make them work, but nothing happened. I heard another soldier say, "Go and get him; he is getting away. Do something, you idiots!"

Seeing the soldiers' guns jamming, the people standing in lines began running out of the factory doors. People were fleeing from all parts of the building as outnumbered soldiers fought in vain against the surging, desperate crowds. Other soldiers stood looking dumbfounded at their rifles, wondering why they would not work.

Reaching the cellar door, I looked back at the group of soldiers coming after me, as I vanished into the darkness below. I shut the door and heard them beating on it. "Bust the thing open. Take your shoes off and beat on the latch."

I sat down in the corner of the darkened room yelling at them, "I feel good. Do you hear me? I feel good." As they beat on the latch, I heard them saying, "What the hell is going on around here? Why don't you do something to open this door?"

Once again I heard the howling wind blowing over the cellar and I knew I was being transported. I silently prayed, "Take me home, dear Lord. Please, bring me back home."

I lay in this darkened room for what seemed like hours listening to the howling wind. When I opened the latch of the cellar door, it was nighttime and I was somewhere in the wilderness. The train station was gone; the soldiers were gone; the factory, everything was no more. There was nothing but stars shining in the darkness.

Still I was not home. The suit that I had worn in Danzig was now turning into threads of dust. I noticed another suitcase and quickly opened it only to find a wrap-around cloth of white linen the size of a large towel. How could I walk around in a piece of cloth barely enough to cover my body? Then I noticed that my body had changed physically; it looked as though I had not eaten for months. My rib cage was but bones pulled over my sagging skin. I touched my face; my jawbone felt like a hollow skeleton. I examined my stomach; it was bloated, looking as if I were a victim of malnutrition. I tied the cloth around my body. I did not have any socks or shoes on, and the rocks and grass felt cool and wet under my feet.

Now I knew what it must be like to be alive and dying at the same time. Oh God, what has happened to my body? I said to myself. Had I escaped the death at the hands of the Nazis only to wake up as a walking dead man? "God," I cried out, "what am I supposed to learn looking like this?" If it weren't for this piece of cloth draped around my body, I would be naked.

There was nothing here but stars and the darkness. As I tried to make my way down a grass-covered hill, each step required so much strength and energy that many times I thought I would fall and not be able to continue. "Oh, God, help me," I pleaded. "Oh, God, help me, please." The brightly shining stars provided some visibility for me, until I realized that I was in some kind of valley. Then I saw them–piles of human bones all around me. Piles of bones, and graves and headstones protruded from the ground as if some great plague had happened here.

As I staggered around I fell down exhausted into the dust. In a brief flashback, I saw a city of people: they were choking each other and destroying one another one at a time. What has caused this great ruin in this terrifying place? Why didn't someone build a hospital to help these people? Why didn't someone organize agricultural schools to teach them to grow their own food? Why didn't someone help them build a water system so that fresh water could flow from faucets? Why didn't someone teach them business skills so they could open a factory to make their own clothes and teach them how to start a bakery? But all the energy and all the gifts given by God were used only to destroy, degrade, and defeat themselves in this last grief of death.

As I touched the soil, I heard a voice saying, "This is the city of wasted lives." Then I knew that time, our most precious asset, was wasted here. Talents, our abilities to bring our thoughts into existence, were wasted here. The power to choose was wasted on those who thought by standing still they did not have to make a decision. The power of cooperation was wasted on those who felt satisfaction in destroying the dreams of others.

Rising from the soil, I noticed more people were alive here. In the distance I saw small fires burning and flickering in the darkness. Everyone was not gone. Hundreds were still alive and keeping warm by holding onto each other.

I stumbled into the camp and fell down near a group of men, women, and children. Cold and exhausted I sat shivering by the light of the fire. It warmed my body. For a long time I did not speak to anyone and no one said anything to me. Slowly I spoke to a woman rocking a baby against her breast, "I am hungry. Please, do you have any food or water?"

"There is food and water in the city–enough for all of us, but we cannot go back there because a civil war is raging there. People are destroying each other. We are the last refugees to leave the city–nomads now wandering from place to place looking for food and water. We are tired and exhausted and cannot walk any longer. We do not even have the strength left to bury our dead. Hyenas and wild dogs follow our procession waiting for someone to die tonight so they can devour the body. Everything is gone now; all the water and a few loaves of bread that we parceled out in meager portions are all gone," she said.

"You seem to be different; you are not of my people," she continued. "I have prayed all night that one of the stars would fall

329

from the skies and redeem us, that our miracle would come tonight to bless and restore our people again."

I told her that my mother once told me before she died that I would be given a special miracle. And I believe that the miracle is to know that life is precious, and that you have the power to choose. The power to bless the land or curse it. The power to redeem a life or destroy it. For we have the keys to this earth. God has made us caregivers of the earth. He has made us responsible.

After that I lay down on the grass and fell asleep. In the morning, the ground began shaking, and the skies began thundering and roaring; but there were no clouds. Everyone rose looking up at the skies, as if a cemetery had once again come to life. Then the clouds, hundreds of them, began moving strangely across the skies. Slowly they came closer to the earth, floating and drifting down near this beleaguered group. A despairing cry erupted from the people and someone began saying, "Angels are coming down to save us. I knew they would come to help us."

Then the white clouds opened up like parachutes filling the skies. And boxes of grain and cereal and dried fruit and powdered milk fell on the earth. Someone had remembered them on the earth and felt their prayer. Someone took an extra step, came out of their darkened house, tied their shoestrings, and was determined to save a life. Someone, somewhere, had remembered them, felt their tears soaking into their heart. Someone had remembered that church was more than sitting in a pew; it was being a force of power and light on the earth.

Food and water can be greater than diamonds for those who are starving. Screams of laughter, cheering, and applauding were given to the benefactors from the skies. Sweeping planes were flying low now dropping even bigger parachutes filled with seeds, tools, and medicines.

I tried to get up, but I was too exhausted to move. I cried out to the crowd, "Please, I need to eat also. Please let me have just a little." I was finally able to stand up. My legs felt feeble and ached with pain.

Just then an old African man came running out of the crowd, his face covered with cornmeal as he praised God for remembering them this day. Then he grabbed both of my hands and laughing said, "Congratulations, Joseph Potter. This is Graduation Day for you, for you have finally gotten off your porch swing. Your confirmation flight has been scheduled. Put your seatbelt on, Joseph; the ride is going to be a lot different from now on." Then he shoved a packet of papers into my arms and ran back into the celebrating crowd and disappeared.

I called out to him, "Hey, you come back. How do you know my name? Help me walk, help me get back. Help me get some food and water. I am so thirsty. Do you hear me?"

Just then I saw a young man in a medical uniform standing over me, cooling my head with a wet towel. I cried out saying, "I am so thirsty. Please, let me have some water." A young girl came running out of her house from across the street with a cup of water. The young man said, "Take small sips slowly, Mr. Potter."

I was in my yard again. "You don't understand. I had died, but I am back again. I have graduated today. I feel good. Do you hear me, young man, I feel good."

As he held my head and checked my vital signs, he said, "I know you do, Mr. Potter. Please, you need to go to a hospital so we can check you out. There is only so much we can do here."

The lights of the ambulance had caused a commotion, and people came out of their houses to see what was going on. A crowd was starting to form in the yard and I heard people whispering, "Old man Potter fell in his yard and he almost died, but some kids helped to save him." One woman whispered to another woman, "The old coot should have died and did everyone a favor."

The medical workers insisted that I go see the doctor, even walking me inside the ambulance; until at the last minute I jumped out yelling that I felt good. I looked at the crowds and started laughing. "I feel good. Do you hear me? I feel the best that I have felt in years."

Some of the people that had gathered in the yard shook their heads, whispering to each other, "See, I told you he was out of his mind. Someone needs to take a bulldozer and knock his house down and put him in the nut house."

Then I realized that I probably did look a sight wearing my dirty robe and my hair looking like a mop that had been left in a bucket of plaster. As I pranced and danced in the front yard with my dust-covered house shoes that were shaped in the form of a duck, I did look a sight. But I didn't care anymore. I was free from hiding, from hurting. Yes, I felt good today. I am back again. I shouted to the people in the yard, saying the HOLEEEE MOLLLLIES ARE BACK AGAIN." I thanked the kids and helped them pick up the fallen apples in the yard and told them they could come back and get more anytime they wanted. Also I told them that I would be cleaning up the yard and the house next week and would need somebody to help me fix it up. I said I would pay them well. I hugged them and said, "Please forgive me, for even grown-ups have to learn things all over again." They assured me that they would be back as they carried away the large sacks of apples.

As everyone began to leave the yard, I felt a clump of papers roll up inside the pockets of my robe. I grasped the papers and saw my name shining in the darkness of the night. It was the papers that the African man had given me when I had died. This cannot be, I tried to reason. This is in my mind. As I held the papers in my shaking hands, I walked into the house, went upstairs to my bedroom, turned on the light, sat down at my desk, and read the letter. It said:

"You must read the enclosed letter for the next forty days, and after that time, you will be instructed to share the knowledge of this letter with those who are on the verge of bankruptcy, those who have lost their homes, those who are being served divorce papers, those who are near taking their life, those who are hiding in their house and are afraid to come out. And they too must read the letter for forty days and pass on the knowledge of these letters to others. This letter is for all of them."

THE LAST WILL AND TESTAMENT OF GOD

DEAR EARTH,

I see inside of you, translucent like the skin of an embryo
      upon my eyelids.
I move through your blood and blink in your eyes.

I felt your breath a thousand light years away crying out
      for me to wash the burning silence of your brow.
To reach in the blackness of your womb and speak to
      and play with your children not yet born.
I have heard an audible prayer rising and filtering from your pores
      and speaking from the depths of the microphone of your
      heart.

Yet you have not seen me, not in all the churches you have built
      with steeples that pierce the blueness of the skies.
For you could not see me in a sunray or in a raindrop or in the
      laughing voice of a child holding the largeness of your
      hand.

I am writing this testament to you because you have not heard
      my prayers; you have not immersed my spirit.

Even though you were baptized and ordained and sanctified by
      men you have not seen me.

You have been like a selfish child playing with my miracles,
      creating and destroying as you wish, regarding little the
      importance of life.

You have deemed all things under you like unto ants to be
      crushed into submission or kept for your entertainment.

You are a spoiled brat; you spill your milk intentionally and
      wait impatiently for me to fill the hollow cups of your heart.

I am not a cosmic bellboy or a court jester or a fool for
      you to mock at your will.

I am God, your Father, and you are my firstborn. I have loved you
      always even in your greatest sins, even when you put holes
      in my hands and gave me vinegar and gall to drink.

You have spent the precious days I gave you trying to destroy
      my stars in the immensity of my universe and uproot my
      trees in the gigantic forest.

I have cried openly for you in the face of every mother that
      beholds her embalmed son sent home from your wars.

Yet you have cried quickly; you have wiped your eyes in fear
      of being different, of the individuality that I breathed
      through you when I pulled you from the womb of the earth.

335

For the oblivion of the burning dream, the indestructible city

of faith which you seek to constantly suffocate and destroy.

And often you hid yourself in your empty rooms until the

plaster was allowed to become hard upon your face.

And you were ready again to make others believe in your lie.

And you have cursed the children I have given you, for you felt

you could not prosper or be successful in your career with

them.

And now you stand upon your mountaintop watching Satan

showing you the kingdoms of the world, trading the sacred

timeless miracles within for an idol of gold decaying in

your hands.

How long shall you cast your pearls before pigs, exchanging the

encompassing power of the miracles of your heart for the

ashes carried in the hands of men?

I have died when my graceful gazelles fleeing in terror were

slaughtered for your sport.

I have died when my affectionate noble elephants were destroyed

for their ivory tusks, for you to wear as your jewelry.

I have died when you hooked my fish and dragged them

unmercifully upon the shore to waste and decay.

I have heard my trees crying, my lilies gossiping, my weeping

willows in continuous grief for the magnificence of the

gigantic forest has become a famished desert.

And the heightening picturesque mountaintops have been

desecrated into dust powder.

And the memory of the roses blossoming in your palms is
forgotten in the embrace of your tears and your restless,
compassionate dream.

Have you not heard, have you not learned, has it not been told
to you since the beginning of time?

Yet in all the thousands of years you have not heard, nor have you
learned, and it has been told to you every day, as I breathe
my dream into your bodies, that you are my greatest
miracle.

You are the flesh of my flesh and the bone of my bones.

And you have passed through my womb a hundred million
times each day yet you say I do not exist, you cannot sense
my omnipotent presence.

Did you not know that it is my power that kept your molecules
together today?

I, God, have become terminally ill with you, accepting the dying of
your childhood dreams that have deteriorated with the
fear of your living.

I, God, have become terminally ill with you, doubting and
receiving your inferior belief that you have not the potential
to turn the mere stones in your hands into diamonds.

I, God, have become terminally ill with you, believing your
sickness is my will and your poverty and destitution is my
spirit.

T. S. Eure

I, God, have become terminally ill with you, letting your talents
become wasted, your uniqueness lost in the cry of the
multitudes.

I, God, have become terminally ill with you, believing you are
saved by your churches, your memberships, doctrines, and
decrees alone, regardless of how you live and treat others
upon my earth.

I, God, have become terminally ill with you destroying your self-
esteem, to be accepted and justified by other men.

Take a deep breath, raise your arms, catch my sunlight with your
lips.

I have never left you, not one second or minute in the
commencement of your existence.

Often you have looked upon yourself weeping in fear, shame, and
disgrace.

And you break the figure of the image you see of yourself and
search like millions before you in the marketplace of life
seeking hope to believe in.

Once you were graceful like an eternal ballerina pirouetting
on a grain of sand.

And once in your quickness and in the form of your beauty you
could outrun my impala and antelope upon the burning
Ethiopia sunrise.

And the brilliance of your mind could calculate the rotations of the
earth around your shadow.

And your tongue was Holy and your word more precious than the
gold from King Solomon's treasures.

Did not I paint the stripes of the zebra, delicately fashion the wings
of the dragonfly?

Each nucleus that divides and splits itself is but my continuous
prayer, testifying through your being.

For truly the brilliant retina of your eyes are greater than the colors
on Michelangelo's brushes.

For the thousand fibers I have placed in your ear are greater than
the strings of the violins of the Masters.

The sound of your voice, its rhythmic cords are greater and more
melodic and harmonious than a thousand flamingos singing
on leafy tropical branches.

Your skin is dark and rich like cocoa butter, and white like the
snowcaps of mountain peaks, or like a sunflower unfolding
in the morning light.

I have written my signature in the furrows of your brow.

It was I with an unseen hand that paired the twenty-three
chromosomes of your father and the twenty-three
chromosomes of your mother in the black womb of space.

Today you shall be married; no longer shall you only worship the
appearance of the flesh.

But you shall be joined to the unseen power that shall build an
eternal mansion unperishing, even if the mountains and the
sea are consumed.

For love shall no more be an indefinable word but you shall be an
      instrument of its force and a preserver of its peace.

And in your pain you shall no more hide your face in the sand like
      an ostrich afraid of the predators of the world.

But you shall stand against the procrastinators and criticizers,
      and you shall overturn the elaborate thrones with the
      purity of your heartbeat.

And as you labor in the fields, there shall be a sacredness in your
      hands.

For your religion shall not be a decorative cup fashioned with
      precious materials that appear to be useful but cannot hold
      water.

For no longer will death be a time to mourn and rent your garments
      and curse the pulsating breath burning like lightning
      through your pores.

For what is death but a small room we enter to exchange these
      garments for the robes of Life and my seamless cloth.

For what is death but to be like your tears vaporized into the sky.

Today you shall be married; no longer shall you forge
      a ring of iron around your husband and wife.

But your love shall ascend higher than the possession
      you heap at the feet of your beloved.

For your inner castle shall be more immaculate than
      towers of ivory and ceilings of gold.

For no longer shall you withdraw into your secret closet

      when love has forsaken and hurt you.

For each tear is a pearl formed from the eminence of your heart.

And in this desert of despair I shall be like unto an orchard over

      these desolate landscapes and uncultivated fields.

And I shall drink from water that shall be thirsty to

      drink into me.

For what is love but the force that directs the course

      of burning worlds.

It is the force that created the foundations of the pyramids.

But in your death pain, you shall not wrap yourself up in a burial

      cloth and worship the elegance of your tomb.

But you shall be called out of this elaborate grave even as

      Jesus called Lazarus out from the palms of death.

For I tell you that you shall be resurrected when you

      touch the womb wet skin of an infant.

No longer shall you fear the legions of kings standing

      with shield and sword before you.

For the prayer within you shall erupt even as a fiery volcano

      dissolves the monuments of men into dust and ashes.

For your prayer alone is stronger than the threats of death

      uttered by men.

For this day you shall be as a skillful carpenter, the rough wood

      shall be evened and measured into usefulness by your

      hands.

This day you shall be a fisherman, you shall cast your lines

      into the deep, and the lights of oceans shall be suspended

      in the twinkle of your eyes.

For truly your labor is but an unspoken sermon, it is a scripture

      interpreted into Life by your sweat irrigating the

      furrows of the fields.

For today your religion shall be more than an altar of gold

      or a shrine of silver.

For your religion shall no longer have physical boundaries,

      no longer shall you only call earthly walls your church.

But you shall worship in that church where your congregation

      becomes the trees of the forest and the mountains lift

      their fingers in reverence towards the skies.

And your testament of my glory shall be even as

      the prayers of the crickets in evening fields.

And your pulpits shall be made with the forgiveness of the

      deceitful.

And your greatest steeples built upon the earth shall

      be human embraces.

For your religion shall be more than a formality to please men,

      it shall be a personal covenant where I write a love letter

      on the membrane of your heart.

This day you shall no longer fear death as a child fears

      the darkness in his bedroom.

For you shall return like a fetus to the black of the womb.

And you shall breathe into my deeper miracle

until you are transformed as a world colliding

and creating an eternal sunset.

For what is death but to inhale my consciousness?

I am writing My Last Will and Testament, for you have

not heard me in all the thousands of years that I have

fashioned flesh around your bones.

You have not heard me when I sent you my Prophets, Messengers,

Wise Men, Dreamers, Saints, and Angels.

What have you done unto them?

For you have only built them mighty graves and have tried

to consume the power of their heartbeat, even as your fathers

before you have killed my chosen servants.

Have you not read my autobiography, the Bible, this flaming

Torah of Life?

Have you not walked among the fields of the Beatitudes

and beheld men come from the valley of desperation and

ascend to the Mount of living fire?

And become a sermon for your children and their children

to believe in?

Have you not read the open letter that I wrote on Sinai,

chiseled with compassionate fingertips?

For my signature, Ten Holy Commandments, did I not write in

the hearts and the minds of the memory of men forever?

Have you not read my scrolls of the sincere heart sealed on the
pages of a human expression?

For you have not heard me when I passed through forty and two
generations to cry out in a woman's body called Mary.

For you have not heard me when I was composed in human flesh
suspended on Golgotha's summit between the compassion of
Heaven and the cruelties of Earth.

For you have not heard me when I died the ninth hour on this cross
forged from the strength and the weakness of your hands.

Have not my Messengers spoken to you of a Kingdom within you
more enduring than the strongest of metals?

And it is a greater treasure than a thousand crowns on the heads
of a thousand Kings.

No longer shall you worship the royalty of families; no longer
shall you kneel in humble submission to the tyranny of a
skeleton king in power.

Today you shall be married, no longer in a circle of fear
placed on your fingers.

No longer will you value all of your meaning on the ceremony
of your marriage.

But you will know and understand that deeper meaning,
that the exchanging of rings has no meaning
if you have not exchanged hearts.

Often we have valued love with a price; we have measured it in
    amounts of the things we can take from those who love us.

But this you should know, that the power of love within you
    can neither be consumed nor destroyed.

It is a tabernacle in your being constructed without human hands.

For truly if a man would ever see me, he would see him only
    in the love that he has for others.

In your pain you have sought to hide in the crevices of the earth.

And the hurting of your heartbeat has caused the mountains to
    tremble and made the hurricanes to move out over the seas.

But you shall stand this day against those whose power comes
    from swords of iron and chains of steel.

For your power comes not from the lavish patios or the spiraling
    crystal staircases held in great esteem by men.

Your power is but my heartbeat tickling through your being.

For verily I say unto you that your labor is your greatest prayer.

For there are too many speech-makers already.

No longer will you fear the tenacity of the knight that stands
    before you in his glistening armor.

For when you open the visor of his helmet you will find that
    it is empty and hollow, and filled only with your own
    fear and torment.

Today you shall be married; the bridegroom shall be waiting in
    anxious anticipation.

The cake shall be decorated in a renaissance of splendor.

The appearance of the bride shall be as morning lilies

on an April sunrise.

For verily I say unto you that marriage shall be the heartbeat

of God encircled around your heart.

For marriage is the indestructible diamond of God, fashioned

with the strength of angels' hands and everlasting as

the cherubims on the throne of Heaven.

Today you shall love without shame or regret, for love shall

be as a waterfall coming from your heart, filling an

invisible sea.

For love this day is the hourglass that continuously refills itself.

For love is the radiance and the brilliance of the red rose

surviving on the desolate desert plains.

For love is my revealed face, the overwhelming

expression of the miracle of birth and the triumphant

celebration of death.

And then I have seen those who quest after power and earthly

authority.

And verily I tell thee that the cemeteries are not filled

with their bodies nor have the dogs been satisfied

with your bones.

These are men that dig graves for men and find themselves falling
in.

For I have given you a body composed of trillions of cells
and each cell being smaller than a centimeter
composed of a trillion released atoms of my power.

It is my prayer that is the force that pushes the molecules
and causes them to divide, reproduce, and give
animation to tissues of flesh.

It is my prayer that moves the rhythmic heartbeat of your
Holy pulse.

For I knew thee even before the bones were formed together
in the womb.

For I knew thee before Moses stood on Mount Sinai
and watched me write my burning love letter in
the sockets of his heart.

For I knew thee before the mountains were formed
and before the hills unveiled themselves like a bride
before her bridegroom.

For I knew thee before the lightning of my power
and the truth of my word was as purifying as
a fire that could not be destroyed in my bones.

Today you shall be married; no longer shall you cast a stumbling
block before your beloved that flees from your
presence like a butterfly before your trembling palms.

And no longer shall you build a cage of gold

      to capture your beloved's translucent heart.

This day you shall chisel the stone in your heart into a

      cathedral of exceedingly earthly beauty.

Today you shall be married; no longer shall you be married only in

      the bone, the skin, and the outward appearance of the flesh.

But you shall love that which extends deeper than what

      your eyes can see and your fingers can touch.

For this power shall diffuse through your being like lightning

      burning through your heart.

For what greater marriage is there than to exchange rings

      with the infinite and breathe through my lips.

For there is no shame in the giving of your love to a

      receptive and receiving humble embrace.

For truly cursed is he that withers the harvest of the fields

      into thorns and thistles.

For he is like a person that has a bouquet of roses in his

      heart yet they turn to ashes and dust in the

      light of day.

For woe unto you that have let love become a plague

      of destruction and an abyss of wastefulness.

For you are not worthy to carry the sacred breath of life

      in the immensity of the black space of your veins.

And it is in your quest for power that you cause

        the poor, the outcast, and the exiled

        to kneel in submission before your feet.

For surely the prophets of this generation are profiteers.

For they are not martyrs for the word of God but they are

        scavengers, using the bones of the weak to build their

        churches.

These are vultures with blood on their mouths crying out

        their innocence.

For truly the calluses upon your hands and the labor

        of their strength are greater than the altars

        built by men.

For verily you are a tree in your ministry of giving;

        children come to climb upon your branches,

        these extended arms reaching out for the

        spacious baptism of the skies.

And in the soundless season of your harvest when your heart

        is a banquet table, many shall come and consume the

        nourishment of the living bread formed out of your

        tears and made from the yeast of your pain.

For as often as you have thirsted to drink my tears,

        I have thirsted to drink into you.

For the forgotten treasure in your soul, if revealed,

        could not be measured by any earthly instruments.

Even as Jesus opened up a spiritual grocery store on a hillside,

> feeding five thousand with two loaves of bread and five
>
> fishes, this bountiful feast in your being shall feed a hungry
>
> people, starving for the taste of eternity.

For surely this day you shall strike a rock three times like

> Moses in the wilderness and water shall issue forth.

For this day you shall stand in the wind and I shall open

> up a bakery in the skies and the bread of Heaven shall
>
> fall into your palms and nourish the womb of your soul.

For I knew thee even as you had no form, sought form.

> For even as you who could not speak, sought to speak.
>
> For even as you who had no hands, sought to touch.
>
> I have composed and written infinite legacies
>
> with the crying of your silence alone.

For I knew thee before the kingdom of Heaven

> was constructed with the power of my love
>
> and the pillars of my indestructible strength.
>
> I knew thee before the wings of the angels were formed.
>
> For even as I gave them lightning speed,
>
> the quickness of your movement was not
>
> even surpassed by them.

For I knew thee before my prophets walked on

> the soft dust of the earth's mirrored summits
>
> and bending slopes. For did I not escort them in burning

chariots of fire, transcending across the starry evening
horizon?

Do you now know Earth, that I, God, your Father, have walked
in the shadows of your evening and felt the wind and the
dust of the afternoon plains against my omnipotent face?

I have moved in your storms and turned upon the peaks of
your mountains in lightning and smoke.

I have come into the gates of your city and my garments
were as the poorest among the poor, even as shrouds
are draped around a dying and exhausted body.

I have walked through your marketplaces and in your temples.

I have seen you cheating and stealing for the worldly goods
that crumble and disintegrate in your hands.

You are the most precious of all my creations, yet you
have reduced yourselves to that of sparrows that fight
over bread crumbs, stale, and tasteless.

Yet you are of much more value than sparrows.

I have seen your children weeping in the streets, crying
out for parents that have left them.
Yet in All Things...........YOU HAVE NOT KNOWN ME.

I have seen you with my all-seeing eye, sitting upon
your elaborate throne, a great multitude surrounding
your presence, singing praises to your name.

T. S. Eure

Believing the power of your greatness and the glory of your being

       is not even surpassed by the wonders of the earth itself.

And many stand gazing upon you as if in the presence

       of an angel or a Holy angelic being, infallible

       in your movement and appearance.

But when I beheld you again, you were alone, poor, and desolate,

       walking the empty streets of earth, begging for bread and

       shelter, weeping because no one knew you and few little

       cared. Even as a slain ghost that walks before men seeking

       the memory of life.

I have seen you again, a mighty conqueror, a great captain of men,

       leading vast uncountable legions at the command of your

       voice.

But when I beheld you again, you were wrinkled, desolate,

       a dried up old man who trembles as he walks, afraid of

       the shadows in his empty heart.

I have seen you standing upon your pulpit, preaching

       before your congregations assembled before you.

The elegance of your words and the power of their strength

       pierce their hearts and comfort their spirit.

And I beheld you fighting the oppressors and deceiving

       preachers that have built their stately mansions with

       the tears and the grief of the poor and the downtrodden.

And those who have been born without hands and legs that cannot climb the golden ladder to earth's fading and diminished

glory.

But when I beheld you again, you were a wretch, a corpse of a

man, sheepishly laying down your life, a servant for fools.

Destroying your self-esteem, embracing ignorance, casting

down your beliefs and principles, sleeping contentedly

among the ashes and cursing the day of your birth.

I have seen you praying in your church, kneeling in your

sanctuary, crying out in your tabernacle.

Believing that your prayer alone is the invisible link,

the inextinguishable flame that eternally binds your heart

with the circle of life burning in the completeness

and the humility of all men.

Extending a thread pulled from the loving fingers

of the Supreme Being.

But when I beheld you again, you walked arrogantly

cursing all men and their faith.

Not truly knowing you have become a grave of despair,

a destructive tomb filled only with sadness and death.

I have seen you, Oh Son of Man, possessing a large house

with many rooms and children playing within your

spacious yard and a wife holding your hands and

caressing your tears.

But when I beheld you again your wife had left your side,
    and your children could not be found.
And you now sit with an empty house trying to rekindle
    the burning torch of yesterday, separated from the soul
    of your mistakes and unfulfilled promises of the past.

For surely you have dried up the rivers of mercy.
You have broken into the storehouse of understanding, an
    undiscovered thief that walks hidden in the multitudes
    of men.
For you have made shrines and towers for selfishness and
    deceit, leaving the greater things undone.
For this cause you shall receive the greater curse.
For you have taught the little ones, the unwise, the unlearned,
    the unknowing and unskilled in the workshop of life's
    survival,

> To Love Without Meaning
>
> To Love Without Hope
>
> To Love Without Power
>
> To Love Without a Friend
>
> To Love Without Sincerity
>
> To Love Without Love
>
> To Love Without God.

And for this cause shall you die alone and forever.
For you are even as a toothpick broken in the teeth of time.

TO LOVE WITHOUT MEANING is to break the perfection of the
Potter's wheel, disregarding the patience of its labor, and the
tears needed to soften the loam clay into living pitchers,
stopping the lips of men from drinking out of the waterfall of
the heart.

TO LOVE WITHOUT MEANING is to forever give unnourishing,
unaffectionate pacifiers to the hungry crying lips of a
newborn baby seeking the warmth of human touch.
It is to abandon and make orphan the heartbeat of a child
from the divine breast of a mother's eternal milk.

TO LOVE WITHOUT MEANING is to walk through the cool,
soft, dimly lit tropical rainforest and behold not a carnation
on the earlobe of the earth, nor the formal gown of
the white and pink magnolia trees conducting living
symphonies in the omniscient wind.

TO LOVE WITHOUT MEANING is to father an unloved child, a
child you cursed in the womb and sought to destroy before
its conception.

TO LOVE WITHOUT MEANING is to marry a woman for her
body and beauty, disrespecting the soul and anatomy of the
spirit untouchable with the lust and decay of your fingers.

TO LOVE WITHOUT MEANING is to invite me to your house
and treat me as an untouchable stranger.
It is to be ashamed to let me eat with you from your lavish,
elaborate banquet table.

It is to forsake me before your friends and acquaintances.

It is to only seek me in your hour of desperation

and tragic need.

And yet you stood cursing me before the impressive ivory

doorsteps of your glory, forgetting that it is only made

of plaster and dust.

TO LOVE WITHOUT MEANING is to destroy the rhythmic

heartbeat of eternity pulsating through the flesh of your

human veins.

It is to curse my resurrective light, shaking the grave

of your thankless, prayerless, loveless existence.

Yet you refuse to rise from your secure, comfortable,

prestigious tomb.

TO LOVE WITHOUT MEANING is to struggle without hope, to

gain without purpose, to strive without excellence, and die

without a testament of love.

TO LOVE WITHOUT HOPE is to abandon the divine staff of

mercy and compassion placed in your hands many centuries

ago by those prophets crucified in your cities, cursed in

your sanctuaries, and left friendless on your doorsteps.

TO LOVE WITHOUT HOPE is to believe that the passing years

of your life have been a desolate grave where your

accomplishments have been as dust, blowing off the

cracked and parched lips of time.

I say unto you, this very moment, reach within yourself. Find
that forgotten, disregarded, disrespected, disowned
Book of Life.

Dust off the blank and meaningless pages, and let this day
become a Masterpiece, a Classic, an Original
composition, an everlasting Recording of the
fingerprint of the Compassionate Creator.

For this day, you shall dip the tip of your pen in the
crucified blood of God and write everlasting books,
cleansed with the tears of the martyrs, the consuming
embrace of the meek, the unselfishness of the
humble, and the undiminished flame rising from the
pure in heart.

For no longer shall you die in your mother's womb, a
stillborn baby never to consume the breath of the
world.

TO LOVE WITHOUT HOPE is to believe that leadership,
courage, faith and achievement are for fools.

It is to believe that a wise man is one who does not possess
honor and greatness, but who has become a cheat and
a liar.

TO LOVE WITHOUT HOPE is to marry a woman and pour out
the labor of your sweat and the wealth of your substance.

It is to adorn her in diamond rings, exquisite pearls and

gold necklaces only to find that her love is a deadly

trap, and her kiss is poisonous.

TO LOVE WITHOUT HOPE is to lose the serenity and the

moving divinity that gives life purpose and meaning.

It is to die without a vision and live without a revelation,

a vagabond on an endless desert without a

destination.

TO LOVE WITHOUT HOPE is to fashion a crown for ignorance

and greed and bow down in reverence, to make them your

king to rule over the corpse of your soul.

TO LOVE WITHOUT HOPE is for great and important men to

parade in a mighty procession of pageantry, yet knowing that

they are the most detestable men upon the earth.

TO LOVE WITHOUT POWER is to love Christ, my redeeming,

everlasting son, only in temples and shrines of gold and

altars of silver and in figures of marble and clay.

It is to believe I am dead and cannot heal your heart.

TO LOVE WITHOUT POWER is to build a great magnificent

church made from all the wealth of the earth.

I, God, have appeared in the bodies of the poor, the sick,

the persecuted, trying to enter your glorious

sanctuary; yet you have refused me entrance into

your soul.

And I say unto you that it makes no difference how loud you
lift up your voice in prayer and song, for your soul is
as a pebble flung by my divine hand into a bottomless
lake.

TO LOVE WITHOUT POWER is to believe that your
compassionate, earth-shaking prayer is lost in the cry of the
multitudes. You are unable to transform your flesh into
angelic wings of Godly beauty rising above the adorned
cemeteries of men.

TO LOVE WITHOUT POWER is to buy a woman a mansion of
earthly beauty, covering her fingers in rings of gold.
It is to sell your very essence on the marketplace of life
to lay endless treasures before her feet.
For verily, you shall find yourself weeping on the streets, a
man without a heart, pleading with someone
to give you a burial.

TO LOVE WITHOUT POWER is to be a husband who makes his
wife into a rag to wash his feet.
It is to make your wife a footstool, caring little if you wear
her out, not appreciating the demonstration of her
unlimited love.

TO LOVE WITHOUT POWER is to believe that you shall always
be as a beggar before the gates of life with your tin cup
trembling, pleading with withered fingers for the

promises of tomorrow to become the realities of

today.

For I say unto you, there are oceans of undiscovered

miracles in your teardrops alone. For I have written my will

and purpose for you in your very consciousness.

Your destiny is my testament, for it is unlike any other

creature that exists. It carries the

resuscitation of life.

TO LOVE WITHOUT POWER is to be a husband that forges

heavy chains of iron around the neck of his wife. For truly,

only the fool would destroy the very light that

illuminates the power of his existence.

TO LOVE WITHOUT POWER is to glorify and give exaltations

to a raging dictator.

It is to carry him on your shoulders and praise him from the

streets.

For surely, in so doing, you build monuments for the

corruptible, images of gold for stupidity, and

memorials for an ignorant and deceitful beast.

TO LOVE WITHOUT POWER is to believe that tradition, pride,

ceremony, formality, fashion, status, prestige or royalty

is greater and more supreme and sacred than the truth.

TO LOVE WITHOUT A FRIEND is to curse the morning tulips
and the brilliant, divinely painted roses that raise their
petals in humble simplicity towards your reaching, seeking,
needing, crucified, and life-worn palms.

TO LOVE WITHOUT A FRIEND is to not have the moving
desire to wash in the liquid communion of nature's
cleansing tears bursting forth from the waterfall womb of a
mountainside.

TO LOVE WITHOUT A FRIEND is to no longer adopt the trees as
your divine, inseparable, sacred brothers.

TO LOVE WITHOUT A FRIEND is to no longer run with the
towering swiftness of my giraffes on the burning Ethiopia
plains.

It is to no longer shake the earth with your footsteps like
my holy and patient elephants.

It is to no longer stalk the dense, teeming, mysterious forest
of your existence with confident strength and
moving stride like the majestic dignity of my noble
lion.

It is to no longer conduct a prayer service with the tiny
crickets in the black stillness of midnight.

TO LOVE WITHOUT SINCERITY is to be a glorified, idiotic
manikin sitting on a pulpit of stupidity and selfishness.

It is to worship this casket of gold that you have
enshrined yourself within.

TO LOVE WITHOUT SINCERITY is to be a husband that brings
orchidsand roses to his wife only after he has committed
adultery with another man's wife.

TO LOVE WITHOUT SINCERITY is to wrongfully give the
emblem of devotion and understanding to the drunkard
husband.

It is to thoughtlessly bestow the badge of honor to a
prostitute and a perverter and despiser of the truth.

It is to give the staff of piercing sacred light to a
demon of darkness.

It is to give the keys of understanding and knowledge to
the slanderous idle mind of a fool.

TO LOVE WITHOUT SINCERITY is to be a wife that curses her
husband as you would a worthless dog that seeks the
crumbs of compassion from the empty table of her heart.

TO LOVE WITHOUT LOVE is to be a diseased-eaten carcass
abandoned and left to perish on the roadside of life by your
beloved.

It is to love someone that has cast you into a bed of
crippling filth and unmovable embalming death.

TO LOVE WITHOUT LOVE is to build a city of gold while
beholding the inhabitants therein carrying hearts made of
stone.

TO LOVE WITHOUT LOVE is to marry for lust rather than for love.

It is to conceive children born not out of devotion and compassion but out of shame, guilt, and fear.

TO LOVE WITHOUT LOVE is to be the worst kind of hypocrite.

It is to be a seducing snake that elegantly counsels and consoles its victims before consuming them.

TO LOVE WITHOUT LOVE is to love an object that has no worth or substance.

It is to manipulate the heart and destroy the self-esteem of someone that believes in the power and salvation of love.

TO LOVE WITHOUT GOD is to sign your own death certificate.

It is to patiently and respectfully fashion your own coffin in ignorant pride and reverent stupidity.

TO LOVE WITHOUT GOD is to be a magnificent, powerful eagle that is content and satisfied to live like a chicken.

TO LOVE WITHOUT GOD is to be as bread without a holding crust.

TO LOVE WITHOUT GOD is to be as water–foul, stagnate and unsatisfying to the famished Sahara in your heart.

TO LOVE WITHOUT GOD is to be as sculptured oak trees, rising like withered hands from the dust, barren of the blossoms of prayer.

TO LOVE WITHOUT GOD is to have the strength of a thousand
men but the mentality of a worm.

TO LOVE WITHOUT GOD is to be as an egg without a
nourishing yolk, possessing only a broken, useless shell.

TO LOVE WITHOUT GOD is to be a king that rules his subjects
with intimidating fear and cowardly glory, building his
throne with the blood of the sons and daughters of peasants.

THIS DAY, appreciate yourself; know that there is no greater
painting on the canvases of men than what I have painted on
the hue of your skin.

No longer shall you struggle helplessly and deem yourself a
crippled bird in the powerful jaws of a lion.

No longer shall you be a slain antelope brought down by the
bow of the hunter's arrow.

No longer shall you be a skeleton that parades in disgraceful
terror before men.

Where is the mighty courage and the supreme grace of your
manner?

Where is the perception and the quickness of your mind?

Where is the understanding of your knowledge, the vastness
of your imagination?

Who are these undetected thieves and robbers who have broken
      without shame into the sanctuary of your soul, leaving only
      empty and discarded shelves?

Where are the strong and powerfully majestic wings of your grace
      and the beauty that once moved upon your countenance
      like a thousand songs sung by a thousand angels with their
      wings stretched out in the gentle morning light?

Let us arrest this fallen and deceitful angel that has betrayed the
      glory of the throne of God to walk in a self-exalted manner
      using the tears of the weak for a pillow to comfort your puffed
      up head.

It has long circled the skies like a disturbing cloud of death with
      the face of a vulture and the heart of a corpse that delights at
      the tragedies of your neighbor.

Yet the identity of this ancient deceiver bears a strange
      resemblance to you.

Do you remember when you lived in your Father's house
      and walked with him through the blowing leaves of time?

And you lay down in the soft blowing pillow of the grass
      beholding the rising and falling shapes of clouds
      taking the appearance of priests, worshipping together,
      in the cathedral of the skies?

And you imagined that the gold from the crowns of a thousand
      kings would be yours in time?

Once you wrote your words in the sand and many would come and
   read what you had written before the waters of the tide would
   come.

And now you stand alone in the street reciting your words to
   those who are deaf.

Also I heard the voice of the Lord saying, "Whom shall I send, and
   who will go for us?" Then I said, "Here am I, send me."

And often you have believed that the ink of the scriptures in your
   heart, if written upon the sand, even the sea could not erase it.

Let us behold the abundance of your gifts and talents.
   Are your handicaps greater than your blessings?

Long have you believed a reassuring lie rather than to wash the
   filth of the ages from your deteriorating carcass.

It is to stand by the burning bush of my candlelight heart
   crying out, but you cannot see.

Your suffering is not my divine plan.

For you have cursed your life, for you have said that you are
   crippled and deformed in your body.

But that which dreams in your body is your greatest beauty,
   the inner indestructible form that moves in the power of your
   smile and the brilliance of your tears.

But verily, how can you build a new house if you do not have
   the proper tools?

For it makes little difference how skilled the craftsman is;

> if he does not have the right tools, his hands and fingers shall move without direction and purpose.

For truly, the greatest workman is he who understands that he

> himself is an instrument held between the fingers of life, used for beauty or destruction.

You are not blind, deaf, speechless, or crippled in your spirit,

> but many of you have pretended to be so.

But I say unto you, those who are deaf, blind, and crippled have

> known greater miracles and shall achieve more than many others, even if they live to be a thousand and one years.

For did not I give you the ability to observe the beauty and the

> pain of the lives of men that parade and stagger past your doorstep?

Have you not learned from the worthless, unaccomplished jealousy

> of Cain who bore the unwashable blood of his brother upon his own hands?

Have you not learned that your greatness comes not in calling

> yourself Doctor, Reverend, Rabbi, Teacher, Your Excellency, Infallible Potentate, Captain, Prince, or King?

Your greatness is in knowing that the dust of your skin makes you

> brother to him who is the poorest of the poor and the richest of the rich.

Have you not learned that your greatness does not come with the
largeness and the heights of your buildings nor by the gold
and silver in the teeth of the dead?

For it is in knowing that the pyramids of pharaohs and the
coliseums and the palaces of emperors now lay in ruins and
their kingdoms are lost forever.

Have you not learned that the scoundrels that sit on plush pillows
and have fashioned crowns of gold for their heads
manipulated the procrastinators?

For their glory is in the multitudes of men, not in the congregation
of the Angelic Host.

Have you not learned that the royal blood of kings is as great as
the blood of peasants in the eyes of the just, eternal creator?

Have you not learned from the betraying, envying, scandalizing
mind of Judas, eating in innocent array from a loving and
majestic Last Supper?

For you are a vulture with filthy wings of death, standing
in false reverence before the King of Glory.

Have you not learned from the uncertain double-minded, wavering
heart of Pontius Pilate, afraid of killing the indestructible
Christ, and afraid of keeping him alive?

Have you not learned that patience is the greatest prayer and
kindness is my visible appearance?

For love is the greatest sermon ever seen.

Have you not learned that Beethoven was deaf, but he could
compose music that those who could hear did not hear?

Have you not learned that Michelangelo painted the ceiling of
the Sistine Chapel, painting but a speck from my eyes that
others have never seen?

Have you not learned that Helen Keller, who was blind, deaf, and
speechless, spoke in a language to multitudes that we have
never spoken and touched thousands we shall never
touch?

Have you not learned that Martin Luther King knelt at the
burning bush and beheld my face and a sacred dream
that we are trying to dream?

Yet I say unto you that your gifts and your talents are
greater than these.

Have you not learned he who murders is often killed a
thousand times over by his own self?

Have you not learned he who steals is often stolen and
lost and cannot be found?

Have you not learned he who lies is often lied to?

Have you not learned he who commits adultery is often
unloved and cannot truly give love?

Have you not learned he who does not honor his mother
or father often beholds his own children not honoring him?

T. S. Eure

Have you not learned he who takes the name of the Lord in
    vain is often found with a vain life?

Have you not learned that he, who covets his neighbor's house, his
    wife, his substance, is often found with truly nothing of his
    own?

Have you not learned that he, who makes other gods before me,
    is often found worshipping himself alone?

Have you not learned that he, who cannot remember the Sabbath
    day, often cannot remember when he had a day of rest?

Have you not learned that he, who bears false witness, is often
    false in his most sincere prayer?

Long have you said the handicaps and disadvantages placed upon
    you have kept you from reaching your success and
    achievements, from touching the golden staircase ascending
    to my heart.

Release these braces from your legs; unlock the burning
    light from your mind.

Stop limping and crawling, degrading and demeaning yourself as
    a worthless worm.

I have given you all the gifts and miracles to save a thousand
    worlds. Then why are you afraid to save yourself?

DID I NOT GIVE YOU THE GIFT OF HAVING

    EXTRAORDINARY ABILITIES AND SUPERNATURAL

    POWERS?

For your LOVE is my greatest testament, my eternal divinity,

    my proclaiming prophecy, my rejoicing announcement, my

    anointed invitation of my presence upon the earth.

For you are the most beautiful, wonderful, and unsurpassed of

    all my creations.

Do you not know in one of your teardrops there is enough

    power to create a thousand universes?

For truly in just your touch there is enough healing power to

    heal all the patients in the hospitals of the world.

For there is a healing in you greater than all the medicines

    ever created.

Do you find that hard to believe?

For you are my greatest possibility, and in your smile

    you can behold the face of your Creator.

For my power is moving in great wonders like a loving, creating

    hand enclosed within your protons and neutrons.

And in your atoms I sing everlasting symphonies.

For not even the strongest of wires or cables of steel,

    not even pillars of the most majestic cathedral

    can outwear the power of your smile.

And the skin that I have tailored for your body is greater

    than the most intricate embroidery of a seamstress, a

    living thread of beauty interlaced around your bones.

BEHOLD THYSELF THIS DAY, you are not dead, your blood is

    still circulating warm in your veins.

Your heart is still pumping with the vitality and the

    pulse of this fleeing existence.

A million nerves and muscles move in precise rhythms even like

    unto a ballerina performing in my silent opera.

BEHOLD THYSELF THIS DAY, your eyes are the open circles of

    the infinite, the microscopes of your soul, revealing your

    slain dreams, crying out to you for life.

Your hopes and aspirations have been like unto angels whose

    wings have been clipped and now only sit on silent hills

    staring at the light of the stars they can no longer touch.

Your eyes are like a crystal chandelier, now hung without brilliance

    in a dilapidated house. Under the retina is kept the memory

    of a time of greatness, where you danced in a wonderment of

    elegance as you twirled in the decorated ballroom of

    life's enchanting splendor.

Your eyes are like cosmic fountains where holy men drink into

    the cleansing baptism of their loving God.

Your eyes can behold the withered face of death staggering

    through the gates of the city, moving in disturbed shadows

across men's faces, taking those who have fallen on the
moving highway of life.

Your eyes can see the whoremongers sleeping contentedly on
the flames of a comfortable hell.

For your eyes can see the prostitute waiting patiently for death,
deeming herself as an object in the hands of empty   men.

For your eyes can see the rich man in his death bed, counting
his coins, wondering if he can stack them together
to make a ladder to heaven.

For your eyes can see the tears of an exhausted body, an athlete,
coming to the finish line in last place, not knowing the
greatest honor is not always being first. Victory is in not
giving up, pursuing and achieving and completing your goal.

Your heart is the restless sea of the universe where solitary
fishermen sit on the shores of your life, seeking to gather
miracles washed against the sands of the pain of your silence.

Your heart is the eternal library where your prayers are recorded.
The times you walked alone and spoke unto the wind and held
interesting conversations with trees.

And you were transformed, even like unto a child playing tag with
the rising and falling shapes of clouds that summon you
to worship in this cathedral that I ordained, where
generations of men from all walks of life, hold hands in
the dust that blows over silent bodies in the earth.

Your heart is a tree whose branches have become praying hands,
   silently worshipping in this swaying sanctuary of earth's
   comforting winds, communicating in a universal language
   to the divine operator of the infinite.

Your heart is a tree where holy men and prophets stop and take
   refuge and eat of the fruit heavy laden on your branches,
   as they journey to the holy mountaintop of Sinai and
   whisper in the ears of the consoling God.

Your heart is a rose that grows alone in the wilderness where
   dust and wind and snows of many winters have discolored
   and withered the fragile petals of your existence.

Yet as you sleep in the rain, the heartbeat of a thousand generations
   shall caress and ignite the flaming candle of your soul, and
   you shall return to the earth in the laughter of children.

THERE ARE THREE DIVINE LAWS THAT YOU MUST
   KNOW, MY DEARLY BELOVED.

The first one is DO NOT BE AFRAID WHEN YOU MUST
   STAND ALONE.

Always be true to your convictions and beliefs.

If there are a thousand men against you and you know in your
   heart you are right, do not betray yourself to attain the
   friendship of others.

I, God, am sick of men and women that cannot be true to what they
believe. It is better for a person to die alone in his dignity,
than to march in a parade with fools.

For surely, when you start believing that you are special,
that you are a miracle, men will curse you and separate you
from their company. For I say unto you, do not be afraid
when you stand alone.

For I have given you a special dream, that no one upon earth
can give meaning to but you. I do not care what force or
power or element comes out against you, keep believing in
your purpose, your destiny, your sacred space, where you
pray alone and your prayers speak back unto you.

There are many cemeteries that are filled with those who
were afraid to dream.

The Caesars, the Hitlers, the Napoleons shall always command
your submission to their wills, that you give your precious
life to build a shrine to their glory.

For there shall be men that will insist and demand you give
them the very light that illuminates from your soul.

It is my desire and my hope that you stand for truth, no matter
what force or power tries to make you kneel before their
demonic throne.

Stand against the oppressors whose kingdoms are made from
the bodies of the poor and the hope of the weak.

Stand against the deceiving dictators that demand your
  respect but do not deserve it.
Stand against the men who have made prestige and fashion
  and status their gods.
Stand against the devouring wolves that sit upon pulpits,
  preaching one thing but doing another.
Stand against the men who try to deny your dreams,
  those who try to make you believe you have no meaning or
  purpose.
Stand against those who are dead, those that lay in caskets
  of stupidity and fear.
Stand against the very powers of hell itself, until righteousness
  is exalted and the hills and the mountains clap their hands
  and become witnesses to thy truth.

THE SECOND DIVINE LAW YOU MUST KNOW, MY
  BELOVED, IS THAT NO EVIL SHALL GO
  UNPUNISHED.
Often you have beheld the wicked standing on pillars of great
  power.
They are even like lions attacking their victims without mercy,
  setting many traps to hurt and degrade those that come into
  their paths, marching proudly without concern for others.

They build mansions for themselves; and they command others to
      live in ruins of poverty, while they live in fields of
      prosperity.

They teach their children to hate and to look down on
      others who are not in their social circle.

They have built elaborate churches of wealth and magnificence,
      yet they have left me standing outside in hungry
      destitution and in nakedness.

They are as snakes that live in luxurious holes.

For they are as wolves who have no fear of the divine shepherd
      that watches over the flock.

Yet, in that day, when they feel so safe and secure, when they
      have gathered all the wheat into their barns, when they are
      sleeping satisfied and contented in their beds,

Then, I, the Lord, will come against them, calamity and
      destruction falling upon them in one day.

And in that day, they shall weep but there shall be
      no one to dry their tears.

For surely, even if men should cast you into a merciless
      dungeon of no escape and you should die of starvation and
      torture, you shall triumph.

For the chains they bind you with, shall be as a golden
      necklace in my eyes.

For surely, even if you are taken, beaten, and dragged through

> the streets for not accepting the idols that the multitudes

> worship and carry, you shall triumph.

For you shall receive greater trophies and honors from me

> than can be awarded and bestowed by men.

For you have graduated from my university where

> I become a reality and not a formality.

For if evil should go unpunished, then fire would stop being hot

> and water would stop being wet.

For if evil would go unpunished, the oceans would break from

> their boundaries and the waters thereof would swallow and

> consume the earth.

For if evil would go unpunished, the stars would fall out of their

> silvery sockets; the sun would fall from its eternal

> celestial orbit; the moon would drip as pouring blood across

> the skies, and the mountains and the hills would shake and

> collide.

For if evil would go unpunished, then death itself would no longer

> hide among the shadows of fallen lives, but would unfold

> its dark wings in tragic splendor, destroying all without

> mercy, and no longer fearing the everlasting guardian who has

> the keys of death and hell in his hands.

So I say unto you, no evil will go unpunished; dry your eyes,

weep no more.

For there is an eternal judge that hears the pleas of his people,

no matter what title or position they might hold in this life.

Even if you are held in great esteem and admiration and reverence

by men, woe unto you that has made evil your god. You have

become as a lump of clay finished by the hands of Satan.

THE THIRD DIVINE LAW YOU MUST KNOW, MY

BELOVED, IS THAT I ALONE AM YOUR GREATEST

MIRACLE AND YOUR GREATEST FRIEND.

For this you should know, my beloved, only I will stand with you

when all others have forsaken you.

Even if your pockets only have pennies and your shoes have holes

in them and you are mocked and ridiculed through the streets.

For I will cause all who have tried to make you dust beneath their

feet to die in a bed of anguish, and I will cause even your

most deadly, hated enemies to come to you and beg you for

forgiveness.

Listen, I say unto you, even your own family will leave you and

your best friend that walked so close to you will abandon

and curse you.

For only you and I will be left again, as we were in the beginning

when I wrote my testament in the womb of your mother.

For some of you have placed too much trust in your leaders,

sounding a trumpet for them and beating many drums.

But when they have deceived you and failed you,

you have gathered up stones against them.

And when you have murdered them, you built memorials to their

names, and told your children to worship the greatness of

their memory.

How long shall you be a puppet entangled in your strings of blind

submission to power-hungry scavengers?

How long shall you be a fool walking in an idiot parade?

How long shall you be a court jester, laughing in sickening

deception?

How long shall you be a dead man without a grave?

How long shall you be a stone being tossed in every direction

by anyone who walks along the path of your life?

How long shall you be a tree barren of fruit-giving branches,

possessing only empty and naked limbs?

How long shall you be a cup without a bottom?

How long shall you be a rose that has cast your petals aside

to become a thorn?

How long shall you be a mole content to tunnel in blind darkness?

How long shall you be an uninvited guest at the marriage

supper of the Lamb?

YOU ARE MY GREATEST MIRACLE. Crowns of gold or emblems of silver, or priceless trophies, adored and worshipped by men, not even the treasure houses of kings are greater than you.

YOU ARE MY GREATEST MIRACLE. The wedding dress of Mount Everest that has endured like pillars of truth and undemanding beauty for thousands and thousands of years, not even this is greater than you.

YOU ARE MY GREATEST MIRACLE. Houses nor property, mansions nor cathedrals, nor the names of the wealthy or great inscriptions on altars of gold, not even these are greater than you.

YOU ARE MY GREATEST MIRACLE. Families who profess to come from royalty, nobility, or puffed-up piety, not even they in all their grandeur are greater than you.

YOU ARE MY GREATEST MIRACLE. The coronation of kings, the glamour of queens, the decrees of governors, nor the regalia of potentates and false prophets, and those that sit in exalted seats of power, not even those are greater than you.

YOU ARE MY GREATEST MIRACLE. Caskets of rich men, nor the tombs of the famous, not even these are greater than you.

YOU ARE MY GREATEST MIRACLE. The terrible force and the unpredictable beauty of the Sahara Desert are not as surreal and moving nor greater than you.

YOU ARE MY GREATEST MIRACLE. The jaguar moving with
unbelievable speed and perfect grace and power is not as
swift or as quick in thought and in mind as you are.

YOU ARE MY GREATEST MIRACLE. The stillness of the
Mediterranean at midnight is not as composed and
contemplative nor greater than you.

YOU ARE MY GREATEST MIRACLE. The ivory swan with its
sculptured wings swimming in the timeless black waters of
evening silence is not greater than you.

YOU ARE MY GREATEST MIRACLE. Yosemite Valley,
this sacred church where crystal waterfalls sing Handel's
Messiah, and mountains become altars where my unbroken
fingers have written commandments in the praying
evergreens, in the meditating poppies that is a mighty
congregation wearing a robe of many colors, is not greater
than you.

YOU ARE MY GREATEST MIRACLE. The indestructible
redwood trees, like prophets in the wilderness proclaiming
my glory in the brilliant loveliness and the beauty and
power of their enduring strength, are not greater than you.

YOU ARE MY GREATEST MIRACLE. The fury of the winter's
blizzard or the dust of the summer's heat, not even all the
wrath of nature's vengeance and the force of its consuming
desolation are not greater than you.

YOU ARE MY GREATEST MIRACLE. The captains of ten thousand men, standing with brilliant swords and gleaming shields ready to conquer and ravish the spoil of any adversary are not greater than you.

YOU ARE MY GREATEST MIRACLE. Even the Grand Canyon or the Sierras as if dug by the hands of some awesome giant are not greater than you.

YOU ARE MY GREATEST MIRACLE. The Toucan bird with its brilliant colors sitting in the blossoms of a cinnamon tree singing a melodic prayer in the sanctuary of a tropical paradise is not greater than you.

YOU ARE MY GREATEST MIRACLE. The glaciers of Alaska, like the gigantic teardrops of a mastodon abandoned by a forgotten world, are not greater than you.

And now, I, God, being of sound and living omnipotent, eternal mind, possessing absolute, unlimited, undefiled, undiminished, imperishable, undestroyed perfect holiness,

I, HEREBY DECREE, MY EVERLASTING, INFINITE POWER to the third planet from the sun, traveling in a divine cosmic orbit, turning in magnificent silence in the still blackness of space.

I, HEREBY DECREE TO YOU, in the presence of saints, angels, prophets, priests, messengers, guardians, and preservers of truth, my last and greatest blessings.

I, HEREBY DECREE TO YOU, an indestructible gift, presented to you this day, a comforter to reassure you of my invincible presence. I restore a new power into you, which shall be a holy light switch turned on in the observatory of your soul.

I, HEREBY DECREE TO YOU, the mountains of gold that rise like an ancient crown from the velvet red clay of the sacred plains.

I, HEREBY DECREE TO YOU, the clear blue lakes that run like holy teardrops into the rushing rapids of dazzling waterfalls that pour out of mountains of gold.

I, HEREBY DECREE TO YOU, the pink and white flamingoes, like a brilliant still-life from the brushes of an artist, a living masterpiece framed forever on the landscapes of life.

I, HEREBY DECREE TO YOU, apple trees that are blossoming with fruit, the air permeated with the smell of cinnamon, and laughing children climbing the branches to behold the last sunlight of the summer's glitter.

I, HEREBY DECREE TO YOU, the goldfish that swim in blue stillness, that glide through a thousand sunlit ripples moving on a pond.

I, HEREBY DECREE TO YOU, the prairies that blossom in orange surprise, where magnificent sunsets caress the landscapes like a mother holding a child against her breast, and where curtains of atmospheric, heavenly lace drape the mountains with the robes of angels.

I, HEREBY DECREE TO YOU, the clouds that take the appearance of men that have conversations with your children in the fields and as mountains of purple mystery cast sacred shadows in eternal canyons where my heartbeat is heard in endless prayers in the wind.

I, HEREBY DECREE TO YOU, talents and gifts so magnificent, so precious and special that I have waited thousands upon thousands of years for you to bring my dream, your dream, into existence, to perfect in you that which is impossible for men.

I, HEREBY DECREE TO YOU, a day where children walk in evening fields, catching lightning bugs with their hands, and where clouds of dust and wind appear as an angelic army, whirling swords of sunlight and shadows on floors of lilac-covered valleys.

I, HEREBY DECREE TO YOU, the trumpet of Louis Armstrong that you might know there is a music that is not learned or composed but is lived with each breath.

I, HEREBY DECREE TO YOU, the jawbone that Samson used to defeat a thousand Philistines that you might know that there is no fire, no flood and no foe that can destroy you. For the gift that I put into you is everlasting and cannot be destroyed in this world or the world to come.

I, HEREBY DECREE TO YOU, the patience and the knowledge
of an ant that you might know that there is a learning not
found in the encyclopedias of men, but there is a learning
that strives for excellence and is not ashamed to work.

I, HEREBY DECREE TO YOU, the baseball bat of Babe Ruth that
you should know that you cannot be content to slide to first
base when you have the potential to make a home run.

I, HEREBY DECREE TO YOU, the body of an elephant that you
should know that your largeness is only respected when
you walk in dignity and humble grace.

I, HEREBY DECREE TO YOU, the slingshot of David for it may
not shine or glitter like the armor of a king, yet no giant
shall prevail or overcome thee.

I, HEREBY DECREE TO YOU, the knockout punch of Joe Lewis
as he dumped Adolph Hitler's champion, Max Schmeling,
in the first round, that you may know right shall triumph no
matter how many millions perpetuate and exalt a lie.

I, HEREBY DECREE TO YOU, the neck of a giraffe so when all
others around you are reaching for the dandelions of deceit
and ridicule, you will not be ashamed to stand tall and to
stretch out your long neck to the trees that are heavy laden
with fruit.

I, HEREBY DECREE TO YOU, the voice of Mahalia Jackson for
you to know that if you use your gift to its greatest potential,

then the song that you sing by yourself in the fields will be sung by the multitudes every day of their lives.

I, HEREBY DECREE TO YOU, the body of a porcupine for you to know that even if you are ridiculed and cursed in the streets, this crown of thorns you wear shall be a testament of your enduring love.

I, HEREBY DECREE TO YOU, the rhythmic syncopation of the orchestra of Count Basie, for you to know that you are a musician that plays music that even the deaf can appreciate.

I, HEREBY DECREE TO YOU, the eyes of Einstein for you to know that there is a universe in your teardrops and in their reflection you can behold my face.

I, HEREBY DECREE TO YOU, the staff of Moses for you to know that seas will not engulf you nor will the chariots of armies slay you with their swords.

I, HEREBY DECREE TO YOU, the legs of Wilma Rudolph, for you to know that my power is swift, for you shall outrun those who sought to hurl themselves against you.

I, HEREBY DECREE TO YOU, the body of a caterpillar for you to know that even if this earthly body perishes you have an eternal body fashioned by a divine tailor of the universe.

I, HEREBY DECREE TO YOU, the twisted and ominous trees in the Garden of Gethsemane, for you to know that when you are overcome with grief, lift your hands and you will blossom in the garden of your life.

T. S. Eure

I, HEREBY DECREE TO YOU, the dancing feet of Bill

"Bojangles" Robinson for you to know that the power of

your feet can carry you above the stars.

IN THIS PERILOUS TIME AND IN THIS HOUR THAT IS

DELIVERED UNTO ME.

NOW, in this infinitely timeless place,

I speak through your pulses in this bountiful existence.

NOW, in this deep silence consuming all, in this contented womb,

I hear your voice.

NOW, in this hour of eternal grace that has burned in my being like

stars that hang in the silent stillness of space for hundreds

of thousands of years.

NOW, in this moving symphony of your heartbeat, as your tears

fall out of my eyes,

AND NOW, my spirit shall flow into your arteries, cells and

molecules–a cleansing, incomprehensible, unconquerable

power rushing through your blood–and your bones shall jump

and your feet shall run with my testament.

Understand me now. Understand yourself.

For nothing can destroy you; mountains and kingdoms shall

fall before you. For nations and dominions and the wealth of

dying men shall fall before you.

And you cannot be killed or destroyed forever, for it is only the
pestilence of spiritual death that can fashion unbreakable
chains around your waist.

For it shall be an everlasting Christmas; you shall smile in wonder
and in anticipation of the gift I have for you.
For you and I have created something very special, a miracle.
For you have become a miracle, and I have touched and
embraced and laughed and cried in you.
For I give you in all humility, in humbleness, in the pureness
of a living fire.
I breathe this, my dream, my miracle, my compassion, my touch,
this something you shall remember, this something I will
remember.

AND NOW I, GOD, BEING OF SOUND MIND, HEREBY
DECREE, MY LAST WILL AND TESTAMENT TO

_____ on this _____ day of _____.
AND GUARANTEE ALL RIGHTS AND PRIVILEGES AS SET
FORTH IN THIS DIVINE HOLY COVENANT, WITNESSED
BY MY SPIRIT, MY BLOOD, AND MY LOVE. I, HEREBY,
NOW LEAVE YOU WITH THIS MY LAST PRAYER, MY LAST
EMBRACE, THE LAST BREATH THAT SHALL PASS OVER
YOUR LIPS. I LEAVE YOU WITH THIS, MY LAST WILL AND
TESTAMENT.

I leave you teachers that will instruct you in godliness and will

ignite the flame of imagination in your cerebrum.

I leave you teachers that will not condemn and criticize

the thoughts of a child, but will sanctify the dream with

learning,nurture it with love; for this is the most precious

gift invested in every human life.

I leave you teachers that know that they too are only children

sitting in the classroom of life turning each page of their

existence in wonder and surprise.

I leave you teachers that instruct their students in understanding,

compassion and humility, for these virtues far exceed the

honors, certificates and trophies bestowed by men.

I leave you teachers that can teach the power of love to the

unloved.

I leave you doctors that believe that there is a greater power that

sees deeper than the microscope, a greater power than any

aspirin that is prescribed to heal the heartbreak of men,

a greater power that can fan away sickness.

I leave you doctors that anoint their patients with the oil of

gladness, doctors that wash and cleanse the scars of the

heart before a band-aid is applied to the torn flesh.

I leave you doctors that prescribe laughter for the terminally ill,

prayer and rejoicing for the incurable, and singing for the

afflicted and desolate.

I leave you doctors that believe that their hands are but extensions to a greater physician who uses the medicine cabinet of my universe.

I leave you doctors that wear stethoscopes of compassion inside their hearts.

I leave you farmers that plant my holiness in the fertile crevices of the earth; that behold the stalks of the fields as my waving hands, blessing your sweat that touches the soil.

I leave you farmers that comb the living strands of the majestic rows with the skillful strength of their plows and the swinging silence of their sickles.

I leave you farmers that bless each egg that is taken from each chicken, that revere the milk taken from cows grazing in the shadows of sleepy meadows.

I leave you farmers that know that each leaf of barley, each ear of corn is but the praying hands of the creator, calling all the multitudes of the earth to stand still and know that I am still creating.

I leave you farmers that speak to their corn in the twilight of morning, saying, "Hello corn, how are you today? I prayed for you last night, that you would raise your leaves to your father in the glory of the skies."

I leave you bakers that prepare the dough with yeast of
   compassion, the oil of humbleness, and shall bake this with
   my tears poured out on the souls of men.

I leave you bakers that have shelves of sweet rolls in their hearts,
   and who will invite many hungry travelers to the dinner
   table of their love.

I leave you ministers that would rather pray with the poor in
   houses of grief than sit on pulpits of selfishness and
   magnificence.

I leave you ministers that would rather be a sermon to someone
   than preach one to them.

I leave you shoemakers that repair the twisted soles of human
   lives, weeping over the shoes of humanity, praying they
   would walk in sincerity, compassion, and unselfish love.

I leave you shoemakers that walk the barren trails and disregarded
   roads encouraging those whose faces weep in the dust of
   defeat.

I leave you street cleaners that take the discarded lives that are left
   upon the roadside, fashioning them into a masterpiece
   of extraordinary beauty.

I leave you street cleaners that pray as they sweep the streets of men, hoping that they can also sweep the filth out of their hearts.

I leave you painters that cover the barren canvas of life with the brilliant pigment of laughter, the hue of humility, covered with the texture of consideration.

I leave painters whose brushes are but testimonies of the beauty of life that they can paint upon others.

I leave you candlestick-makers that have made their hearts torches that shine through the thick darkness of human tragedy.

I leave you candlestick-makers that lead men with storm-cloud hearts into the bright sunlight of hope.

I leave you tailors that sew the scars of contempt with the thread of comfort, replacing the rags of ridicule with the robes of righteousness.

I leave you tailors that labor in the midnight hour sewing torn hearts into living tapestries of beauty.

I leave you carpenters that take the discarded wood of life and build an altar for all men to worship upon.

T. S. Eure

I leave you carpenters that carve hollow and dead trees and

      useless stumps into a redeeming masterpiece that will bring

      beauty for thousands of years.

I leave you dishwashers that wash the filth off the plates of the

      wealthy, wishing that their hearts were just as clean.

I leave you dishwashers that reach their hands into the dirty

      waters of shame and fallen lives and wash

      and cleanse a thing of beauty.

I leave you judges that are able to judge between sincerity and

      hypocrisy, and that are able to discern between a false smile

      and a lie.

I leave you judges that know that the wolf that cries out like a lamb

      is still a wolf; and a snake will always be a snake, no matter

      how dignified he speaks or how well he dresses himself.

I leave you mothers that are not afraid to breastfeed their babies,

      mothers unafraid to change a diaper or to wash their

      children's faces with their tears.

I leave you mothers that sing their children to sleep rather

      than curse them to sleep.

I leave you fathers that carry their children on their shoulders
    to behold the twilight of the evening stars falling on the
    shadows of mountaintops.
I leave you fathers that teach their children to kneel and
    pray rather than teach them to drink liquor.

I leave you junkmen that travel through the alleys of life and
    find treasures in those lives that men have thrown away.
I leave you junkmen that find beauty in broken hearts and shattered
    dreams, knowing that these pieces form the jewels inside my
    heart.

I leave you poets that fill their pens with the blood of prophets
    killed in your cities for preaching to dead and embalmed men.
I leave you poets that hold candles in their hearts and
    waterfalls of magnificent power moving in their eyes.
I leave you prophets that cry out in the streets, whose lives
    are but a prayer that all men can speak.

If there ever comes a time that you forget my touch or can no
    longer hear my voice, if the weariness of seasons seek to
    destroy you, or the disappointments of life have caused you
    sorrow, take a deep breath and know that you are my greatest
    miracle.

T. S. Eure

I hereby decree unto you the power to believe with a might so great

that you will know that anything that is destroyed wrongfully

is born over a thousand times again.

I hereby decree unto you the power to pray with such compassion

until your heart unfolds unto a temple of everlasting beauty.

That even your enemies will humble themselves before your

presence.

I hereby decree unto you the power to believe that all that is good

and wonderful has been presented to you this day.

I hereby decree unto you the power to pray until angels come down

from their angelic mansions to bring a divine report from the

throne room of the eternal king.

I hereby decree unto you a breath of life to fill your body

with an invincible dream.

I hereby decree unto you trees that cover you with shade in

the sunlight of summer's silence.

I hereby decree unto you the laughter of children to fill the

emptiness in your heart.

And finally I give unto you this day the most precious of all my

gifts, the power to love.

It is your ability to love that sets you apart from any living being

that exists, for nothing is greater than the power to love.

I place this power in your hands this day; and if ever you feel

I have abandoned and forsaken you, act upon the power to

love, and you will see your heavenly Father loving through

you.

For nothing is greater than the power to love.

For nothing is stronger than love demonstrated.

For nothing is more sacred than sincere love.

For nothing is more lasting than love that is humble.

For nothing is more holy than love that is shared.

For nothing is more lovely than love that is kind.

For nothing is more understanding than love that can listen.

For nothing is more compassionate than love that is giving.

For nothing is more powerful than love that can pray.

For this is the miracle of living.

I leave you with the knowledge that your love can save the world.

After I read this letter over the next forty days, it was revealed to me that I should sell everything that I had and have a yard sale. Before the sale I hired workers to replace the broken roof and gutters, and painters and cleaners to freshen every room until it shined and sparkled to perfection. I paid the young boys a hundred dollars each to help me cut the grass and trim the hedges. Also I gave them sacks of groceries that I had horded for years.

I was able to sell the house for a substantial amount. I posted a huge sign that read, "Everything for a dollar." Once again my neighbors thought that I had lost my mind when they saw oak tables, bookcases, china cabinets, dishes, silver trays, and plates all selling for a dollar. I packed up all of Claudette's clothes and sent them to her aunts out of town.

When everything was done and every room in the house was empty, I packed all of my belongings into a duffle bag. Now I was determined to find my sister Sarah, go to Africa, and have Christmas dinner with David's children. On the journey I would share the messages from the last letter from God to all that needed to hear it.

The day I left I went to the front yard and spoke to the apple tree and said, You make sure you keep putting out apples, for the new residents have five children that might need some apple pies every once in a while. It was early spring and already the leaves were starting to shoot out blossoms that had small pink and blue flowers.

Recently I received a letter from Papa Jacob in which he said that once again he did not think he would have the strength to go on after hearing about David's death. Everything within him wanted to revert to depression and withdrawal from his work with the immigrant workers. But that Papa Jacob had died long ago, and David's life work would not be wasted with his grieving for him. For you see, life is not about hiding, it is not about feeling sorry for yourself. David was meant to go to Africa; he was meant to make a difference.

Papa Jacob said that he awakened one morning to find a note that Mama Flo had written that said,

Dear Dr. Jacob,

Please forgive me for leaving so quickly without saying goodbye. My work with you has also healed me in many ways. But once again God has given me a new assignment. The new assignment is at a critical level so I must go to do what I can. You need no more healing: you have become medicine for all those around you. And you have learned the most important lesson in life: to look for miracles in your own backyard.

Your caregiver, life motivator,

Mama Flo

Papa Jacob walked towards his bedroom window and looked out. The morning sun had streamed down through the valley below, and to his surprise never in the history of the valley could he recall the grape fields blooming with pink and blue flowers.

About the Author

T. S. Eure was born in Omaha, Nebraska, graduated from Central High School in 1972 and the University of Nebraska-Omaha in 1986 with a B.A. in History and a minor in English Literature. As an exchange student in Bancroft, Iowa, during his sophomore year in high school, he began writing poetry. He became an ordained minister in 1980 and started writing *Dear Joseph* in 1982. As a youth care team leader, he motivates and encourages adolescents to change their behaviors.